Until Jax

Aurora Rose Reynolds

Dedication

Natasha may everyone find a friend as crazy as you.

Table of Contents

Until Jax

Love isn't always what we want,
but it's always what we need.

Prologue

Ellie

BY THE TIME I arrive at the hospital and get put into a room, I'm at my wit's end. My body is exhausted from having nothing really substantial to eat or drink over the last couple of days, and my mind is a mess from what I have just survived. On top of all that, I need to get to Hope.

"I'm really okay," I repeat for what feels like the hundredth time to the doctor, who has been checking me over since coming into my room a few minutes ago.

"Ruth, let's start an IV," he says, looking over my head at the nurse, once again ignoring me and pulling my arm towards him, prodding It with his fingers.

"I need to get to Hope," I whimper, yanking my arm out of his grasp when the nurse walks around the bed with the needle in her hand.

"Let the doctor put in the IV, Ellie," the guy named Jax says, taking my other hand in his and smoothing his thumb over my palm. He hasn't left my side since I walked out of the woods. I've been trying to ignore him, but am failing miserably. He's a giant, and intimidatingly good-looking, which makes it nearly impossible to be in his presence without acknowledging him.

"You don't understand. Hope needs me," I cry as the doctor takes my arm again, placing the needle into my skin, causing tears of frustration to fill my eyes.

"Hey, don't cry. I'm sure your dog is okay," Jax says softly, running his fingers over the back of my hand.

"Ex-excuse me?" I sputter, turning my head towards him.

"Cat?" he asks, frowning.

"Hope is my daughter," I hiss, pulling my hand from his grasp.

"Daughter?" He pales, searching my face. I'm not surprised by his reaction. That's the normal response I get from men when they find out I have a kid, but something inside of me whimpers from his response.

"Daughter," I affirm, lifting my chin, and then look at the doctor to glare. "I need to get out of here *now*," I growl through clenched teeth.

"Fuck me," Jax mumbles, but I ignore him and continue to shoot daggers at the doctor, which does nothing as he places the IV bag on a hanger above my head.

"I'm sorry, Mrs. Anthony, but you're severely dehydrated and we're going to need to keep you here for at least a few more hours before you're released."

"I'll drink some water," I tell him, tempted to rip the IV out of my hand and stab him with it.

"Get some sleep." He ignores me once more then walks away to speak with the nurse.

"This cannot be happening," I mumble, falling back against the bed and feeling my eyes suddenly grow heavy, making me wonder if they put something else in the IV.

WAKING TO THE sound of whispering, my eyes blink open slowly. The room is dark, with the only light coming from a TV in the corner, casting a blue glow throughout the room. As my eyes focus on the TV, I double blink. Jax's uncle, Nico, is standing with a group of officers in front of the house I had been taken to, and the woman in front of the camera is speaking, but the volume is so low I can't hear what she's saying as the cameraman pans from the woman to the truck that had been driving after us. Sitting up, I find the remote next to the bed and turn up the volume.

"The two women were then chased by this truck while trying to get away on a four-wheeler they took from one of the assailants. One captor is dead and the other is still missing. If you have any information regarding the whereabouts of the suspect, please call the number listed below," the woman says before the scene is gone.

Replaced by a man and woman sitting behind the desk at the news station, announcing, *"Tonight, you can watch Dan Seagan's special report about sex trafficking in the Nashville area."*

Pulling my eyes from the TV and sitting up, I reach for the phone next to the bed, dialing the only number I can think of that will lead me to Hope.

"Hello?" my aunt answers on the first ring.

"Aunt Marlene," I get out through a strangled breath, holding the phone closer to my ear. "Have you seen my mom?"

"Did, but she's gone now," she mutters, and I hear her light a cigarette. I'm sure she's sitting in her recliner, where she always is, with her feet propped up, smoking cigarette after cigarette and watching TV.

"Where's Hope?" I close my eyes, praying my mom didn't take her with her.

"Hope's with me. When are you coming to get her?"

"I'm in Tennessee," I whimper, not knowing exactly how far away I am from Kentucky.

"I know. Your mama was here when the news came on," she tells me.

Tears fill my eyes, but I refuse to let them fall. I refuse to let these people hurt me anymore. I wasn't surprised my mom told my aunt what happened or that she didn't care. My mom stopped caring about me when my dad died, when she no longer had to pretend my brother and I mattered to her more than her next high.

"I'm on my way. Please tell Hope I'll be there soon."

"I gotta work tomorrow night, so keep that in mind," she says right before the line goes dead. Setting the phone in its cradle, I rub my eyes.

My family is what most of America would classify as trailer trash. I hated that term growing up, but we were poor and lived in a trailer. There was a time in my life when I was okay with the kids at school calling me that, because I knew I might've lived in a trailer and been poor, but at least I had my family. Then, when I was seven, my dad died in a coal mining accident, leaving my older brother and me alone with my mom, who had an addiction to pain pills. Even though she was sick long before we lost my dad, we never suffered because of it. My dad always made sure we had food and clothing. We didn't have much, but we had each other. After he passed away, we lost everything.

"You're awake."

Looking over my shoulder at the open doorway, my gaze connects with Jax's concerned one. I don't know what to make of him. I still don't understand how someone who has just met me could show me more care in just a few hours than the people I have known my whole life ever have.

"I need to get to Hope," I say, placing my fingers on my throat, which I'm just noticing is dry and scratchy.

"I know, baby. I'm gonna take you," he says, stepping into the room.

Baby? Why do I like that? Why do I get warm all over every time he calls me that?

"Thank you." I close my eyes in relief then open them, saying, "I'll pay you back as soon as I get home."

"No," he rumbles, making me jump, which seems to cause his jaw to grind. "I mean that's not necessary," he says gently, shoving his hands into the front pockets of his jeans giving me a chance to really look at him.

I wasn't kidding when I said he's a giant. His shoulders are so wide I'm pretty sure I could fit twice between them. His hips are lean, his thighs thick, and his legs are long.

His head is covered in a ball cap, drawing attention to his eyes that seem hazel in the dark, and he has an angular jaw, full lips, and an almost perfect nose that has a slight tilt to it. "My mom and dad are here. Mom brought you some clothes if you want to change before we leave," he informs me, taking a step towards me then stopping and pulling his ball cap off his head, giving me the opportunity to see his dark brown hair for the first time, which is short on the sides and longer on top.

Standing and running my hands down the front of my dingy jeans, I look over his shoulder into the hall, where there's a woman with red hair standing next to a man who looks like an older version of Jax. The moment my eyes connect with hers, she steps into the room.

"Honey," the woman calls softly, "why don't you go wait in the hall with your dad while I help Ellie get changed?"

"Mom." He shakes his head, not taking his eyes from me.

"Come on, bud," the man, who I'm assuming is his dad, says, stepping slightly into the room.

Jax pulls in a breath then releases it, looking at me like he doesn't want to leave. Weirdly, I don't want him to either.

"I'll be right outside," he says after a couple beats.

"Sure," I whisper, fighting myself from going to him and begging him to stay.

"You can come back in once she's dressed," his mom tells him softly as he moves past her out of the room.

Once the door is closed, the room becomes even darker, but then the light comes on, causing me to squeeze my eyes closed in surprise.

5

"Oh crap, I'm sorry. I didn't even think," the woman mutters, and I see through my closed eyelids when the room goes dark once again.

"It's okay; you can turn it on."

"Are you sure?" she prompts.

"Yeah." When the lights turn back on, it takes just a moment for my eyes to adjust, and when they do, I watch Jax's mom step closer to me.

"I know my son didn't introduce us, but I'm Lilly, and you're Ellie, right?" she asks, studying me.

"Yes," I croak out and she frowns, walking to the bed. Picking up a pink cup off the side table, she brings it towards me, holding it out for me to take.

"Just take sips, honey," she says gently, with her hand under mine like I might drop the cup. "Is that better?"

"Yes, thank you," I say, surprised to hear my voice crack again, but this time with emotions from having someone look out for me.

Nodding, she takes the cup back and sets a bag on the bed.

"Jax said you were small, so I just grabbed some of my yoga clothes for you."

"Thank you," I mumble absently, watching her pull out a pair of black yoga pants and a tank with a jacket to go over it.

"Do you want to wash up a little in the bathroom?"

Following her gaze to a door I hadn't even noticed, I nod. Taking the stuff, she helps me into the small room murmuring, "I'll be out here if you need me," closing the door behind her.

Turning on the water I don't even look at myself in the mirror above the sink as I strip off my clothes and grab a few paper towels, soaking them. Scrubbing myself from head to toe, being careful of my hands, which are still sensitive from carrying a two-by-four around as a weapon.

Once I'm as clean as I'm going to get without a shower, I catch my reflection in the mirror and cringe. My dark hair is matted, my skin pale, and my brown eyes are sunken in, I look like hell run over. "You're alive," I remind myself, pulling on the yoga pants that are a little too long, but they are clean and thankfully fit. Putting on the tank, I cover it with the jacket, zipping it all the way up before slipping my sneakers back on and running a hand through my hair, watching as dried leaves and dirt fall to the floor. Giving up on getting the knots out, I pull it all up on top of my head and spin it into a bun, tucking the ends in so it stays in place.

"Everything fit," I say when I step out of the bathroom, finding Lilly sitting on the bed with her head bent, like she's deep in thought.

"I'm glad." She smiles softly then her head tilts to the side, studying me. "Jax said you have a daughter."

"I do." I nod, taking my old clothes to the waist basket and dropping them in.

"And your mom did this to you?" she asks, catching me off guard with her question, making my body go solid in response.

Licking my lips, I turn to look at her. "She did."

"Does she live near you?" she questions softly, looking me over.

"About twenty minutes away, with my aunt."

"So...your daughter's father?"

"He's dead," I say, feeling tears fill my eyes at the thought.

Hope isn't my biological daughter. Edward, my brother, and his girlfriend, Bonnie, were hit head-on by a drunk driver. Both died on impact. Hope survived with only a few scrapes. I was granted custody of her the next day on my ninetieth birthday, when she was just four weeks old.

"I'm sorry," she whispers quietly.

"It was a long time ago," I say, wrapping my arms around my waist, trying to keep myself together.

"Do you have a job back home?"

My body stiffens further and I feel my eyes narrow. I know people make assumptions about me all the time because of where I live and how I grew up, but I went to school and got my hairdressing license right after highschool and have been on my own since then. I've worked hard at making a life for me and Hope, so her future will be brighter than Edward's and mine. I know that's what he wanted for her, and for me.

"I do hair," I reply, just because I don't want to be rude after how nice she has been.

"I know this is going to sound completely outlandish, but have you ever thought about moving and starting over somewhere else?" she inquires softly.

Sure, I had thought about it, but as a single mother, I was only able to save a few dollars here and there. Having a child isn't cheap, and I refuse to use government assistance. My mother did it for years, even though she could have worked. "I'm only asking, because this is a nice place to live, a good place to raise a child."

"Maybe someday," I mutter, feeling uncomfortable.

"I was a single mother for awhile," she says, surprising me. "I know how difficult it is to raise a child without having people around you can lean on. Not that I'm saying you don't have that, but—"

"All I have is me," I cut her off. Yes, I have a few friends, but no one I can trust. Not really, anyways, and family…I don't have that either. It's always been just Hope and me.

Her eyes go soft and she stands from the bed. "You could move here. My friend owns a salon in town. He's always looking for help, and Jax already said you could stay with him until you got on your feet. He's hardly home anyways."

Stay with Jax?

Yeah, no thank you.

"We would all feel better knowing you're here—at least until the other guy is caught."

Oh, God. How did I forget about him? I don't know if he knows where I live, and what if something happens to Hope? Closing my eyes, I rub my forehead, feeling a headache coming on.

"I know you want to keep your daughter safe, and my son will make sure of it."

"I don't know." I open my eyes. This is too much to handle right now.

"Sometimes you have to jump off the ledge with both feet, honey. I know this is a scary time to be making big life changes, but I believe everything happens for a reason, and maybe…just maybe…you're supposed to take a chance on something new." She reaches out, rubbing my arm.

My grandma before she died told me, *Devour life without chewing, and pray that you don't choke.* Could I do that now? Take a chance and pray for the best? "Are you sure your friend needs help?" I hear myself ask without even realizing it.

She smiles then nods. "I'm positive."

"Maybe I have a concussion," I mutter, surprised I'm really thinking about doing this. It's not like me to take unnecessary risks.

"I'll be here for you whenever you need me, and I know my husband and daughter will do the same, along with Jax."

Oh, God. Jax. I'm not sure what to do with him, but I need to keep Hope safe, and the farther I get away from my family, the better, not only for her, but for me as well.

"Okay," I state.

"Okay?"

"Yes, I need to make sure my daughter is safe," I explain softly.

Her arms wrap around me in a hug and she mutters, "I promise things are going to be better now."

I'm not so sure about that. I feel like I just went from the frying pan into the fire.

Chapter 1

Jax

"THANK YOU AGAIN for taking me." Pulling my eyes from the road for a brief moment, I look at Ellie. Her head is resting against the window, her legs pulled up onto the seat, tucked near her ass, and her arms are wrapped tight around them. One thing I've noticed about her over the last few hours is she's always wrapping her arms around herself or tucking her body into a tight ball. It's like she's forcing herself to stay together.

"I told you I got you, baby," I say gently, wanting more than anything to take her hand in mine, but every time I touch her, she freezes up like she's waiting for me to strike out at her, and I would be lying if I said that didn't piss me the fuck off. It does; it feels like a slap in the face every time it happens.

"I know," she whispers, and the tears I hear in her voice cause a sharp pain in my chest.

Fuck.

"This is the turnoff." Her feet go to the floorboard and her hands to the dash as she sits up taller, moving her face closer to the windshield. We drive up a long dirt driveway with forest and the occasional broken down car on each side. When we make it to the top of the hill, a singlewide trailer comes into view, with junk cars and garbage piled up out front.

As soon as I come to a stop, she opens her door and hops out before

I can tell her to keep her little ass in the cab. I don't even know how I'm going to deal with the range of emotions that have settled over me since seeing her for the first time.

"Fucking Boom," I mutter, getting out behind her and doubling my steps until I'm able to reach her side, where I wrap my hand around her waist and pull her closer to me. She's so fucking tiny that the top of her dark head sits right at my chest. So fragile, from her too soft skin to her petite size. *And she's mine.*

"Took you long enough," a very large woman says, opening the front door to the trailer. Her thin blonde hair is pulled away from her face with a headband, and her large, round body is incased in what looks like a baggy dress with long sleeves. I know right away this must be Ellie's aunt Marlene, her mom's sister.

"Where's Hope?" Ellie asks from my side as I wrap my hand tighter around her to keep her in place.

Taking a puff off her cigarette Marlene tosses the butt into the yard while stepping back into the trailer as we come up the creaky wooden steps that lead inside.

"Where's Hope?" Ellie asks as we step into the small living room. Feeling a shiver slide through her and I give her side a squeeze reminding her that she's not alone.

"Hope's asleep in the back bedroom." Her aunt points down a long hall then looks at me. "Who's him?" she asks, but Ellie pushes past her and rushes down the hall, ignoring her question.

"Who you?"

Jesus. It takes everything in me to keep my mouth shut. Crossing my arms over my chest, I wait for Ellie, ignoring the woman, afraid of what I'll say if I speak.

"You a cop?"

Fuck me.

"I'm not a cop," I growl, wanting to tell her she shouldn't look relieved by that.

"That niece of mine has always acted like she's better than all of us. Figures she'd meet a guy who thought the same."

My fists clench and drop to my sides. I don't know much about Ellie, but there isn't a doubt in my mind that she is better than this dump and her fucked up family.

"Jax."

My gaze goes toward the open mouth of the hall and collides with Ellie, who is holding a little girl in her arms; her face is pressed to Ellie's chest, her long, dark hair hanging over Ellie's arm, and her legs wrapped around her side.

"What is it, baby?" I question, closing the distance between us.

"Can you hold her while I get her stuff?" she asks in a hushed tone.

"Sure," I mutter, and she slips the sleeping little girl into my arms. Her small, warm body presses close to my chest and I lift her higher, adjusting her against me.

"Hurry, baby," I tell Ellie as her eyes stay fixed on me. "Babe," I say, and she blinks then turns around, heading back down the hall, and my eyes drop to the tiny girl. I know she's three from the info Ellie gave me. Her skin is the same cream color as her mother's. Her cheeks are slightly rosy from sleep, her lips are in a small pout, and her long, dark lashes fan out across her cheeks. She's beautiful, and she hasn't even opened her eyes.

"Her dad never even seen her grow up," Marlene says, putting another cigarette in her mouth.

Looking down at the little girl in my arms, I imagine her being mine and never seeing her. The thought alone causes my heart to bleed and my arms to tighten around her. "Don't light that," I growl when she lifts a lighter to the cigarette hanging out of her mouth.

"It's my house."

"I don't give a fuck. You can wait until we're gone."

Her face screws up, but she pulls the cigarette out and closes her hand around it.

"Ready," Ellie says, carrying a large bag over one shoulder then a smaller diaper bag in her other hand. Taking the large bag from her and being careful not to wake Hope, I carry her outside to the truck. Once I have her buckled in the car seat I had my mom pickup when we were still in the hospital, I lift Ellie up into the cab and pull her seatbelt around her.

"Jax."

"Yeah, babe?" My hands stop and my gaze meets her beautiful brown eyes that are surrounded by long dark lashes.

"I can buckle myself in," she whispers, and my eyes drop to her mouth. She has a gap between her front teeth that I have become obsessed with since meeting her. Really, I'm obsessed with her mouth. Her lips are plump, the bottom; slightly fuller than the top, the pink so dark that I want to lean in for a taste, just to see if they're as soft and sweet as they look.

"You owe me for watching Hope," her aunt says from behind us, breaking the moment and causing a growl to vibrate my chest.

"Stay put." I growl, clicking her seatbelt into place, stepping back and slamming the door. Once I'm a few steps away, I set the locks and the alarm so I'll know if Ellie tries to get out then storm up the few stairs into the trailer. Pulling the door closed behind me, the small room turns almost black, the only light coming from a small window in the living room, and a smaller one above the sink in the dirty kitchen.

"What are you doing?" Marlene asks, and I can hear the nervousness in her voice as she backs away from me.

"I'm going to give you a chance to be honest with me. I'm going to ask you where Ellie's mother is, and I want you to tell me the truth. If you don't tell me where she is now and I find out later on that you knew her whereabouts and kept that from me, I'm going to make you pay for that mistake."

"You ain't the law. You can't talk to me like this," she says, putting her hands on her wide hips and looking toward the door.

"You're right. I'm not a cop, and that information should lead you into doing the smart thing," I snarl.

"She's my sister."

"I don't give a fuck if she's the fucking Pope. Tell me where she is."

"I don't know," she says quietly after a long moment.

"You sure you want that to be your final answer?" I ask her, turning toward the door.

"It's the truth."

"Remember I warned you," I say, opening the door and stepping down the rickety stairs to the grass.

"What about my money?"

"Get it from your sister," I tell her, clicking the alarm for my truck and swinging up inside. I'm so pissed that I can actually feel my heart pounding in my neck. I want to take a can of gasoline and light her damn trailer on fire.

"What did she say?" Ellie asks quietly from my side as I pull out onto the main road. Pulling my eyes from the asphalt, I look over at her quickly, seeing a sadness in her gaze that makes my fist tighten on the steering wheel.

"Nothing, baby."

"Jax."

"Ellie," I say in the same tone, feeling my lips twitch.

"I don't know what you could possibly think is funny right now," she huffs, and I see her cross her arms over her chest out of the corner of my eye, the action making me smile. *Fuck but she's cute.*

"So annoying," she mumbles under her breath, making me chuckle.

"Mama," I hear, and I look over my shoulder at Hope, whose eyes are open and locked on her mom in the front seat.

"Angel baby." Ellie pulls off her seatbelt, gets up on her knees, and leans over the backseat. Pulling off the side of the road, I put the truck in park, walk around, to help Ellie out, but before I get there, she's out and has the back door open, trying to get Hope from her car seat.

The moment she has Hope unbuckled and in her arms, sobs begin to wrack Ellie's small frame. Without thinking, I wrap my arms around both of them as a feeling of rightness settles in my gut.

"It's okay, Mama." Hope pats her mom's back, making Ellie cry harder.

"I know, Angel," Ellie says, pulling her face away from Hope's neck and kissing her forehead. "I missed you."

"I missed you too. Gwama said you were workin'," she says, putting her hand on her mom's cheek and looking into her face.

"I was, Angel, and guess what."

"What?" Hope asks, and my heart does another tug when both their faces light up with smiles so bright they steal the air right out of my lungs.

"Mommy has a new job."

"Yay!" She laughs, and Ellie places her hand on the back of Hope's head and dips her backwards, whispering in her ear.

"I love you, Angel baby."

"Lub you, Mama," she says then her eyes come to me and she tilts her head to the side.

"Hope, this is Jax," Ellie says, and I watch her cheeks get pink as she realizes her body is pressed against the length of mine. "Jax, this is Hope." She steps away, turning so Hope is facing me.

"It's nice to meet you, Hope."

"You too, Ax." She smiles, showing off a gap between her front teeth that makes her even more beautiful.

"All right, Angel, get back in your car seat," Ellie tells her, and she climbs up into the seat then locks herself in place, like she's done it a million times before. Not trusting her, I check to make sure it's secure then tap the end of her nose, making her smile before I shut the door.

Once I'm back behind the wheel, I head towards Ellie's place so we can pick up her stuff. Do I feel shitty I told my mom to find a way to get Ellie to Nashville, even if she had to use her fear against her? A little, but at the end of the day, she will be under my roof, so fuck it. All's fair in love and war, right?

"Turn here," Ellie says, bringing me out of my thoughts. Frowning, I turn and enter a large trailer park. I know places like these; rent's cheap, making it easy for everyone and anyone to live here. Following Ellie's directions, we pull up in front of a small singlewide trailer. Just from the outside, I can tell she is one of the few people in the park who takes pride in her place, judging by the flowers on her small front porch, which have died in her absence, and the colorful floral flag hanging off to the side of the front door, welcoming anyone who might come for a visit.

Shutting down the truck, I hop out and round the hood, taking in my surroundings. Two trailers down, there are a group of guys sitting outside in lawn chairs, drinking beer. A little farther down from them, I watch a man pass a small bag of something off to a kid who's probably no older than seventeen.

"From now on, wait 'til I open your door," I tell Ellie, taking a sleeping Hope from her arms.

"Why?" She frowns, shutting the door.

"Because my mom would kick my ass if I didn't."

"Oh." She presses her lips together like she's trying not to smile, making me want to lean in and kiss her.

"Ready?" I ask knowing I cant do what I want, not yet anyways.

"Ready." She sighs, going to the porch, lifting the edge of the mat, and pulling out a key.

"Are you kidding me?" I growl, looking at the key in her hand.

"What?" she asks, opening the door and stepping inside.

"Ellie, baby, you do not leave a key to your house in such an obvious place. That's basically an invite to anyone who comes over to walk inside and steal all your shit."

"Nothing has ever happened before." She shrugs.

"Thank fuck but there's a first time for everything," I tell her, trying to gentle my voice, which is hard to do considering how pissed I am, knowing a single mother is living in a place like this with a key under her motherfucking doormat.

"I won't do it again," she says, reading my face.

Nodding, I lay Hope down on the small couch by the door then look around.

The place is small but clean and homey. A small flat screen TV sits in front of the couch on a stand with tons of picture frames scattered across the surface, most containing shots of Ellie and Hope, but in a few, are pictures of a man holding a baby. There's one with the same man, but this time his arm is wrapped around a woman as she looks down at the small bundle in her arms while he smiles at the camera. I wonder absently if that was Ellie's ex, but still can't drag enough courage to the surface to ask.

Pulling my eyes away from the photos, I take in the rest of the space. A stylish chair sits in the corner, adding color to the room, and it matches the drapes on the windows. In the kitchen is a small dining table, with two chairs that are old but still fit with the decor.

"I don't know what I should bring," Ellie mumbles, walking into the kitchen and looking around.

"Whatever we don't take now, we can come back for," I tell her softly, moving to her side. "My place has everything you'll need for now."

"Are you really sure about us staying with you?" she asks, tucking a piece of hair behind her ear. "I know your dad said he could get us an apartment in town."

"I'm sure." I feel my chest vibrate in annoyance. I don't want her or Hope out of my sight. And God, I love my dad, but I was ready to pummel him when he suggested that. "Like my mom said, I'm hardly home. I work a lot, and my place already has security set up. It's the safest place for you both."

Her eyes go to the couch, and I know without Hope there wouldn't be a chance in hell Ellie would be moving in with me.

"I really do appreciate it."

"Baby," I murmur, watching her eyes slide half closed, "I'm glad I can help."

Licking her lips, her eyes go soft then move to the couch again.

"Hope will want her bed."

"Show me where it is and I'll put it in the truck now, while you get your clothes and stuff packed up."

Nodding, she heads down a short hallway and stops at a room that is smaller than my closet at home. There isn't much in the space, just a small, child size bed and a white dresser, along with stuffed animals scattered over a pink rug. "I'll get this; you go start packing," I rumble, rubbing her arms. Looking over her shoulder at me, her lips part when she realizes how close I am.

"I...I'm g-gonna start packing," she stammers then slips under my arm and heads down the hall. Following her with my eyes until she's out of sight, I smile. She may not want to admit it, but I know she feels the same pull I do.

Heading into Hope's room, I pull her pink bedding and mattress off her bed then pick up the frame and move it out to the living room, checking to make sure she's still sleeping before taking it to the truck.

Once we get started, it doesn't take long to get everything packed up and in the back of my truck. We will have to come back in a week to clean the rest out but we got everything they will need for now.

"Baby, we're here," I whisper, running my finger down Ellie's cheek, not really wanting to wake her up. She had fallen asleep with her head on my thigh ten minutes after we left the restaurant we stopped at after getting gas. I don't even think she realized what she was doing when she laid down. I know she has to be exhausted after everything that happened.

Blinking up at me, she wipes the corner of her mouth then sits up quickly, looking around.

"This is your house?"

Looking out the front windshield, I wonder why she looks so scared. It's not the nicest house on the street, but when it came on the market a year ago for a hundred grand under market value, I had to buy it, and have been slowly fixing it up since then. "Yeah."

"It's really nice." She swallows then looks at the other houses on the block, which look similar to mine.

"It's your home now too," I say softly, wanting to get rid of that look on her face, the one saying she feels like she doesn't belong here.

"Until I have enough money to get somewhere else," she murmurs, rubbing her eyes.

Ignoring that comment, I grit my teeth and get out of the truck before I can tell her there is no way in hell she's ever moving out.

"Get a grip before you scare her the fuck off," I growl under my breath, opening her door and helping her out. I then open Hope's door and grin when her face lights up.

"You wiv in a castle!" She smiles, unhooking her belt, catching me off guard when she throws herself at me.

Looking back toward my house, I guess it kind of does look like a castle. The old grey brick Victorian with two round rooms on each side of the house gives the look of towers, the white scalloping along the edges, and in the middle is a window that resembles a lookout point.

"I guess I do," I tell her, setting her on the ground.

"Sooo cooool," she breathes, peering up at me with her big brown eyes, making my chest ache.

Pulling my hat off, I turn toward Ellie. "Why don't I take you guys inside and you can look around, while I bring everything in?"

"Are you sure?" she asks, picking up Hope then looking in the back of the truck at all of her stuff, most of which is in black garbage bags.

"I'm sure. Plus, you really should be in bed resting after everything that has happened," I say quietly, taking her hand and leading her up the front steps, letting her go long enough to open the door and walk over to the keypad to shut off the alarm. "The code is zero-four-zero-three. I want the alarm on anytime I'm not in the house with you." Watching her nod, I take her hand again and lead her through the house, showing her the living room, kitchen, and downstairs bathroom before moving her to the stairs. "You can have your pick of rooms."

"Where's your room?" she asks when we make it to the second-floor landing.

"At the end of the hall." I nod my head toward my room and she looks in the opposite direction. Dropping my hand, she sets Hope on the ground, opening the door in front of us, almost the farthest from mine, which makes me bite back a smile. A few feet and a couple doors between us isn't going to matter in the long run, but I'm willing to give her the sense of space for now. "We'll take this room."

"There's plenty of space for Hope to have her own room," I tell her softly.

"I'd feel better if she was close, at least for now," she replies just as quietly, taking the piece of hair that is constantly falling out of the bun on top of her head and tucking it back behind her ear.

"Mama, I wanna wiv in the tower like a real pwincess."

Turning my head, I see Hope has opened the door at the opposite end of the hall from mine, the second room that has a round section that juts out into the front yard, with large windows, and a seat underneath them.

"You don't want to sleep with me?" Ellie asks her, and Hope's face scrunches up adorably like she's trying to think about it then she shakes her head.

"I'm not a baby, wemember?"

"No, I guess you're not." Ellie sighs then looks at me, biting her bottom lip. "Are you sure you don't mind us taking up two rooms?"

"Positive." I smile, and she looks toward the end of the hall at my door then back toward hers, and my smile gets bigger. I can practically hear the wheels in her head turning. "Why don't you guys get cleaned up while I bring everything in?" I say, opening the door to the bathroom.

"Bafftub! Bafftub!" Hope jumps up and down, squealing, making me laugh.

"I'll bring your clothes up first. That way, you'll have something clean to change into afterward."

"Thanks, Jax," Ellie whispers.

"No problem, baby," I tell her then look down at Hope when she grabs my hand, tugging on it.

"Mama's not a baby." She giggles then runs into the bathroom, making me laugh.

Leaning on the doorjamb, I watch as the two of them turn on the tub then pull myself away, closing the door when they both take off their shoes.

I have never really put much thought into having kids, but I could get used to hearing Hope giggle. Moving downstairs, I pull out my cellphone and press send on my mom's number when I see she's called a few times.

"Don't you know how worried we've been?" she scolds after the first ring.

"You knew I was driving." I know my dad isn't really included in that 'we'. It's all my mom; she's always worried.

"You have Bluetooth," she mutters, sounding annoyed.

"Ellie and Hope were sleeping, and I'm not gonna answer the phone with the girls in the truck."

"Oh, God, it's really happening, isn't it?" she whispers, making me frown.

"What's happening?"

"Nothing," she says quickly. "How's Ellie feeling, and what's Hope like?"

"Ellie's tired, but I think she's okay. Hope is cute. You'll love her."

"I wish it wasn't so late," she grumbles, making me smile.

"You can come over tomorrow. If I know Ellie at all, she's gonna want to head over to the salon in the morning."

"I can take her," she says immediately as I pull two of the bags from the back and take them inside.

"Thanks, Mom," I say sincerely.

"I'm happy to help."

"Where's Dad?"

"He's right here. Hold on," she says, and I'm sure she is sitting on my dad's lap, or tucked into his side, where she always is.

"Hey, bud," I hear his deep voice come over the line.

"Hey, Dad. You busy tomorrow?"

"Nothing's on the schedule. What's up?"

"I need to get Ellie some wheels. You got time to go with me?"

"Sure, I'll bring your mom over in the morning, since I can tell she's chomping at the bit to meet Hope, and we'll head out from there."

"Thanks," I mumble, taking the two bags up the stairs and setting them in bedroom Ellie chose.

"Anytime. Get some rest and we'll see you in the morning."

"See you then," I say, hanging up and heading back outside. My phone vibrates again, and I look at the screen and shake my head when

I see Mellissa's number pop up, with the emoji of a butcher knife that my sister Ashlyn put next to her name. Mellissa and I dated in high school, and hooked up over the summer one time. I thought maybe she had changed with age and college, but she was a bigger bitch now than she was back then. Pressing ignore on her call, I put my phone in my pocket and take the rest of the stuff into the house. Once I get everything upstairs, both girls are in Ellie's room lying in bed.

"Thank you for bringing everything in," Ellie says sleepily.

"No problem." I shrug, watching as she gets out of bed, and that's when I realize she's only wearing a shirt that hangs down to the middle of her thighs. My eyes track her as she walks toward me. Taking in the creamy expanse of her legs and the way her hair looks down over her shoulders, I can picture her walking toward me naked, her hair brushing the tips of her breasts.

"Ax, I wuv your bafftub," Hope says, bringing me out of my perusal of her mother.

Clearing my throat, I look around Ellie to Hope, who is now standing on the bed and bouncing.

"I'm glad, sweetheart," I say, and she smiles then hops off the bed, luckily landing on her feet as I rush towards her, feeling my heart in my throat. Picking her up off the ground, I mutter, "Be careful." Which only seems to make her laugh.

"No jumping on the bed, Angel," Ellie says, and Hope grins then wiggles out of my hold, running out of the room, past her mom.

"She's a handful," Ellie mumbles, looking from the door to me again.

"She's sweet." Besides, I was already getting the feeling I was going to have my hands full with both her *and* her mother. "You look beat."

"I am, but Hope wants to sleep in her bed, so I'm gonna go get it set up for her," she says yawing turning towards the door.

"Already done," I say to her back.

Stopping, she turns to look at me over her shoulder, and something works within her gaze, but her head dips before I'm able to decipher it.

"Thanks," she mumbles, walking out of the room. Following her to Hope's door, I stop behind her. "She's already asleep," she whispers, tilting her head back to look at me. Tipping my chin toward her, I place my hand on her shoulder then reach around her with my other hand to shut off the light. "You even found her a nightlight," she whispers, almost like she's in awe.

Roaming my hand down her arm, I rest it on her waist, giving her a squeeze. This time she doesn't flinch, but shivers. "Go to bed, babe you need to rest."

"Okay." She swallows, and I notice a pinkness to her cheeks that wasn't there before as she stops at her bedroom door.

"I'm right down the hall if you need me. Do you remember the code for the house?"

"Zero-four-zero-three," she says, nodding.

"Good girl." I smile, reaching up and running my finger down her cheek, watching her eyes slide half closed from my touch. "Mom and Dad will be here in the morning."

"Oh."

"Mom said she would take you to the salon if you want to go."

"I do." Her face brightens.

"I had a feeling you would want to." I smile as she yawns again. "Get some sleep."

"Goodnight, Jax," she says quietly, walking into her room.

"Night, Ellie," I murmur, watching her door close before heading down the hall to my room. The minute I'm inside, I kick off my boots and take off my jeans and tee then go into the bathroom. Something inside of me settles into place…something I didn't even know I had been looking for all along.

I knew about the 'Boom'; every man in my family knew about it from the time they were little. Most of us chalked it up to some old wives tale, but that doesn't mean I hadn't been hoping it would happen to me one day. I grew up watching the way the men in my family were with their wives, knew the strength of their relationships and the bonds they shared, how rare it actually was to have something run so deep, something that nothing could ever come between.

I know I now have that under my roof; I just need to convince Ellie of the same thing. I need to show her our future could be beautiful if she'd give it a chance. With that thought, I go to bed hoping that one day Ellie will be climbing into bed next to me while our kids sleep down the hall.

Chapter 2

Ellie

OPENING MY EYES, I close them again when I realize I haven't been dreaming. I'm really at Jax's house in Tennessee. Sitting up and putting my feet on the floor, I stretch before standing. I don't want Hope to wake up Jax, and my daughter—though I love her more than anything in this world—is loud. I don't think she has ever gotten the concept of her *inside voice*. Opening my door and looking down the hall towards Jax's room, I see his door is open, but he's not awake. At least, I don't think so.

His chest is rising and falling steadily. His arm muscles are flexed, one over his head, the other draped across his bare abdomen. All I can see is beautiful golden skin over muscle…lots and lots of muscle. Pulling my eyes from him and tiptoeing down the hall, I make it to Hope's room and go inside, shutting the door.

Seeing Hope asleep in her bed on her tummy with her hand pressed under her cheek, I walk to the only other piece of furniture in the room, an old rocking chair, and sit down. My life with Hope hasn't always been easy, but we've always been happy. I have always made sure she has what she needs, and a little extra when I could afford it, but last night, when we pulled up in front of Jax's house and she whispered to him that he lived in a castle, I knew I needed to do more. She deserves to live in a house, not a trailer park where drugs are dealt right outside her bedroom window. She deserves a backyard and a good school, with friends who are good kids. I'm not sure what is going to happen with us living in Tennessee, but I vow I will work harder to give Hope a life completely different than the one I had growing up.

"Mama?"

"Hey, Angel." I smile, opening my arms to her as she walks sleepily toward me. "Did you sleep okay?" I ask, tucking her head under my chin and wrapping my arms around her, rocking her gently.

"Like a pwincess." She smiles, tipping her head back to look at me. "I'm hungwy."

I know Jax said to make ourselves at home, but I still feel awkward using his stuff when he isn't around. It feels personal...*way* too personal. "Can I have pancakes?"

Crap. I'm not gonna starve my daughter, so I need to pull my big girl panties up and get over whatever reservations I have with being in Jax's house, especially since this is our home for the time being, too.

"You have to be very quiet until we get downstairs. Can you do that?"

"Like a mouse," she whispers, making me smile.

"Okay, little mouse, let's go," I tell her, standing up and taking her hand in mine.

"Jax is sweepin'," she loudly whispers when we step into the hall.

"Remember, quiet as a mouse," I say, and her nose scrunches up and down a few times like a mouse would do, and I grin.

Getting to the kitchen, I lift her up, set her on the counter, and then look around.

Jax's house is nice, but you can tell he's slowly trying to fix it up. Cans of paint and different tiles sit in the corner next to a backdoor I hadn't noticed last night. The upper cabinets don't match the lower ones, and the linoleum floors are peeling up, completely gone in some spots. The fridge is new, stainless steel, with some kind of computer on the front, but the other appliance are old and white. The one thing that's completed is the countertops. They aren't granite, but look like concrete that has specks of glass imbedded in them. Looking around, I can tell that one day, when he gets around to finishing everything, it will be amazing.

"What are you doing?" Hope giggles, bringing me out of my perusal of the kitchen.

Smiling at her, I shrug then begin opening the cupboards one at a time until I come across the stuff necessary to make pancakes.

"Are you ready to be my mixer?" I ask her, putting some flour in the bowl and handing her a spoon.

"Yep." She grins, stirring the flour, causing it to fly up out of the bowl and hit us both in the face. "Uh oh." She covers her mouth with the spoon still in her hand, flinging flour at me and dumping some on her in the process. Then she begins to giggle louder, her little body shaking with the force of it.

Narrowing my eyes, I set my hands on my hips. "You did that on purpose."

"I didn't. I pwomise."

"You did." I laugh then tickle her while kissing her all over her face, making her squirm in my arms.

"Looks like I'm just in time." Freezing in place, I lift my head and meet Jax's sleepy gaze.

"We woke you. I'm so sorry," I mumble, standing to my full height. I try to ignore the fact he's shirtless and his hair is rumpled from sleep, giving me a visual of what it would look like if I were to run my hand through it.

You do not need that visual, Ellie, I scold myself.

"You didn't. This house is too quiet; I could get use to waking up to the sounds I heard this morning." He smiles, and I feel my cheeks heat up when his eyes drop to my legs. I know I have shorts on, but the shirt is so long that it hides them. His eyes turn darker then travel up, meeting mine again before dropping to my mouth when I pull my bottom lip between my teeth.

"We're makin' pancakes, Ax," Hope chimes in, and his eyes go to her, the heat disappearing, and softness enters them.

"I love pancakes. What's your favorite kind?"

"Ones wiff syrup." She grins.

"I like chocolate chips in mine," he tells her, making her eyes light up like he just told her there is a real life unicorn in the backyard and she gets to ride it.

"Chocowate chips," she repeats then looks at me and frowns. I have never made her pancakes with anything in them, and apparently she thinks I've been holding out on her.

"We can make them with chocolate chips another time, after I have a chance to go to the store," I promise her.

"We have chips, baby." Pulling my gaze from Hope, I meet his again. "Like I said last night, use anything you want," he says, picking up a dishtowel and smiling while wiping off my face then Hope's.

"Thank you," I murmur. I swear the only words I have really spoken to him have been thank you. He's constantly doing things that are sweet and catch me off guard. I'm not use to anyone being nice.

"So can I have chocowate in my pancakes?" Hope asks, making me laugh.

Leaning in, I kiss her chubby cheek and whisper, "Yes, you can have them in yours."

"Yay." She smiles, rubbing her face against mine like a cat.

Feeling something strange coming from Jax, I turn my head, seeing a look in his eyes that sends a shiver through me. It's tender and dark, but so soft, and I wonder what caused it.

Clearing his throat and running his hand over his jaw, he walks across the kitchen and pulls down a bag of chocolate chips from the cupboard, handing them to me.

"Thanks." When I smile, his hand lifts and he runs his fingers down the side of my face then looks at Hope, tapping the end of her nose, making her grin before he moves to the coffee pot and starts it up.

"Do you want a cup of coffee?"

"Sure." I nod, watching as he pulls a mug down from above the coffee maker. Forcing myself to look away from him, I go to the fridge and pull out milk and eggs to add them to the bowl. Once everything is mixed, Jax sets a large griddle on the counter and plugs it in.

I raise a brow at him and he smiles then shrugs. "My sister comes over for breakfast quiet a bit, and we always have pancakes.

"You gots a sister?" Hope asks.

"Yep, her name is Ashlyn. She works at the dentist office in town. I'm sure you'll meet her soon."

"I wanna sister," Hope says, looking at me then back to Jax, the corners of her mouth lifting mischievously.

Is my three-year-old seriously trying to hook us up?

"Maybe one day, sweetheart," Jax rumbles, raking his eyes over me, causing my pulse to spike and the space between my legs to tingle.

"Jax."

Jumping at the sound of a woman's voice, I turn to find a beautiful brunette wearing a button down silky-looking shirt, a tight skirt, and heels striding into the kitchen as she looks in her purse. When her head lifts, her eyes stop on me.

"Ellie," she breathes, catching me off guard when she wraps her arms around me. Unsure what to do, I pat her back awkwardly as she rocks us back and forth.

"I... Do I know you?" I mumble, frowning at Jax, whose body is shaking with silent laugher.

"Oh, God, I'm sorry." She pulls away. "I'm Ashlyn. I probably should have said that before I mauled you, right?," she lets out in one breath while laughing.

"It's okay. It's nice to meet you."

"You wook wike a pwincess," Hope breathes, and Ashlyn's body turns toward her and her face lights up.

"You must be Hope." Hope nods and Ashlyn steps forward. As she runs her hand over Hope's hair, she tells her, "I think you're the one who looks like a princess."

"I have a princess bed, and now a princess room in a castle," she informs her, smiling from ear to ear.

"You're a very lucky princess."

"I know, and now we're having chocolate chips for breakfast." Hope bounces where she sits on the counter.

"Chocolate chips?" she asks, looking at Jax.

"Jax just told Hope that his favorite pancakes have chocolate chips in them, so now Hope wants to try them," I explain to her while Jax moves, giving my side a squeeze before pulling down another coffee mug from the cupboard.

"Ahhh. Well, chocolate chip pancakes are my favorite too. Do you mind if I stay and have one?"

"Mama, can—" Hope pauses then looks at Ashlyn again.

"Hope, this is my sister, Ashlyn. Ashlyn, you already know Princess Hope," Jax introduces them.

"I do." Ashlyn curtsies, making Hope giggle and me smile.

"Here, Ash." He hands her a cup of coffee, which she takes and nudges his shoulder with hers, muttering, "Thanks."

Watching the two of them, I know that if things had been different, if my brother had lived, this is what our lives would have been like. We were always close, and after my dad passed away, we came to depend on each other even more.

"Mama, can Ashlyn stay?" Hope asks, pulling me from my thoughts.

"Of course." I smile at her, dipping the ladle in the mix and pouring it on the griddle.

"The key to the perfect chocolate chip pancake is the sprinkling of the chips," Jax tells Hope, picking her up off the counter, holding her on his hip. "Do you think you can help sprinkle them?"

"Yes." She nods vigorously, sticking her hand into the bag. She dumps a handful of them on one pancake before he can show her what to do, making him chuckle.

"Like this, sweetheart," he says quietly, making a smiley face on one, and then a heart on another. Watching, she leans her head on his shoulder, and my heart flutters inside my chest so hard it feels like a bird beating against my ribcage.

"My mom was saying you're a hairstylist."

Pulling my eyes from Hope and Jax, I look at Ashlyn, who is leaning with her elbows on the countertop, her coffee cup between her hands.

"Yeah, for a few years." I nod, picking up my cup and taking a drink of coffee, wondering how Jax knew exactly how I liked it without even asking me.

"You have great hair." She smiles, and I self-consciously run my hand down my tangled strands.

"I'm sure it looks crazy right now. I didn't take the time last night to find my blow dryer after I washed it," I mumble, and she shakes her head.

"It looks sexy, wild," she assures me, which catches me off guard. Most of my life, I have been surrounded by women who are quick to cut you down or give a backhanded compliment. But there was no malice in her eyes when Ashlyn spoke. I'm getting the feeling the Mayson's are all just very good people, and I really need good people in my life right now.

"Thank you," I say for what feels like the billionth time in the last seventy-two hours.

"Just speaking the truth, girl." She grins then looks at Hope, who is laughing at something Jax said. "She's really adorable, and seems to have already wrapped big, bad Jax Mayson around her tiny little finger," she whispers, winking at me.

Looking at Jax talking softly to Hope, I wonder how often he does this kind of thing. *For all I know, he could have women with kids over all the time*, I think, while something I don't like settles in the pit of my stomach.

"Who's ready for pancakes?" Jax asks.

"I am!" Hope yells loudly, making him chuckle.

"What happened to my little mouse?" I ask her, and she wiggles her nose at me over his shoulder.

"Inside voice, Angel," I remind her softly.

"Okay, Mama." She sighs.

"Do you have a table?" I ask Jax, looking around and trying to remember if I saw one last night when he showed us around the house.

"No. Shit," he mutters, setting Hope back on the counter.

"You said a naudy word," she tells him.

"I meant crud," he says, trying to look mollified but failing.

Her head tilts to the side, studying him, then she looks at me. "Mama, is crud a bad word?"

"No, Angel." I shake my head at her, pressing my lips together to keep from laughing when she starts mumbling "crud" under her breathe over and over again, making Jax grimace. One thing I learned early on is never tell a three-year-old not to say something, because suddenly that becomes their favorite word.

"I don't have a dining table."

"It's okay; we can eat here," I assure him, watching as Ashlyn goes to one of the cabinets and pulls down plates.

"I'll pick up some stools for the island today while I'm out with my dad," he says then looks around, his eyes going to the stuff on the floor.

"And I'll get this stuff cleaned up too."

"Jax," I say softly, waiting for his eyes to come to me. "It's really okay. Please, don't do anything. You've already done too much."

"Ellie—"

He starts to say something, but is cut off when, "Honey!" is yelled through the house.

"Fuck, I need to take everyone's keys back," he grumbles, making me laugh, causing a smile to twitch his lips.

"You said a naudy word," Hope pauses then adds, "again."

His chest expands on a deep breath and his face softens when he looks at her, muttering, "Sorry, sweetheart," as his parents walk into the kitchen.

"Ellie," Lilly says in greeting, giving me a warm hug.

"Hi." I smile then turn slightly to receive a hug from his dad, Cash, whom I met in the hospital before Jax took me to get Hope.

"How are you holding up, honey?" he asks gently while Lilly moves to Jax, kissing his cheek.

"Good," I say sincerely then pick Hope up off the counter. "I would like you guys to meet Hope. Hope, this is Jax and Ashlyn's dad and mom, Cash and Lilly."

"Hi." Hope smiles shyly, leaning her head on my shoulder.

"It's nice to finally meet you, Hope," Lilly says with a soft look on her face while reaching out, running her hand down Hope's cheek.

"Hi, Hope." Cash wraps his arm around his wife's back, pulling her closer to his side.

"Ax said naudy words," she tells his parents, and I pull my bottom lip into my mouth as Ashlyn starts to laugh at my side and Jax groans, tilting his head back.

"He did, did he?" Lilly frowns over her shoulder at her son.

"Two times," she says, holding up three fingers, the third one coming up because her little fingers are so chubby.

"Are we supposed to tattle?" I ask her, and she frowns while shaking her head. "Good, now are you ready to eat?" I lift a brow and she nods, so I set her back on the counter, since there is no table, and cut up her pancake, placing it next to her.

"Here, sweetheart," Jax says, giving her a Solo cup with orange juice in it.

I give him an appreciative look, and he shrugs then asks, "Are you going to eat something?"

"I'm going on a diet, so I'll have a banana or something," I tell him absently, watching Hope eat.

"Why are you going on a diet?" He frowns, checking me out and making me blush as his eyes get darker. "You look perfect."

"I realized how out of shape I was when…" I stop and look at Hope, not wanting her to hear what happened. "I just need to get into better shape," I whisper.

"I can teach you some self-defense stuff," he says quietly.

My eyes run over him and I feel my cheeks heat again. He's not just in good shape; his body is perfect. I doubt he has an ounce of fat on him. Pulling my eyes from his abs, I look into his eyes.

"I just want to be able to run without feeling like I'm having a stroke," I say, watching his jaw clench.

"You won't need to run again," he growls.

"That may be true, but I need to know for myself that I can," I tell him, reaching out and squeezing his bicep. His eyes drop to my hand and his body relaxes.

"I'd still like to show you some stuff," he presses.

"All right," I mutter then look around the kitchen, seeing everyone watching us. My eyes stop on Lilly, whose eyes are on my hand, which I didn't realize is now against his chest, over his heart. Pulling it away quickly, I mumble an apology and step away from him, going to Hope's side.

"Are you finished, Angel?" I ask her, needing to get away from Jax.

"Yes." She smiles with chocolate around her mouth.

"Let's get you cleaned up." I laugh, pulling a paper towel off the holder and wiping her face.

"Can I have a baff?"

"Tonight," I tell her, picking her up off the counter and turning to face the room of people, who are still watching us. "We're gonna go get ready."

"Sure, honey," Lilly says getting a coffee mug while Cash nods, and Jax just stands with his arms crossed over his chest and a frown on his face.

"It was nice meeting you, Ashlyn." I smile as I pass her.

"We'll have coffee sometime soon."

"I'd like that." I nod and head up to the second floor, where I get Hope ready first, in a pair of leggings, a sweater dress, and her ballet flats. Going to my room, I dig through the garbage bags of clothes until I find my trusty black jeans that always look perfect, a black t-shirt that scoops in the front just enough to give a hint of cleavage, my black ankle boots, and a chunky silver and turquoise necklace that makes the outfit look more dressy.

"Let's go brush our teeth and hair." I hold out my hand to Hope, who is sitting on the bed, playing with her favorite doll.

Walking across the hallway, I notice Jax's door is closed, but I can hear him talking loudly to someone on the other side. Closing the bathroom door, I give Hope her toothbrush while I fix her hair into a French braid. Once she's done, I brush my teeth while looking myself over, seeing sleep has done wonders. The bags under my eyes are gone, and Ashlyn was right; my hair actually looks good with crazy waves. Taking my hair serum, I squeeze some into my palm, using it just on the ends to tame them a bit. All I use on my face is some mascara and a little blush.

"Can I have makeup?" Hope asks, watching me.

"How about lip-gloss?"

She nods, pulling one of the pink ones from my makeup bag and putting it on herself, so I bend to her level and let her put some on me as well. "What do you think?"

"You look pwetty." She smiles, patting my cheek.

"So do you." I tell her giving her a kiss.

When I open the bathroom door, Jax is standing in the hall leaning against the wall with his phone in his hand, frowning at something on the screen. When his head lifts and our eyes meet, I look down at Hope.

"Why don't you go grab a couple of your dolls to take with us, Angel?" I say, and then watch as she heads to her room before looking at Jax again and asking, "Is everything okay?"

"Yeah, baby, I just wanted to see if you need any money before I take off."

"What?" I ask, feeling something strange creep over me, making my insides turn with unease.

"I know your purse is gone, and it'll take a few days to get a new card from the bank. I don't know if you need to get anything from the store for you or Hope."

"Oh," I breathe out. "I didn't even think about that. I need to see about getting a new ID. I have the debit card from my savings account that has about four thousand dollars in it, which can hold us over until I get everything else worked out," I mutter absently. I can't believe I forgot my purse is gone. I didn't have much in it, maybe forty dollars, my cellphone, and my wallet with my bank card. I don't even have a credit card in my name.

"Are you sure you don't want some cash just in case?"

"I'm sure," I say, shaking my head, when Hope comes out of her room with her doll and doll stroller. "Millie wants to go for a walk,

Mama."

"Well, you're gonna have to wait until we get back here later to take her for a walk."

"But she really wants to go," she pouts.

"Hope," I say her name in my 'mom voice', tilting my head to the side and waiting for her to take the stroller back into the room before shaking my head and meeting Jax's gaze again.

"Are you gonna be okay with my mom?" he asks, reaching out and touching my hand so briefly I wonder if it even happened.

"Of course, your mom seems really nice."

"If you need me, just call."

"I'm sure we'll be okay, and that won't be necessary," I assure him.

"I know, but call anyways."

"You know I don't have a phone, right?" I ask softly.

"Sh—" His eyes move to Hope, who walks out to stand next to me, and then his eyes sweep up to meet mine again. "I mean, I'll get you one today."

"I can get my own phone."

"You're gonna be busy. I don't mind getting one," he says gently.

Pulling in a deep breath, I let it out slowly. I'm not used to anyone looking out for me, but maybe it's time I learn to accept help from other people.

"Okay, but I'll give you the money back for it when I get home. Can you make sure it's not more than fifty? I need to stick to a budget."

"Sure," he agrees immediately, making me feel like that was way too easy. I don't know Jax very well, but I'm getting the feeling he's the kind of guy who's used to getting his way, even if it's by plowing you over.

"Also, here," he says, handing me some kind of bar in a shiny wrapper.

"What's this?" I frown, flipping it over and reading what's in it.

"You need to eat."

"This has almost a thousand calories in it," I tell him, holding it back towards him. If I'm going to get in better shape, I'll need to lose a little bit of weight. In order to do that, I will need to keep under around thirteen hundred calories a day. Eating that bar would leave me just a few messily calories for the rest of the day.

"It's good for you."

"Thank you, but I'll just grab a banana on the way out," I say, holding the bar closer to him until he takes it back.

"Ellie, you need to eat," he insists.

"I will."

"You need to eat something more than a banana. Your body needs protein to run more efficiently."

"You're annoying," I mumble, snatching the bar from him, ripping it open, and taking a large bite, which I chew twice before shoving the rest back at him and running to the bathroom, spitting it out in the toilet. It tastes like chalk and peanut butter—not a good combo, if you ask me. How anyone would willingly eat that, I don't even know.

When I step back out into the hall after rinsing my mouth out and brushing my teeth again, both Hope and Jax are laughing hysterically.

"Do you eat that crap?" I ask Jax, and he grins, his body still shaking with laughter.

"Yeah, before workouts." He chuckles.

"Why in the world would you waste perfectly good calories on that garbage?" I ask, and he places his hand on his stomach and laughs harder while Hope giggles.

Rolling my eyes at them, I ask Hope, "Are you ready to go?"

"Yep." She smiles, taking my hand and tugging me toward the stairs. When we reach the first floor, Cash and Lilly are waiting at the bottom, both smiling strangely at us.

"Is everything okay?" I ask, grabbing Hope's coat and then mine.

"Perfect." Lilly smiles then turns to kiss her husband when he tells her that he and Jax are gonna head out.

"We'll do dinner here tonight, babe," Jax says, and I turn to look at him.

"Uh...sure," I agree, even though I don't know how I feel about dinner with Jax. This situation is already feeling way more intimate than I'm ready for.

"Also, here's your key, and you remember the code, right?"

"I do," I say, placing the key in the front pocket of my jeans.

"Have a good day, baby." He smiles, making my stomach do something strange.

"Later," I murmur, watching him tap the end of Hope's nose, making her beam before walking out the door.

"Ready, honey?" Lilly asks, standing in the open doorway.

"Ready." I smile, taking Hope's hand in mine and following her outside. "Wait, I need to get Hope's car seat."

"Jax already took care of it."

"Oh," I mutter, and she smirks, opening the backdoor to her car. Picking Hope up, I get her buckled in and hand her doll over before getting into the passenger seat.

"How far is the salon from the house?" I ask Lilly.

"About a five minute drive."

That's good; I could walk to work. I still need to work out a babysitter for Hope, but I'm hoping I can find a child care program she can go into while I work, since that's what she did before and she loved it.

When we pull up in front of the salon, I take in the area around it. It's in a shopping plaza, which would mean a lot of walk-ins, and since I needed to build a new clientele, that would be perfect. In Kentucky, I owned my chair at the salon I worked in. I enjoyed it, because I made my own hours and only worked when I had someone coming in. Here,

I will be starting from the bottom until I have enough of a base that I could maybe open my own place or rent a chair from someone.

"I'm really nervous," I blurt as Lilly turns off her car.

"You're gonna be great. Frankie is really sweet. You're gonna love him, and the girls who work with him are all really nice too."

"I know you're probably right, but I've never really done this. The salon I worked at is the same one I interned at while I was in school. I don't even remember what it's like to interview."

"You've already got the job, honey. You're just going to meet him. I'll be out here with Hope if you need me."

"You're not going in with me?" I ask, feeling like I want her to hold my hand, which is strange, since I have never had anyone around to hold my hand before.

"I can if you want. I just figured you would want to go in alone." Lilly shrugs.

"No, you're right. I should go in by myself," I mumble, looking at the shop.

"He knows you're coming. I sent him a text when we left the house. It'll be okay, honey. Take a breath."

Pulling in a breath, I let it out slowly then put my hand on the door handle. "Wish me luck."

"Good luck, Mama," Hope says from the backseat.

"Thanks, Angel," I whisper as Lilly encourages, "Go get 'em."

Opening the door and closing it behind me, I pull my coat tighter around myself as I walk across the sidewalk. When I reach the salon and go inside, I'm bombarded with the familiar smell of hair products. Looking around, the place is more than nice. The décor is simple but high class. A large, dark purple couch sits in front of the shop windows, scattered with white pillows that have gold streaks through them. In front of the couch is a mirror-top table, two small kid-size chairs, and a stack of coloring books and crayons.

"Can I help you?" a beautiful woman with long, almost-white blonde hair asks when I get to the front desk.

"I'm here to see Frankie," I say softly, feeling suddenly uncomfortable. The salon I worked at back home wasn't even half as nice as this one, and the women I worked with were much older. I'm not sure how I will get along with women my own age.

"Do you have an appointment?"

"Yes, I'm Ellie. Lilly sent me," I say, and her face goes soft, seeming to make her even more beautiful.

"I'm Kimberly, but everyone calls me Kim. It's nice to meet you. Frankie's with someone right now, but if you give him five, he'll be done."

"No problem." I smile, taking a seat on the couch.

"I'm sorry about what happened to you," she says, catching me off guard. "Frankie filled us in on what went down, and then I saw the news report. I hope they catch the other guy. Have you heard anything?"

"Um, no, not yet," I say, feeling a chill slide over me. I don't want to think about him still being alive, or the fact I could still be in danger.

"I'm sure they'll catch him."

"I hope so," I reply then think about Jax, and something deep within me knows he will make certain Hope and I are safe.

"You're going to love it here. Frankie's the best, and Mickey, Ian, and Kendal are all really great too."

"Have you been here long?" I ask, jumping on her change of subject.

"I just moved into town a month ago, and this was the first place I stopped." She shrugs, but I still catch something flash through her eyes before its gone.

"Are you a stylist?"

"Yep, and we all work the front desk between clients, except week-ends. Then Becka comes in to help out, 'cause we're all normally booked."

"Cool," I mutter, watching a woman a few years older than me walk toward the front. She's stunning, with big green eyes that stand out against her dark, almost-black hair and pale skin. Her eyes scan over me and her lip curls up at the corner, not a smile, but like she smells something bad as she flips her hair over her shoulder and turns, dismissing me to face the counter.

"Kim, can you take care of Mellissa for me?" I hear from behind her.

"Of course." Kim smiles, but it's nothing like the smile she had on earlier directed at me. I can tell it's the kind that has been rehearsed.

"Ellie?" Pulling my gaze from Kim, I turn and come face-to-face with a very pretty man wearing jeans and a plain tee. His face is contoured with makeup, his eyebrows sharp, his lashes long, and his lips lined and glossy. *Yes, very pretty.*

"That's me." I smile as he sticks out his hand.

"Frankie. It's so nice to meet you," he says, smiling back.

"It's nice to meet you too."

"Why don't we go back to my office and sit down for a few minutes."

"Sure," I reply, and he places his hand at the small of my back, leading me through the salon, which I notice has six booths, all clean and tidy with dividers between, offering a little bit of privacy for the stylist and their clients. When we reach his office, he takes a seat in a hot pink chair behind a white desk with a mirrored top. Sitting across from him in one of the two stylish turquois chairs, I cross one leg over the other.

"So, tell me about yourself and your experience," he asks casually.

Leaning back in the chair, I do just that. I tell him about myself and what has happened to make me move to Tennessee. I tell him about my experience as a stylist and what I want for Hope's and my future. I tell him everything, and when it's over, I feel like I have just spent an hour with a psychologist, rather than twenty minutes applying for a job.

"Where do you see yourself in five years?" he asks, causing visions of Hope and me living with Jax in his castle in our own happily ever after to fill my brain. "Do you have any goals?"

Clearing my throat and the vision of me with Jax and Hope out of my head, I say, "Yes, I see myself with my own salon or managing one. I see myself and my daughter in a nice house I provide for us. I see a different childhood for her than the one I was raised with, and a much brighter future."

"I see that for you too, girly," Frankie says softly, sitting forward in his chair. "I'll see you Monday."

"Wait, what?" I ask.

"Take the weekend and get things sorted with your daughter, and I'll see you Monday."

"So I have the job?" I ask, just to clarify.

"Girly, you already knew you had the job. You just proved you're worthy of working here."

"Awesome," I breathe, standing when he does.

"See you Monday, Ellie, and tell Lilly I said hi."

"I will," I promise with a smile, heading out of his office, feeling better than I have in a long time. When I reach the car, Lilly is standing with Hope on her hip, who's wearing a purple tutu she didn't have on earlier. She's talking to Mellissa, the not-so-nice girl from the salon.

"Oh, there she is," Lilly says as I get close enough for Hope to move from her grasp to mine. "How did it go, honey?"

"Really great, I start Monday." I grin and then turn when I feel eyes drilling into me from my side, where Mellissa is standing. "Sorry, I'm Ellie," I introduce myself.

"Mellissa," she says then looks at Lilly. "Tell Jax I love him and to call or come over whenever he has a few minutes," she says as something ugly crawls over my skin.

"Sure." Lilly frowns.

"Thanks, Mrs. Mayson, and nice to meet you, Ella," she says, turning on her heels and walking away before I have a chance to reply or correct her about my name.

"I'm hungry," Hope says, and I look at my daughter and kiss her cheek, knowing she is the reason I'm doing what I'm doing and that I need to remember that.

"How about we stop for brunch?" Lilly asks, breaking into my thoughts.

"Sure," I agree, and we hurry to get into the car.

"PERFECT TIMING, LOOKS like the guys just got here too," Lilly says, looking in the rearview mirror. Turning my head, I look through the back window, seeing Cash is driving Jax's truck and Jax is driving a white Range Rover. After we stopped for brunch, where I ate waffles, eggs, and a fruit salad, I vowed I would start my diet tomorrow. Then we went to the DMV and I got a new driver's license before heading to the bank for a new card.

Getting out of the car, I open the backdoor. As soon as I do, Hope is out and running towards Jax, yelling, "Ax!" at the top of her lungs. She stops midway and spins in circles, showing him the purple tutu his mom bought for her while I was in the salon. She got it from a woman named Liz's store, called Temptations.

Smiling, he picks her up, saying something that makes her laugh before setting her back on the ground and walking toward me. Suddenly, yelling, "Catch, babe!" tossing something to me.

Catching a set of keys I hold them out in front of me, frowning. He already gave me the house key this morning, so I have no idea what these are for. "What's this?" I ask, holding the keys out toward him.

"I got you a car." He smiles bigger, jerking his head over his shoulder towards the white Range Rover parked behind his mom's car.

"You got me a car?" I repeat just for confirmation as anger and something ugly turns in my stomach.

"I know you're gonna need some wheels to get around, so—"

"You did not buy me a car," I murmur, looking from the car to him then back again.

"I did." He grins.

"Yay, Mama! You got a car!" Hope cries, dancing around me.

"I cannot believe you," I hiss, throwing the keys at him, which he catches before they smack him in his stupid face. "I'm not a charity case."

"Uh oh, Mama's mad," I hear Hope say from behind me as I storm toward the house. I'm angry, but I also feel extremely vulnerable. So much so, I feel my throat closing up with tears.

Not wanting to be rude, I turn to look at Lilly, who is frowning at her son. "Thank you so much for taking me today," I croak out.

"Anytime, honey," she says gently. I nod and wait until Hope catches up to me to go into the house and close the door, wishing I knew how to change the code so I could lock Jax out. Going to my room, I make sure Hope is settled while I start to put away my laundry.

"Ellie, I need to talk to you for a minute." Jax says lightly tapping on the door.

Gritting my teeth, I get off my bed, making sure Hope is distracted by her doll before opening the door and stepping into the hall then to the side when Jax takes a step towards me.

"I never said you were a charity case," he says, and the urge to punch him in the stomach hits me so hard I have to fist my hands at my sides to keep from doing just that.

"I never asked for a car, and if I wanted a car, I would have found a way to get one for myself."

"I'm just trying to help you, Ellie."

"Well don't, and please take the car back, Jax," I say, crossing my arms over my chest.

"I bought it cash, so you're gonna have to suck it up and accept it."

"I'm going to have to suck it up?" I repeat, just to make sure I heard him correctly.

"It's paid for." I have no idea how much a car like that costs, but I have a feeling it's *a lot* of money, and there is no way in hell I would take a car like that from anyone. Definitely not from an almost stranger, even if he is just trying to be nice.

"I don't want it. Take it back."

"Too bad, it's yours," he growls at me. Yes, *growls*, like he has the right to be pissed off at me for not accepting it.

"We're done talking," I announce, turning and walking back into the room, hearing him growl again as I shut the door. I don't even care if it seems like I'm acting like a child throwing a temper tantrum. I'm thankful for his help, but no way in hell am I taking a car from him. *And he can't make me,* I think immaturely as I walk to the bed and plop down next to Hope, deciding then the only way Jax and I will be talking again is when he takes the car back to wherever he bought it from.

Chapter 3

Jax

M<small>Y HEAD LIFTS</small> as the backdoor opens and Ellie whispers, "Jax?" loudly, stumbling into the kitchen. She's holding onto Wes, whose body is bent almost double from her weight.

"What the fuck happened?" I ask, getting off the stool I was sitting at, working on a case for a client while waiting for Ellie to get home so we can talk, whether she wants to or not.

"Her, July, and all the sisters and cousins decided to have an impromptu bachelorette party at the compound," he says, chucking when Ellie says something about loving July and going on runs with her.

"And you didn't think to call me?" I growl, pulling Ellie away from him and tucking her into my front, smelling tequila mixed with her sweet scent.

"Sorry, man." He shakes his head. "July told me if I called I wasn't gonna be sleeping in bed with her tonight. I'll do a lot of shit, but no way am I taking the couch over some shit that's not my concern."

"I'm not talking to Jax," Ellie cuts in, looking at Wes then up at me, pointing a finger then going cross-eyed when she stares at it, muttering, "I'm not talking to you."

I know this, since she hasn't talked to me in almost a week. I had no fucking idea women could use silence as a punishment, but Ellie does and it fucking sucks. This shit has been going on since the day I drove up in the Rover, which is still parked out front of the house, because I refuse to take it back. Ellie needs something safe to get her and Hope around in, and I know eventually she will see it my way.

Or at least I hope she will.

For the five days, anything and everything Ellie felt necessary to tell me, she did it through text messaging, including the fact July asked her to be one of her bridesmaids at her wedding this weekend. After what happened with July getting kidnapped, Wes told her they were going to get married now, rather than in a few months. Aunt November refused to let July get married at the courthouse like she did, and she pulled my mom and aunts together and planned a wedding in just a few days, which apparently included an impromptu bachelorette party tonight, since tomorrow night will be the wedding.

I also learned through text that Harlen would be escorting Ellie at the wedding. Though that text came from my cousin, who I'm pretty sure was just saying it to piss me off. And it worked. That day, I found my ass at the Broken Eagles Bike Shop, where I had a talk with Harlen about his hands and what would happen to them if even one touched Ellie in a way that I didn't like.

"My wedding's tomorrow. Any other time, I would have called, but my girl needed tonight, so I gave it to her."

"That's 'cause your sweet...and hot," Ellie slurs, looking at Wes, which causes my chest to vibrate in annoyance, but the feeling abruptly ends when she presses her face into my shirt while wrapping her arms around my middle.

To say I'm over this shit is an understatement, but now, seeing Ellie drunk and cute, I'm completely the fuck over it. We need to talk, and whether she wants to or not, it's happening. Maybe not tonight, because she wouldn't likely remember any of it, but it would be very soon.

"You should have called me to come get her."

"Like I said..." He shrugs then looks at Ellie in my arms and raises a brow.

Shaking my head, I ask, "Where's Hope?" while pulling Ellie's hands out of the back of my shirt, where they had wandered. I was already hard from seeing her in the tight jeans and tighter tee with her body pressed against mine, but her hands on my skin would send me over the edge.

"Your mom took her home with her for a sleepover when the girls decided they were gonna drink and hang out."

My mom is in love with Ellie and Hope, and completely backed Ellie in her silent treatment, so it doesn't even surprise me that she wouldn't call to give me a heads up about tonight. Still, that shit pisses me off too. *What happened to loyalty?*

"If you're good, I'm gonna head out. July's in the truck," Wes remarks.

Lifting my chin, I walk with Ellie, who's still glued to my front, to the door and lock it behind him.

"It's so hot," she gripes. Tilting my head down, I see she's peering up at me. I close my eyes for a moment, praying for strength. "I need to get out of these clothes." Opening my eyes, I watch as she pulls from my grasp and drops her coat to the ground, her shirt coming up and over her head, leaving her in a dark purple lace bra and jeans.

"Jesus," I hear myself hiss under my breath, knowing I should stop her, but fuck if I can do or say anything as her hands go to the buttons of her jeans and I see dark purple lace is there too.

"Ellie," I growl, needing her to stop.

"What?" she asks, tilting sideways, but before she can hit the floor, I pick her up bridal style and head for the stairs.

"I'm too heavy for you to carry. I suck at being on a diet; I don't even like vegetables," she murmurs, pressing her face into my neck, where I swear I feel her tongue touch briefly.

"You don't need to diet, Ellie. You're perfect the way you are, and I could run laps with you in my arms just like this."

"Really?" she whispers, pulling her face away from my neck to catch my eyes.

"Really," I grunt, feeling my zipper imprinting on my dick just from her weight in my arms, her skin against mine, and the view of her tits in her lace bra.

"Can I see?" she asks, wrapping her arms around my neck as I head up the stairs.

"Another time." I chuckle from the serious look on her face.

"Fine," she pouts, laying her head back against my shoulder. Once we make it to the second floor, I lead her to my room and set her on the bed. I know I should probably put her in her own bed, but I tell myself I need to be close in case she gets sick and needs me during the night.

"Why are we here?" she asks, sitting up and looking around.

Ignoring her question, I walk to the dresser and find a shirt before going back over to her and answering, "In case you get sick, my bathroom is closer than if you were in your bed and would have to go across the hall."

"Oh." She smiles, flopping down on my bed and raising her arms above her head, giving me a visual of her spread out just like that for me to enjoy. Shaking my head, I lift one of her feet then the other and pull off her boots and socks then help her sit up. I slip the shirt on over her head, and as soon as she has it on, she does the shit girls do and puts her hands behind her back, unhooking her bra and slipping it out the sleeve of the tee.

"I hope Mellissa doesn't get mad that I'm in here," she mutters, lifting her head to look at me.

"Mellissa?" I frown, wondering how she could possibly know about her.

"Yeah, Mellissa…the one who loves you," she singsongs, making my eyes narrow.

"Babe, Mellissa and I dated back in high school," I rumble.

"Well, she loves you, and even told your mom to tell you that."

"I don't love her, and I'm not with her, or anyone else," I say, knowing I'm going to have to repeat this shit when she's sober, because I'm sure she's not even comprehending anything I'm saying right now. "Jeans off, babe, and get under the covers," I order, turning around toward the bathroom, so I can grab the garbage can, but I stop when she sits up and bolts past me to the bathroom, landing on her knees in front of the toilet.

Pulling her hair away from her face, I rub her back, waiting for her to finish being sick before grabbing a washcloth and turning the water to cold. Placing it on her forehead, I wait a moment until I know she's good then wipe her mouth. I help her sit up then grab a toothbrush from the holder. Muttering, "Open," I move it around her mouth while her head tilts back and her eyes close. Once I'm done, I get her to the sink to rinse her mouth before picking her up and carrying her to bed, putting my knees on the mattress with her in my arms and laying us down, tossing the covers back over us.

"Jax?" I hear her whisper as I hit the remote for the light to go out.

"Yeah, baby?"

"Thank you for taking care of me."

"I'll always take care of you, Ellie," I say softly, listening as her light snore fills the quiet. Wrapping my arms tighter around her, I fall asleep with her weight against me, knowing this is how it's supposed to be, and there is no way I'm ever going to give it up.

Waking up, I feel my hand on something soft and smooth before it registers that Ellie is with me, her ass pressed to my morning wood, my hand holding onto her stomach, and my other arm dead from being underneath her. I lay there, enjoying it for a moment, and know exactly when she wakes up, because her body goes solid against me and her hand goes to her head. Turning she looks over her shoulder, her sleepy eyes meeting mine, and a dark blush creeps over her cheeks.

"Morning." I smile, trying to ease whatever embarrassment she's feeling.

"Um…" she mumbles then looks around. "I…what am I doing in here?"

"You got drunk last night," I remind her, and she nods then rolls to her stomach and blinks. "Wes brought you home and you got sick."

"You took care of me," she says softly, closing her eyes like she's remembering. "I'm sorry you had to do that."

"Baby, taking care of you isn't a hardship for me. Plus, now I can say you owe me one, and you can take the Rover, and the silent treatment can be done."

"I don't want the car, Jax." She frowns.

"What if I say it's my car and you're just borrowing it?"

"Jax." She shakes her head against the pillow.

"I want you and Hope to be safe, Ellie, and I know you can get a car for yourself, but until you do that, please use the Rover," I plead.

"I looked up the price of the phone you got me, Jax," she says, narrowing her eyes.

SHIT.

"I bought it off someone for fifty dollars, Ellie," I lie, and she closes her eyes.

"I hate feeling like I owe people. I have always done everything on my own, and it's really difficult for me to accept help," she confesses then opens her eyes, dropping her voice. "You and your family have been so amazing, and I don't want to feel like I'm taking advantage of your generosity."

"Baby," I wrap my arm around her waist and pull her closer to me, as close as I can get her, before her body freezes up, "have you asked me for anything?"

"No," she whispers, looking at my throat.

"Have you asked my family for anything?"

"No," she repeats, and I give her a squeeze, bringing her gaze back up to meet mine.

"Then you're not taking advantage. If it makes you feel better, we can say the car is on loan from me to you, and when you're done with it, I can sell it off. But until then, please use it."

"Have I told you that you're annoying?" she asks then huffs when I smile.

"A few times."

"You're annoying. Bossy. And annoying."

"You already said I'm annoying." I grin.

"It needs repeating," she mumbles under her breath.

"No more silent treatment," I tell her on a squeeze, dipping my face closer to hers. "I don't like it."

"Well, I don't like you buying me expensive phones or cars, so we're even."

"One more thing we need to talk about," I warn.

"What?" She frowns.

"Last night, you brought up the name Mellissa," I say, watching as her face loses color and she tries to pull away. "Stop," I growl, pulling her back to me when she attempts to tug my arms from around her.

"You have a girlfriend. We shouldn't," she cries in distress.

"Ellie, listen to me," I state firmly, and her body stills and her eyes go to my throat again. "I do not have a girlfriend, not yet anyways." I gently nudge her, feeling her stiffen further. "And when I do have one, I guarantee you will be the first to know."

"I have a headache." She breathes out a puff off air that hits my chest.

"I'll get you some aspirin and some food in a minute, but only after you tell me that you understand what I just said."

"I understand," she wheezes out as her nails dig into my arm.

"Good." I give her a squeeze, dip my face, and brush my mouth across hers before rolling out of bed and heading to the bathroom.

Walking back into the room, I'm not surprised to see that Ellie is no longer in my bed. I'm sure she's down the hall freaking out about what happened this morning. Instead of giving her time to think too much, I go to her door and knock twice. It only takes a moment for her to open the door, and when she does, her eyes meet mine then drop to my mouth before moving to my throat, when she mutters, "I think I'm just going to get back into bed."

"You're going to take these," I say, handing her two Advil, "and then we're going to have breakfast. After that, we'll go pick up Hope from my parents, so get dressed. We'll head out in fifteen."

"I… We're not going to eat here?" she asks, tugging at the bottom of my shirt.

"Best hangover food you'll ever have is extra greasy and from a place called Jones' on Main."

"My diet—"

"Babe." I shake my head, cutting her off before she can say more, while roaming my eyes over her. I have no idea where this diet shit is coming from, but no way in hell does she need to lose weight. She's perfect. "You do not need to diet." When my eyes travel up to her face, her cheeks have a pink hue that wasn't there before and her eyes have gone soft in a way that makes it really fucking hard not to lean in and kiss her. Clearing my throat, I turn on my heels and growl over my shoulder, "Get dressed and meet me downstairs." *Before I do something like push you back to the bed and show you with my mouth how beautiful I think you are.*

Hearing her mutter, "Annoying," as her door closes, I smile and head to the kitchen, picking up her coat and shirt from the floor before sending a quick text to my mom, telling her we'll be there to pick up Hope in an hour or so. Then I send a text to Sage, asking how his meeting went this morning with our client. My cousin hates being the one to give bad news, and the news he was delivering this morning was definitely that. The man's wife was having an affair with her co-worker. Obviously, since he hired us to check into her, he had his suspicions, but thinking it may be happening and seeing proof are two completely different things.

Getting a response from my mom almost immediately makes me smile, because all it is, is a sad face. Sage's response takes longer, but his message lets me know he had to talk the guy down from going over to his wife's co-worker's house and going postal after he saw the photo evidence. I can't imagine what the guy is feeling. He and his wife have two kids, both under the age of five, at home, and he now has to think about what to do regarding his marriage.

Typing a quick response, I let him know to check in with me once he is done filing the paperwork and closing out the case, then tell him I will be out with Ellie having breakfast. To that, he responds almost immediately with, *Is she talking to you again?* to which I responded, *Fuck off.* My cousins and Evan had been giving me shit all week about Ellie's silent treatment, most of them staying out of my way, because they knew I was likely to blow at any minute.

I know she's downstairs before I see or hear her when her smell wraps around my lungs. I've been with women who wear perfume like a coat of armor that's overpowering and covers up their natural scent, but not Ellie. Her scent of vanilla and cherries is so subtle that I crave getting closer to her, wanting to pinpoint where the scent is located on her body, so I can breathe more of it in.

"Ready," she says, walking into the kitchen then frowns, going over to the counter where I sat her coat and shirt. "How did this get here?" she asks, holding up her shirt.

"You took it off last night when you came home," I say with a shrug, not wanting her to be embarrassed, but not wanting to lie either.

"I took it off down here, wi…with you here?" she whispers in horror, balling the shirt up in her hand.

Moving toward her, I take the shirt from her, laying it on the counter while placing my fingers under her jaw and tilting her head up until her eyes meet mine.

"I didn't see anything more than what I would see if we went to a pool and you wore a bikini."

"I don't wear bikinis." She closes her eyes. "I don't even know how to swim."

"We'll add learning to swim to the list of things I'll teach you," I declare quietly.

"This is so embarrassing," she murmurs with her eyes still shut, moving her head back and forth and causing her hair to slide over my hand.

"Would you feel better if I took off my shirt?" I ask, pulling on her chin so she opens her eyes.

"I've seen you without your shirt," she mutters as her cheeks turn pink.

"Well then, we're even." I smile. "Now, are you ready to go have breakfast?"

Pulling in a lungful of air, she lets it out slowly then nods.

"Good." Smiling, I lean in before she can stop me, placing a soft kiss on her mouth. I move away without acknowledging her quick intake of breath or the way her eyes go half-mast, even though I really want to do it again to see if I can get the same reaction.

Handing over her coat, I grab the keys from the counter and head for the door, holding it open for her to go out before me. Then I wait, watching as she pulls her bottom lip between her teeth, pulls her jacket on, and then slides past me out the door, ducking her head as she moves to my truck.

"You're driving, baby." Her body turns toward me and I toss the

Rover keys to her. She catches them, muttering something under her breath before stomping to the driver's side, popping the locks, and getting in behind the wheel. Sliding into the passenger seat, I fight back my smile and the urge to pound my chest like some kind of caveman as she looks around the car. Her eyes sparkle with excitement and happiness, even though she tries to hide it as she starts up the car and moves her hands along the steering wheel.

"Do you think this would be a good time to tell you I don't have my driver's license?" she asks, putting the car in reverse, pressing the gas then braking hard, causing me to lurch forward before slamming back against my seat. Feeling my heart pound in my chest, I'm about to tell her we'll add driving to the list, when she breaks into a fit of laughter that causes my chest to tighten.

Without thinking, I wrap my hand around the side of her head, tangling my fingers in her hair, and pull her towards me roughly, covering her mouth with mine and swallowing her laughter down my throat as I thrust my tongue into her mouth. Her hands on my chest that had started out pushing me away wrap around my shirt and pull me closer. Groaning as she whimpers, I start slowing down the kiss, swiping my tongue across hers once more, then pull her bottom lip into my mouth, giving it a tug and soft peck before reluctantly pulling my mouth away and placing my forehead against hers. Opening my eyes, I notice hers are still closed.

"That...that was wow," she whispers, opening her eyes slowly and swallowing when our gazes connect. "Is it always like that?" she asks in a whisper.

Placing my other hand on the underside of her jaw, I mutter, "Never, baby."

"We...um..." She looks away. "We should get breakfast," she states after a long moment, slipping from my grasp, her eyes going to the windshield before looking at me once more. She shakes her head and places her fingers against her lips, taking a breath then shaking her head again.

"You taste like you smell," I tell her, not wanting her to forget I'm here with her, that I'm still in the car, that just because my mouth isn't on hers doesn't mean I can't still taste or feel her lips against mine, her hands wrapped around my shirt. Putting the car in reverse, she begins to back out without acknowledging my comment, which only eggs me on. I know she wants me as badly as I want her, and I refuse to let her ignore this thing brewing between us just because she's afraid.

"I wonder if the rest of you tastes like that." I smirk as she slams on the brakes, jolting the car. "You okay to drive, baby? I don't mind taking over if you need time."

"Jax," she warns, turning to glare at me.

"Baby, unless you're gonna give me something to eat at home," I drop my eyes to her lap, "then take me to get food." Lifting my gaze to hers, I watch her cheeks turn an even darker shade of pink that starts to spread down her neck.

"You really like embarrassing me, don't you?" She frowns, breathing heavily, something that says she's not embarrassed, but turned on.

"If you're asking if I want to lick over the pink your skin turns to see if it has a flavor, then the answer is yes."

"Oh, my God," she whispers, covering her face with her hands.

Laughing, I pull her hands away from her face. "Okay, baby, I'll stop." Bringing one of her hands to my mouth and kissing it, I mutter, "Scout's honor," while holding up two fingers.

"I doubt you were ever a boy scout." She rolls her eyes before looking over her shoulder and backing onto the street.

When we arrive at the restaurant, the place is packed, like it normally is on Saturday morning. You can tell by the crowd that most of the patrons were up late partying. Almost everyone has on sweats, and half are wearing sunglasses and holding coffee cups in their grasp, praying it cures the hangover they are suffering from. Placing my hand against Ellie's lower back, I move us through the small restaurant to the back, where there is a free table for two, sitting close to the counter where you can watch the three cooks on the grill.

"Jax," Jones, the owner and my friend, calls from behind the counter, where he's stationed flipping eggs. Jones and I went to school together. He played football with me; his short, stocky build ruled the field every time he stepped onto the turf. He was our secret weapon. Hell, he still is.

"How's it going, man?" I ask, pulling out Ellie's chair for her to sit before taking my seat across from her, which gives me a view of the whole place.

"Can't complain too much." He smiles.

"You know you owe me ten on the Giants game, right?" I remind him, watching as he shakes his head, grinning.

"You're really gonna make me pay up?" he asks, pointing at himself.

"Fuck yeah, you would've had my ass behind that grill if I lost."

"You're right." He smiles. "You want coffee?"

"Yeah, two," I tell him, watching as he signals for one of the busboys to bring us two coffees.

"How's Sylvia?" I inquire, talking about his wife.

"Good, she'll be in soon. Who's your friend?" he asks, dipping his head towards Ellie, who is looking over the menu while simultaneously trying to hide behind it.

"This is my girlfriend Ellie," I announce, watching a few heads in the room swivel my way as she hisses, "Jax," while kicking me under the table.

"Baby, this is Jones, the owner," I say, ignoring the look in her eyes that promises retribution.

"Nice to meet you," she says, plastering a smile on her face.

"You too, beautiful." He smiles then laughs as Ellie tries to kick me again, narrowly missing my junk.

"I told you you'd be the first to know if I had a girlfriend," I remind her.

"I'm too hung over and haven't had enough coffee to even contemplate how the hell I ended up in this situation," she murmurs, taking another sip from her mug.

"Fate, baby...this is fate," I tell her seriously, wondering how crazy she would think I am if I told her about the Boom.

"Jax?" Pulling my eyes from Ellie, I groan, seeing Felicia walking toward our table. Felicia has been one of my regular hookups for the last year. Unlike what my family thinks, I don't sleep around with just anyone. Most of the women I'm with are people who don't have time for relationships or just don't want one. Which was perfect for me—that was, until Ellie. "You haven't been returning my calls," she says with a fake pout while crossing her arms under her chest.

"I'm off the market," I tell her with a shrug, hoping she gets the point and moves along. She's a nice woman, who is very intelligent when it comes to books, but common sense, not so much.

"I saw Mellissa at the nail salon and she told me you two were back together, but I honestly didn't believe her," she mutters as my teeth grit and Ellie's body grows stiff in front of me, her fingers wrapped around her coffee cup turning white.

"I'm not with Mellissa," I growl, annoyed that I fucking have to call her and make clear the status of our relationship. That being we don't fucking have one.

"Oh." She tilts her head. "Who are you with?"

"I'm going to the restroom," Ellie says, standing suddenly, causing Felicia to jump back from the table and me to stand with her, trying to grab her arm, which she pulls from my grasp.

"Fuck," I clip, watching Ellie rush across the room and out of sight.

"I'm sorry. I didn't know," Felicia says as I scrub my hands down my face. "It's okay, but I'm serious. I won't be calling you again," I tell her, hating that I feel like an asshole, but knowing I need to make it clear to everyone, not only her, that I'm off the market.

"Sure, I understand. Take care, Jax," she says, turning to leave, but not before I catch something in her eyes that sets my nerves on edge and has me instantly on guard.

"You're gonna have your hands full, my friend," Jones says, pulling my eyes from where they were glued on the bathroom door and turn to look at him. "You know I love you, man, but some of the girls you've been with are," he rolls his finger around his ear, "*muy loco*, and that girl...your girl looks scared of her own shadow."

"She's been through a lot," I tell him, and he points the spatula in his hand at me.

"I know, and that's why I'm telling you to close down shop on these bitches, so they don't think they have the right to fuck with her. 'Cause, homie, whether you want to face it or not, they will fuck with her, and until your relationship is solid, you can't have that shit."

"I know, man." I let out a deep breath then stand when Ellie comes back to the table.

"You okay?" I ask, pulling out her chair again.

"Yeah, fine, sorry," she mumbles, picking her menu back up.

"You know what you want, beautiful?" Jones asks, and I try not to let it annoy me that he's calling her beautiful, but it still does.

"What's good?" she asks him, setting down the menu, turning her body toward him.

"Everything, but if you trust me, I'll make you something special," he says, giving her the smile that had women dropping panties left and right before he got married to Sylvia.

"Sure." She shrugs.

"You want your usual?"

"Yeah, man," I say then look at Ellie, who has her eyes on her coffee cup in front of her. How the hell I'm going to prove to her that she's it for me, I have no idea, but I know there is no fucking way she won't be mine.

"YOU MAY NOW kiss the bride," the pastor says, and Wes bends July backwards over his arm, kissing her in a way that I'm surprised Uncle Asher doesn't get out of his seat, storm up the aisle, and take her from him.

"Oh, God," my sister sitting next to me cries, and I look down at her as she wipes her eyes while wrapping her arm around mine. "They are so perfect for each other," she says then looks at me, smiling before standing up when everyone else does.

"Ax," Hope calls from my other side, and I pull my eyes from my sister and hold my breath as Hope smiles up at me.

She looks like her mom...her mom, who has taken up my every thought since meeting her.

"What's up, sweetheart?" I ask softly, still unsure of what to do with a three-year-old little girl.

"Can you pit me up so I can see Mama?" she asks, and my chest gets tight, similar to the way it does every time I look at her mom.

"Sure," I say, and she holds her hands up to me. I pick her up in her big poufy pink dress then lift her onto my shoulders so she can see her mom walk down the aisle behind July, holding onto Harlen's arm, which causes a different kind of tightness to fill my chest.

She looks beautiful today. Her long brown hair is tied up with a white ribbon that is woven through a braid, which is wrapped behind her ear with small pieces framing her face. Her body is incased in a dress that is so formfitting I know just from looking that her breasts would fit perfectly in my hands. Hell, her body fits perfectly against mine. I know this, because every chance I get, I have her close. Since we had breakfast this morning, I have made a point to show her I want her and that she's the only woman I think about.

She's mine. She may not understand it—hell, I don't even know if *I* understand it—but she was made for me.

Taking Hope with me, I meet Ellie at the end of the aisle and take her from Harlen, who just grins when I pull her from his grasp with a hand around her waist.

"Mama, you wook so pwetty," Hope says as she moves from my hold into Ellie's arms.

"Thank you, Angel," Ellie says then looks at me. "I can't believe how many people are here." Looking around my uncle's backyard, I have to admit there are a lot of people for such a spontaneous wedding, but I'm not surprised. The women in my family are determined if nothing else.

"I'm starving," Hope says dramatically, leaning her body way back until she's looking at me upside down.

Smiling at her, I mutter, "Let's get you girls something to eat," before placing my hand against Ellie's lower back, leading her through the crowd towards the food that has been laid out. Once we each have a plate, I head toward the table my parents are sitting at with my sister.

The moment Hope spots my dad, she yells, "Gwampa!" and runs to him. He picks her up, tossing her in the air, causing her large, poufy dress to float up around her as she laughs loudly. Then she looks at my mom and smiles, yelling, "Gwamma, look! My pwincess dress fits me!" making Mom's eyes go soft as she says something I can't hear.

"I don't know when she started calling them Grandma and Grandpa," Ellie whispers, stopping a few feet from the table.

"My mom probably bribed her," I tell her, wanting to get the look of unease off her face. And that probably isn't a lie—I know my mom and dad both love kids. They would've had more than my sister and me if things had been different, but after being apart for so long, I know they wanted to focus on our family.

"Hope has never really had grandparents. My mom, as you know, is crazy, and my dad, who would have adored her, died long before she ever got a chance to meet him." She pauses. "She already loves them," she says softly, and before I have a chance to ask her about Hope's father's family and why none of them are around or involved in her life, she steps away from me toward the table, taking a seat. I follow and sit next to her, watching her face as she watches Hope, who is now sitting on my mom's lap and babbling about something to my dad.

"They're already in love with her too," I say, nudging Ellie's shoulder with mine to get her attention. When her eyes come to me, I dip my face closer to hers and tell her gently, "You have family now. Both you and Hope do."

Her lips press together, and that tightness fill my chest again, making me uncomfortable. Taking her hand from the table, I wrap it around my thigh, placing my hand over hers. It might take some time, but one way or another, she will learn to accept she isn't alone anymore.

Chapter 4

Ellie

AFTER PUTTING AWAY the rest of Hope's clothes in the closet and making her bed, I head downstairs to the kitchen. Since Ashlyn picked Hope up this morning, I have no possible reason to stay up here any longer, and I'm sure Jax, who knocked on my door thirty minutes ago and told me he needed to talk to me, isn't going to give me much longer to avoid him.

It's Tuesday, three days since July's wedding, and I haven't seen much of Jax since then. On Sunday, the day after the wedding, I had to work, so Jax's mom watched Hope, and then Jax picked her up and made her dinner. He sent me a text at work asking if Hope could have ice cream, to which I told him not before dinner. I can see now that my girl has him wrapped around her finger.

When I got home, I had a quick dinner, and luckily Hope was just as tired as I was, so we had an early night. Yesterday, Jax worked, so I only saw him for a brief moment when he stopped at Hope's bedroom door. His eyes collided with mine as we stared at each other until he rumbled, "Goodnight," quietly and left the doorway. Hope had long since fallen asleep, but I couldn't leave her, and if I'm honest with myself, I used her like a shield to protect myself from Jax.

I know I find him attractive. I know the kiss he gave me in the car stole more than my laughter. I know the way I felt when he told his friend I'm his girlfriend. I know that at the wedding, when I shared a slow dance with him and he held me tight against his body, I felt like the only women in the world. I know the way I felt watching him hold my daughter, who had fallen asleep in his lap as he laughed with his family, all while keeping a firm grip on my hand. I know I want more than anything to believe it's my turn to find happiness, but I also know how I felt having a beautiful woman shove reality in my face and down my throat while I sat across from Jax in a restaurant.

I hate the way I feel about Jax being with other women. I don't expect any man in this day and age to be a virgin or to have waited until marriage to have sex. But I can honestly say the idea of being with a man who looks like Jax, and who has his dating history, is worrisome. I don't only have myself to think about; I have a daughter who watches everything I do. I don't want to show her at an early age that some men are assholes and can't be trusted.

Moving down the stairs, I pause. Even my lungs freeze up when I hear Jax ask, "When was she taken?" My heart beats hard against my ribcage and my legs begin to get weak. *Another woman was taken.* Could it be the same guys who took July and me? The same guys who had drugged that girl then brought her back so doped out of her mind she didn't even know who she was?

I hate that one of them lived, and I hate more there are others no one knows about. I don't want to live in fear, but I'm afraid. I can't help but think they will come after me again. The first time they took me, I had just gotten off work at the salon and was heading for the bus stop, when their van pulled up, opened the side door, and hefted me inside like a scene out of a movie. I was so stunned I don't even think I screamed until I realized what they were doing, that they were actually wrapping tape around my wrists, and then they told me my mom sold me to them. What kind of parent sells their only living child into sex trafficking? How does anyone even know how to get into contact with people who do traffic? The whole thing disturbs me, but one thing I do know—I have Jax now, and though I may feel conflicted about the status of our relationship, I know deep down he will protect Hope and me.

Tiptoeing toward the entryway to the kitchen, I try to be silent as I walk, so I can try to hear anything else. It does no good though, and I know Jax is still somehow aware I'm near without me ever making a sound, when he tells the person on the phone I'm there and he will see them in the office later.

"Hey," I say softly, avoiding his eyes and moving to the counter to the coffee pot, where I pull down a mug from the cupboard, pour myself a cup, and then go to the fridge. I grab the cream, put a splash in before moving to the counter, pull a spoon from the drawer, and scoop three heaping spoonsful of sugar in then stir.

"Are you gonna look at me?" he asks.

I really want to say no, but instead, I say, "Hmm?" taking a sip of coffee and closing my eyes, letting the taste and aroma work its way through my system. I pray that I'll magically teleport to another dimension, where I can look at Jax but not have to talk to him, where I can be invisible.

"You've been avoiding me since the wedding."

Knowing I have no choice, I turn my head and look at him. "I know," I agree rather than lying, which causes his eyes to open wider in surprise.

"You know?" he repeats as his brows pull together, causing two wrinkles to form between them.

"I could lie and say I haven't been avoiding you, but you would know I'm lying, and I suck at lying, so I may as well just tell the truth," I rattle out before taking another sip of coffee, trying to keep my mouth occupied.

"I appreciate that. I don't like games," he says as his face softens.

"Me neither," I agree, even though I have never played the kind of games he's probably talking about.

"So why are you avoiding me?" he asks, leaning back against the counter behind him and crossing his bare feet at the ankles. How can someone make leaning look hot? I do not know, but if I had a camera and took a couple pictures of him right now, with his still slightly damp hair, dark blue tee that's straining against the muscles of his arms, his jeans hanging low, the warn material tight enough to show off the thickness of his thighs, I could probably sell those images for a lot of money to a catalog for whatever brand it is he's wearing.

"I like you," I blurt then bite my lower lip in punishment.

Why the hell did you say that?

"I like you too," he states simply, picking up his cup from the counter and taking a sip. "That's why I want to spend more time with you and get to know you better, and you avoiding me doesn't really allow me to do that."

"You've dated a looooot," I drag out the word, telling him something he should know already, because obviously my filter is malfunctioning and I'm spewing out anything and everything that comes to mind.

Watching him closely, I'm surprised when I see regret in his eyes. "I've dated a lot." He nods, and I nod back, because what the hell else am I supposed to do? "But—" He starts to say something else, when there's a loud knock at the door then the doorbell goes off. "Fuck," he mutters, looking towards the door then back to me. "I'll be right back. Just drink your coffee," he says before prowling out of the kitchen toward the front door.

Taking a sip, I frown when I hear a loud groan and something rattling and banging against the wall. Moving to the kitchen doorway, my heart drops into my stomach before picking up speed and banging hard against my ribcage.

The blonde from the restaurant wearing skinny jeans, cowboy

boots, and a sheer blouse has her body wrapped around Jax, her long legs around his hips, her arms around his neck, and her mouth on his…or his on hers, I don't know. But I do know that his hands are on her ass as he leans back against the entry room table.

Stepping back into the kitchen, I set my mug on the counter, absently feeling the hot liquid hit my skin before shaking it off, grabbing my coat and keys, and then leaving through the backdoor.

Getting in the Rover Jax got me, the Rover that up until that moment I had not once been truly grateful for, I back out of the driveway, narrowly miss the car parked behind me, and then turn onto the street.

I can't recall ever feeling like I do right now, like I have just been stabbed in the chest, which makes no sense, because Jax is not mine.

Parking in Ashlyn's driveway, which is just a couple blocks away, I make my way to her front door and ring the bell, trying to get my breathing to even out, so I don't sound like I just ran a race.

"Hey!" She smiles, opening the door, then frowns when she sees my face. "What's wrong?" she asks, grabbing onto my hand.

I want to tell her everything. I want to tell her I like her brother waaay too much and that he was just mauled by a blonde but looked like he was enjoying it before I ran out of the house. I want to ask her if this pain in my chest is normal, if I should feel this way for someone I hardly know. I want to tell her all of this, but instead, I say, "Another girl was taken."

"Oh, no," she whispers, covering her mouth.

"Yeah, I'm sorry to do this. I know you guys were going to spend the day together, but do you mind if I take Hope early?"

"Of course." She nods as her cell phone begins to ring somewhere in the house.

"Mama," Hope yells excitedly, running toward me. "Wook at my makeup!" she cries happily, showing me a pink kids' makeup set in her hands that Ashlyn obviously got for her.

"So cool, Angel baby." I smile, picking her up, seeing Ashlyn frown when her house phone starts to ring.

"Tell Ashlyn thank you, Angel," I tell Hope, leaning down and grabbing her bag that's sitting right inside the door.

"I'm weaving?" she pouts.

"Yes, but you can come back again another time," I assure her softly, really needing to get out of here.

"Thanks, Aunty Ashwyn," Hope says, blowing her a kiss.

"Bye, Princess Hope." Ashlyn smiles then looks over her shoulder when the phone that just went silent rings again.

"You get that and we'll see you soon," I tell her, but I can see in her eyes that she knows something else is going on.

"Are you sure you don't want some coffee? I just put a pot on." Feeling tears choking me, I shake my head.

"Call me if you need to, honey," she says gently as I step away from the door, and I carry Hope to the backdoor of the Rover, put her in, and make sure she's buckled before getting in behind the wheel and backing out of Ashlyn's driveway.

Looking at the house, I see Ashlyn standing in her open front door with the phone to her ear and a worried look in her eyes. Giving a slight wave, I finish backing out and then try to figure out what the hell it is I'm doing.

I live with Jax, so I can't avoid him forever, even if I wish I could go pick up my stuff from his place and head back to my trailer. My eyes go to the rearview mirror, and I see Hope is watching me and I swallow. No, I don't wish that. We're in the best place for us; I just need to get my heart out of the mix.

"What do you say me and you spend the day at the zoo, Angel baby?" I ask.

"Zoo?" she whispers, and then yells, "Yay! Zoo!" making me laugh.

Heading through town, I get on the highway, and it only takes about twenty minutes for us to get to the zoo. Once we park the car, I rent one of the strollers they have available, even though as of right now Hope wants to walk. I know in a couple hours she's not going to feel the same way, and I can't carry her like I could when she was a baby.

Walking into the zoo, I stop at one of the shops and grab an apple juice for her and a coffee for myself, along with a map.

"Where to first, Angel?" I ask her, getting down on my haunches so she can look at the map with me.

"What are those?" she asks, pointing at one of the pictures on the map.

"Those are flamingos," I tell her, watching her face as she studies the image.

"Dey're pink," she says, pointing out there color.

"They are. That's their real color."

"Can I see them?" she asks hopefully.

"Yes," I agree, taking her hand in mine, using my other to push the stroller as we walk along the trails, stopping every once in awhile when we pass something that catches her attention.

"Ax!" Hope yells, pulling her hand out of mine where we have stopped to look at some bison that are roaming in a large open field.

My eyes meet Jax's before he drops to one knee, catching Hope, who throws herself into his arms. Our eyes stay locked and I swallow. He looks pissed...or whatever emotion is worse than pissed.

"Hey, sweetheart." He smiles, kissing Hope's cheek before setting her to the ground and taking her hand.

"Uhh..." I breathe as my heartbeat accelerates and he gets closer to me.

"Mama, Ax is here," Hope points out happily, and I open my mouth then close it again, because nothing comes out.

"Hey, baby." Jax bends his head toward me, touching his mouth to mine. Once again, I notice the way his lips feel—the way they are so warm, the way the top feels softer than the bottom, the way even his lips taste like cinnamon and mint, and the way I want to lean in and get closer.

"Uhh..." I stutter, opening my eyes and looking up at him.

"We're gonna see fwamingos," Hope tells Jax, tugging on his hand, not mentioning he kissed me, like it's completely normal for him to do it.

"Sounds good, sweetheart." Jax smiles, and Hope grins back then gets into the stroller, pulling the sun visor over her head, which in turn leaves me alone with him.

I swear my kid is too damn smart for her own good.

"Let's go see the flamingos, baby," Jax says, pulling me out of my stupor by wrapping arm around my waist and then shoving his hand down the back pocket of my jeans.

"Jax," I hiss under my breath, twisting my hips to try to dislodge him.

"*No,*" he snarls under his breath near my ear. "You left me. I can't even tell you how badly I want to bend you over something and spank the shit out of you right now." He sounds almost pained as he growls the words at me, causing my heartbeat to thump in my ears.

"You were kissing another woman," I whisper-yell, feeling that pain in my chest once more, and he stops the stroller, turns me, putting my back to him, and wraps his arms around my body.

"You know I fucking wasn't, Ellie, so do not even try to pull that bullshit card with me," he growls into my hair. I'm sure that to passersby, we look like a couple embracing. His body tight to the back of mine, one arm around my waist, the other hand up and wrapped under my jaw, holding my head to the side. I couldn't move, even if I wanted to, and I can honestly say I don't want to. I know he's right. I knew when I pulled out of the driveway, but I'm so scared. *So damn scared,* I think as I close my eyes.

"Feel this?" he asks against my ear, pressing his erection into my back. "This only happens for you. No one else, baby, and that's the fucking truth. You have unknowingly ruined me for all other women."

Shaking my head, I whisper, "Jax," while dropping my head until my chin rests on his arm.

"I was going to tell her to leave when I opened the door, but she ambushed me like a fucking spider monkey, catching me off guard. I swear I would never fucking do that," he whispers against my neck as his hand moves to spread against my abdomen, holding me even closer to him.

"I hated it," I tell him honestly.

"I'm sorry," he breathes against my skin, causing the fine hairs on my body to stand on end and my body to lean back into his as my head tips to the side, wanting to feel that sensation again. "We'll talk about it, but first, we gotta take Hope to see the flamingos," he says, kissing that spot he just whispered against before turning me again and placing his hand back into my jeans pocket, anchoring me against his side as we walk.

"What just happened?" I ask him quietly as we take a trail up a dirt path through a bunch of trees that give the path shade.

"We just had our first fight."

I feel my face scrunch up as I turn to face him, and he smiles, kissing my nose. "Okay, but how did you know I was here?"

"Your car has a tracker." He shrugs like it's no big deal while my heart gets warm. My stupid heart thinks it's hot that he's a stalker.

"It has a tracker?" I repeat, and he must recognize my tone, because he slows down and turns toward me again.

"It has a tracker, Ellie." He nods then adds, "You and Hope are in that car. You both are coming to mean something to me, so if you want to be pissed about it, you're going to just have to get over it. It's gonna stay, and there isn't anything you can say that will make me take it out," he says causally, like we're talking about the things he needs to pick up from the grocery store.

"You're crazy," I whisper, taking a deep gulp of air. "You're seriously cuckoo. Like, white coat, padded room crazy," I ramble, looking at him.

"Wasn't crazy before you, so if I get diagnosed as mentally unstable, that's all you, baby." He grins and I cover my face.

"I'm going to tell your mom about this," I tell him, knowing his mom is probably the only person on this earth that he's scared of. *Hopefully she can help me fix her son, or get him medicated,* I think as we begin to walk again.

"Baby, she's had a tracker in every car she's owned since she and my dad got together."

"So this is obviously genetic. Your dad is crazy too," I tell him then feel myself slow down when I see Jax grinning. "What?" I question, tilting my head and studying him.

"Nothing. You're just really fucking cute when you ramble."

"I don't ramble. Sometimes I have a lot to say about stuff, but I don't ramble," I gripe, knowing damn well I ramble. I have done it since I can remember. I tend to over share or say too much, when I should just shut up.

"Fine, you don't ramble." He smiles again then leans to the side of the stroller, looking in on Hope. "She's out."

"She had an early morning," I say as we start walking again. "How mad at me is Ashlyn?" I ask after a long moment of silence.

"She's worried," he says quietly, pulling me a little closer to his side. "She knows how I feel about you. She also knows that women can be bitches, so she's worried you're gonna freak and leave all of us behind if something like this happens again."

I want to tell him I won't leave, that I'm brave and strong, but I know that's a lie, so I keep my mouth closed and my side pressed tight to his as we move along the shaded path.

"I know we just met, Ellie, but I need you to know that, while we're figuring us out, I'm all in."

"I have a daughter, Jax," I remind him quietly.

"So? What does Hope have to do with this?"

"I have a kid. Dating me is not as simple as dating a girl who has no responsibilities. I have a human that counts on me for everything, a mini person who lives, breathes, eats, and needs loads of attention," I tell him, and he stops walking and turns me to face him.

"I know this, Ellie." He smiles, leaning in and kissing my forehead before whispering there, "I know this, and I'm still here with you right now. If I wanted to be with someone else, I could be, but I'm not. I want this. I want you and Hope."

"You scare me," I admit, leaning my forehead into his chest.

"You scare me too, baby," he says, taking my hand and placing it over his heart. "Do you feel that?" he asks as his heart beats against the palm of my hand.

"Yes."

"Twice, you've taken it. The first time I saw you looking so afraid, like the world was against you when you walked out of those woods alone, I gave it to you. Today, when you pulled away from the house, you took it. It knows it belongs to you, so it willingly went with you when you left. It's yours, Ellie, if you want it."

"You're really good at this kind of thing, aren't you?" I ask him, lifting my eyes to meet his.

"Never done anything like this before," he confesses, making my breath catch and my body melt deeper into his.

"There's so much…" I pause and lean my forehead against his chest again while locking my jaw. I don't know why I haven't told him about Hope's dad. Well, I guess I do. When people find out she's not my biological daughter, they have a tendency to act like she shouldn't call me her mom, that I shouldn't consider her my daughter. They don't understand that she's mine. No, I didn't give birth to her, but I have taken care of her since she was just a few weeks old. I was the one who endured sleepless nights, endless diaper changes, and bottle feedings. I was there the first time she rolled over, her first step. I will be there for every first she has. She's the one person in this world who loves me, really loves me, unconditionally. She was my brother's Hope for a brighter future, and now she's mine.

"You know the thing about time?" Jax asks softly, wrapping his hand around my jaw until my eyes meet his.

"What?" I whisper, seeing the look of longing and optimism in his gaze that has my heart beating a little harder.

"There's always more of it. It's one thing that will always be available, one resource that will never diminish. We have time, Ellie. I just need a chance."

Could I do that? Give him a chance and risk being hurt again by someone I care about? I don't know if I can, but my stomach hurts when I think about not trying, when I think about not seeing if, for once in my life, I can have what other people have, a future with someone, someone in my corner and at my side when I need them, someone to lean on when the road gets bumpy. I know Hope adores him, and he's someone I trust with her.

"I want to try, but we have to take this slow. I haven't..." I pause, taking a breath. "It's been a long time since I've dated, and we live together." I pause again, looking away, and say, "Until I can get a place for me and Hope..." His fingers tighten on my jaw, where he's still holding me, causing my head to turn back toward him. "I don't want it to get awkward," I finish on a whisper then swallow from the look of raw determination in his eyes.

"Just tell me you're in this with me."

I can't believe I'm doing this, that I'm taking this kind of risk, but I really don't want to fight this pull I feel anymore. "I'm in," I get out right before his lips crashes down on mine, pulling the air from my lungs as his tongue thrusts into my mouth, tangling with mine. My hands grip his shirt tightly, feeling the material between my fingers as his hands move, one sliding across my body right above my ass. The other drifts into my hair, where he wraps it in a fist so he can deepen the kiss before slowly pulling back, nipping my bottom lip one last time, leaving me panting for breath. When I open my eyes, his are on me, and there is no denying the happiness I see in their hazel depths.

I just hope he doesn't regret this. I've never dated—okay, I did in high school, but it was two different boys, and all we ever did was kiss, so I don't even think that really counts. Right after high school, I started cosmetology school and worked full time, so there was never an opportunity for me to date during that time. Then I was granted custody of Hope, so I was left with even less opportunity, and I didn't want to bring random guys around my daughter.

Now, I'm a twenty-four-year-old virgin, with a kid and no dating experience. *What the hell do I know about dating a guy like him?*

"Now, let's go see the flamingos," he says, pulling me from my thoughts by putting me in front of him, my back to his chest, and placing his hands on the outsides of mine, which have automatically grasped the bar of the stroller in front of me. As we begin to walk again, I wrap my hands tighter around the bar so I don't fall on my face as Jax walks behind me, occasionally nuzzling my neck, sending sensations through my body that cause my core to throb. Reaching the area where the flamingos are, I bend and check to see if Hope is still sleeping, which she is.

"Let's just come back here when she wakes up," I tell Jax over my shoulder.

Nodding, we move down the pathway, following a sign to the goril-las. When we reach the bottom of a small hill, there's a rock formation that looks like a large cave. Going inside, there are three large glass panels, where you can watch the gorillas that are out lazing in the warm fall sun. On the other side, there are benches lining the walls, so you can sit in the cool air.

Moving the stroller to a bench, I sit next to Jax when he pulls me down to his side, and then I adjust Hope's stroller in front of us, so we can keep an eye on her. Leaning my head on Jax's shoulder, I watch the families coming and going until one of the large gorillas comes to the glass across from us, looking directly at me.

"I think you've got a new admirer, baby," Jax grunts against my ear, making me smile. Getting up from the bench, I walk toward the glass, keeping my eyes on the large creature in front of me and the way he backs away then stands up on his legs and pounds his chest.

"I can see why he's fascinated by you. You're very beautiful." Jumping at the voice next to me, I turn my head, coming face-to-face with a very handsome man about ten years older than me, with caramel-colored skin, dark hair, and startling green eyes, holding a young boy in his arms.

"I...thanks," I mutter, taking another step away from him as I notice something in the way he's looking at me is off.

"Baby, c'mere." Turning to look at Jax, I see his eyes are on the man next to me. "Babe," he repeats, holding out his hand. Ducking my head, I walk to him and place my hand in his. As soon as I'm in his grasp, his hand goes around my waist and he moves me to the other side of his body, the side farther away from the man and his son, then leads me outside while pushing the stroller with one hand.

"Are you okay?" I ask, feeling the muscles of his body draw tight.

"I'm good," he says, giving my waist a squeeze as we move back up the hill we just came down. "I didn't like the way that guy was watching you before he approached you."

"I didn't see him," I admit.

"I know; you were watching the gorilla when he came in, but it wasn't like he came in to see them. It was like he came in to watch you. I don't even think he knew I was there until I called you over," he says, sending a chill through me.

"I heard you on the phone this morning. You said another girl was taken," I confess quietly while leaning over to make sure Hope is still asleep.

"Yes, another girl was taken. Her family contacted me. The police can't do anything yet, because it hasn't been more than seventy-two hours. She was hoping we could look into it."

"What are you doing here? You should be out looking for her."

"All of my guys are on it, and at the risk of sounding like an asshole, baby, you're more important to me than any of that. I needed to come make sure you were okay," he states.

"Jax, I'm okay, but you have to help her. Do you know how scared I was when I was taken? I prayed over and over that someone would find me, that someone would be looking for me, but I knew I was praying in vain, 'cause the people who should have informed the police I went missing were the same people who set me up to be taken in the first place."

"I'm so fucking sorry, baby," he says, letting out a ragged breath and holding me a little tighter.

"You have to find her," I repeat, feeling my throat close up with emotions.

"We're working on it, and so are Wes and the guys."

"Wes is helping?" I ask with a frown. I know Wes and a few of his friends own a repair shop, but I didn't know he helps Jax out, and July never mentioned it.

"Since July was taken, he's been on a mission to find the guy who got away."

"Are you guys any closer? Do you know who he is?" I ask, hearing the hope in my voice.

"We're getting closer," he says, but I notice he doesn't fully answer my question, which makes me wonder what he's trying to keep from me or if I'm in danger.

"Nothing is going to happen to you, Ellie. No one is going to get close to you or Hope; you have my word."

"You can't promise that, Jax," I whisper as fear creeps over me.

"I can promise you that," he growls. "You and Hope are mine, and anyone who even thinks about harming either of you will wish they were never born."

"Jax, you're not a cop," I remind him.

"I don't answer to the law, Ellie, and that makes me their worst nightmare," he snarls, wrapping his arms so tightly around me that I have a hard time taking a breath. Huffing heavily, I do a face plant against his chest, praying he can keep both Hope and me safe.

Chapter 5

Jax

PARKING IN FRONT of my office, I growl when I see Mellissa is standing out front, holding two cups of coffee and her eyes on me. *"Fuck."*

I know she got my text. I knew she was going to ignore it and the fact I told her to call me when she had a few minutes, so we could talk. I also know her well enough to comprehend she would show up here so she could attempt to have it out with me face-to-face.

I don't want to deal with her shit today, not when I left Ellie and Hope at home eating pancakes that I made them for breakfast, both my girls still looking sleepy as I kissed them each goodbye, so I could come into the office and deal with a phone call I had to make this morning.

Getting out of the cab of the truck, I slam the door and pull my office keys from my front pocket.

"Hey, stranger." Mellissa smiles as I get close, handing me a cup of coffee that I take then walk four steps to the garbage can on the corner of the street and dump it in.

"That was rude." She frowns, watching me as I step up to the building and open the door.

"I told you to call me, Mellissa. I didn't tell you to stop by and bring me coffee." I know I'm being an asshole, but this chick only *understands* asshole. If I try to go about this playing the roll of the good guy, she will read that signal wrong and think I want back in there, which I don't.

"I figured we could talk over coffee," she pouts.

"We don't need to have a sit-down, Mellissa. All I want is for you to understand that we fucked once five months ago. You're not my girl. You haven't been my girl since we were kids. I don't want to be with you, and I'd appreciate it if you'd stop giving my mom messages to give to me. She's too nice to tell you that she thinks you're a snob, and will kick my ass if I even thought about getting back with you."

"Is this about that bitch with the kid?" she asks angrily, throwing her cup of coffee on the ground at my feet, causing the hot liquid to come up, soaking the bottom of my jeans.

Taking a step closer to her, I growl, "That's my woman, so tread very lightly, Mellissa. I don't give a fuck who your dad is."

"She's trash, Jax."

"I suggest you leave," Sage says, coming from across the street. "You don't, and I'm calling *my* dad, Mellissa, and let's just say if he searches your car, you're going to jail, and I don't think *your* daddy would be very happy with you if that happened."

"I don't have anything in my car," she says, crossing her arms over her chest, glaring at my younger cousin.

"You don't?" he asks then looks over her shoulder toward her car. "Saw your car parked outside of a house on fifth last night, the same house that got raided this morning. The house was clean, but I doubt your car is," he says, and I watch her face pale. Then, without another word, she moves to her car, hops in, and speeds off down the street.

"What was that about?" I ask him, and he shrugs.

"Lucky guess. I know she's been hooking up with a guy named Benji. He's a low rank drug dealer, but this week, a large supply of meth came through, and the rumor is he was going to begin selling it. The cops raided his house this morning, but found nothing, not even a joint," he says as I open the office door, and then he asks, "Why was she here?"

"She's heard about Ellie, and has been spreading rumors that we're getting back together to anyone who will listen. I told her to call me so I could tell her to cut the shit, but she showed up here instead."

"You got the magic stick, Cuz." He grins, following me down the hall.

"You're an idiot," I say, shaking my head. I head across the hall to my office, leaving him in the kitchen area to put on a pot of coffee.

Tossing my keys on the desk, I pull out my cell and pick up my desk phone, calling back the number that was texted to me this morning while I was making the girls' breakfast.

"Jax?" my friend since high school, Mav, answers, picking up on the second ring.

"How's it going, man?" I ask, picking up the mail and sifting through it.

"It's going. Alexa is getting ready to pop at any minute. I'm hoping to close down this case in time to get home, so I can be there to watch my daughter take her first breath."

I can't imagine doing what he does. Living with the scum, working undercover, having to be away from my family for weeks on end, missing important events and life moments. I don't think I could do it, but I respect Mav, because he does. All I know is that because of him, there are families that sleep easier at night.

"So, what new info do you have for me?" I prompt.

"Yesterday, Deborah Anthony was taken into custody on drug charges. There should be a call going through sometime this afternoon regarding the case of Ellie Anthony, and the roll Deborah played in her kidnapping."

"That's good, but I don't understand why you're calling me. You know my uncle would have gotten this information to me."

"You're right, but before she was taken into custody, she had a conversation with one of my informants about a way to make twenty grand easy," he says, and I take a seat, feeling my brows draw together.

"How is that?'" I ask, not really sure if I'm ready to hear what he's going to tell me, especially if this information has anything to do with Ellie.

"She told him all he had to do was find a virgin, and then tell Deborah who the girl was. The girl would be abducted, and they would get the money and could split it fifty/fifty."

"She's selling virgins?" I ask in disbelief.

"She's selling virgins, and when my informant told her she was full of shit, she explained to him that she knows it's legit, 'cause the first one she sold was her daughter."

"You know Ellie has a kid, right?" It's something he knows; he's read the police report. He knew I was taking Ellie up to Kentucky to pick up Hope.

"She doesn't have a kid, Jax. I'm not saying she doesn't think of Hope as hers, but Hope is her brother's daughter. He, his longtime girlfriend, and Hope were in a car accident. Ellie's brother and his girlfriend died on impact. Hope survived with minor injuries, and Ellie was granted custody of her shortly after she was released from the hospital."

"You're kidding, right? She looks just like her," I say, feeling something sour settle in the bottom of my stomach.

"They're family," he says quietly, understanding the distress in my voice.

"Jesus." I rub my chest, feeling a stabbing pain where my heart is.

"She never told you? I figured she would have said something to you about it," he mumbles, sounding distracted.

"She never told me," I confirm.

"Sorry, man."

"Is she still on their radar?" I ask, knowing if they were paying that much for her, chances are they won't give her up that easily.

"This is still an open case, so the guys are still out there, but if I had to guess, I would say no. These are not dumb men, and they know her story made the news. They are not going to want that kind of attention."

"Thanks, man."

"Still keep vigilant," he warns.

"Will do, and let me know if you want me to go check on Alexa."

"I will never send you to check on my wife, Mayson."

"You know she loves me."

"Don't remind me," he jokes then mutters, "We'll talk soon."

"Talk to you soon," I agree, hanging up and sitting back in my chair, raising my arms above my head, locking my fingers together and putting them behind my neck, closing my eyes and trying to figure out what I'm feeling right now.

Hope isn't Ellie's daughter. I don't even know if I should confront her about this, or if I should just wait until she comes to me with the information.

"Jesus." Shaking my head, I pull off my hat, toss it on top of my desk, and run my hand through my hair.

She's a virgin? What the fuck is that about? And is it even true? She's gorgeous, and I have a hard time believing she's never had a relationship. I don't even think I've ever had sex with a virgin.

"Fuck," I growl, feeling myself get hard. Apparently my dick likes the idea of her still having her virginity.

Getting up, I grab my hat and go across the hall to the kitchen, finding Sage and one of my new guys, Evan, talking quietly. Noticing the look on Evan's face, I ask, "What's up?"

"I just asked Evan to check into this new guy June is dating," Sage says, and I look back at Evan, feeling my brows pull downward when I notice the look in his eyes from moments ago is gone, now replaced with a blank expression.

"Why are we looking into June's new man?" I ask.

My cousin is going to college in Alabama, and I know she's planning on moving home as soon as she graduates. I haven't heard anything about her having a boyfriend, but that doesn't surprise me. The females in my family have a tendency to play their cards close to the chest, and they sure as hell don't tell us about the men they are dating.

"I overheard Willow and Harmony talking about him and didn't like the vibe I got." Sage shrugs.

"You're looking into him based on a vibe you got from an overheard conversation?"

"I can't explain it, and Evan's mom still lives in the area, so I asked him to check in on it the next time he was up there to visit."

"Are you good with that?" I ask Evan.

"Yeah, it's no trouble. I should be up there this weekend, so I'll ask around while I'm there," he says casually, but I notice a tic in his jaw that wasn't present before.

"You know the girls hate it when we interfere," I say, slipping my hat back on and putting my cell in my back pocket.

"Yeah, but they always get over it." Sage smiles.

"Well, this one's on you." I move to the door. I had enough drama when I was dealing with July and Wes when they got together.

"I'm stepping out for a couple hours, but I'll have my cell on me," I tell them over my shoulder, getting two chin lifts before I close the door behind me.

Getting in my truck, I back out, first thinking about going home, but I know I can't do that yet. I need to take some time to cool off. I don't know if I should tell Ellie I know about Hope, or if I need to let her come to me. Feeling conflicted, I drive, and before I even realize where I'm going, I pull up in front of my parents' house.

Staring at the house I grew up in, I feel my gut get tight as I'm bombarded by happy memories. Without thinking, I shut down the truck, get out, and head up the front walk, tapping twice before opening the door.

"Mom?" I call into the house as I walk through the living room.

"In here, honey," she calls back, sticking her head out the laundry room door that's off the kitchen. "Give me a minute. Did you have breakfast?" she asks, and I hear the washer start up.

"Yeah, I had a protein shake," I tell her, watching her face scrunch up as she walks into the kitchen.

"I have no idea how you drink those things; they taste like dirt," she says, making me smile.

"You eat dirt often, Mom?" I joke, taking a seat at the island across from her.

"No, but I'm sure that's what it tastes like." She smiles, but then her eyes search my face and her smile disappears. "What's wrong?"

"I don't know," I sigh, pulling my hat off my head and setting it on the bar, and then I scrub my hands down my face. "Hope isn't Ellie's daughter," I blurt, needing to get it off my chest.

"Yes, she is," she replies immediately, frowning.

"She's not. Hope is Ellie's brother's daughter. He and Hope's mom died in a car accident when Hope was just weeks old, and Ellie was granted custody shortly after that when she was nineteen."

I watch tears from in her eyes then slip silently down her cheeks as she studies me. "You're not my blood, Jax," she whispers softly, and I feel my throat close up. "I love you as if I gave birth to you, but you don't have my blood pumping through your veins."

She tilts her head back as more tears fall from her eyes.

"No one...no one could ever tell me you're not my son. I love you with the same fierceness I love Ashlyn with. You're my boy. This is where you belong to me," she says, pointing at her heart.

Swallowing, I choke on the emotions that seem to be suffocating me as I look at the woman who raised me, the woman I have called mom since I can remember. Watching her eyes light with a fire for me has my vision going cloudy.

"Hope is Ellie's daughter, honey," she says quietly, and I blink until I can see clearly again. "You don't have to give birth to a child to love it as your own."

Nodding, I swallow again, get up from the stool I was sitting on, walk around the island, and then take my mom into my arms as she cries.

"She's so strong, Jax, so strong, and beautiful, and she loves Hope with everything she has inside of her." She leans back, placing her hand on my cheek. "Please, understand that before you go to her with what you found out. If she thinks you feel like Hope isn't her daughter, it will really hurt her." She shakes her head, closing her eyes, and I can hear the anguish in her voice as she says, "She's was just a baby herself when she took on the responsibility of raising a child that she didn't give birth to. That tells me everything I need to know about the kind of woman Ellie is, and I hope you understand the amazing woman you have sleeping under your roof right now."

"I understand," I say quietly, kissing her cheek then letting her go, moving back to the stool I was sitting on. "Should I let her tell me?" I ask quietly, still unsure of what to do with the information.

"Let her tell you, and know that when she does she's trusting you. I don't think she has really trusted anyone in a long time."

"She trusts you," I point out. Ellie is very picky with who she allows to watch Hope, and so far, that list only consists of me, my mom, and my dad. Even Ashlyn had to pass inspection before Ellie allowed her to take Hope with her to her house.

"I think a lot of people have taken advantage of her," she says softly, grabbing my hands from across the counter. "I don't know why she trusts me, but I love her like a daughter. I would jump in front of a bullet for her or Hope, the same way I would do for you or Ashlyn. I want to be someone she trusts, someone she can depend on. I don't want her to feel like she's alone, and that girl I met at the hospital was alone," she confides, crying again, which causes my chest to hurt.

I know a lot of this sadness stems from her and my father's past. She had my sister on her own for years, thinking my dad had abandoned her to be with my biological mother. She had no idea my dad was suffering just as badly as she was.

"I'm falling in love with her…her and Hope," I admit, watching her eyes close.

"Then be there for her, and when she tells you her story, understand she's believing that she's safe with you, that her heart is safe with you."

"Thanks, Mom. For everything, not just this."

"I will always be here anytime you need me, honey."

Nodding, I let her hand go and lean back. "Do you have time to make me breakfast?" I ask, watching her face go soft.

"Of course." She straightens her spine, wiping the tears off her cheeks, giving me a smile before moving to the fridge.

Breathing a little easier, I sit back on the stool and watch her move around the kitchen as she makes me breakfast.

"Do you want me to keep Hope for you and Ellie one night?" she asks. Caught off guard by the question, my fork is in the air with a piece of fluffy pancake hanging off the end, syrup still dripping onto the plate below it. "Honey, I'm not dumb, and I remember what it was like when me and your dad got back together and had both you kids at home."

"Mom," I groan, and she laughs.

"What? Your dad is a very attractive man."

"You can stop." I shake my head, setting my fork down, my appetite suddenly gone.

"Well, just remember that I offered." She smiles, and I throw my hands up in the air, giving up on finishing my pancakes.

"Thanks for ruining my breakfast," I tell her, watching her laugh.

"You have to leave anyways. Ellie's bringing Hope here in," she looks at the clock over my shoulder, "fifteen minutes."

"Are you kicking me out?" I ask with amusement.

"Yes, Hope likes you more than me, so when you're not here, I get her to myself." She smiles.

"She does like me more then you, doesn't she?" I ask smugly.

"Don't rub it in," she says, kissing my cheek. "Now go, and you know I'm always here if you need anything."

"Thanks, Mom," I mumble, slipping my hat back on my head then pulling my keys out of my pocket. "I'll be here to pick up Hope before dinner, so don't let her trick you into giving her ice cream."

"Honey." She rolls her eyes, putting her hands on my arm, giving me a gentle shove toward the door.

"Love you, Mom." I smile, kissing her cheek before walking out to my truck, feeling the weight's gone from my chest.

"THANKS FOR PICKING up Hope from your mom's," Ellie says quietly as she takes a seat next to me on the couch, tucking her legs underneath her.

She came home an hour ago, but as soon as she walked in the door, Hope was on her, so all I got was a quiet greeting before she disappeared with Hope upstairs to put her in the bath then into bed.

"You can thank me with your mouth," I tell her, wrapping a long piece of her hair around my finger then watching as her cheeks turn a dark shade of pink.

"Jax," she murmurs, ducking her head, which causes her thick dark hair to fall in front of her face.

"C'mere," I say, pulling her hand until she's pressed up against me, with her hands against my chest and her big eyes looking up at me. "You okay?" I ask, running my thumb over her bottom lip.

"Yeah," she breathes quietly as her eyes roam over my features. "I like when you don't wear a hat."

"Why's that?' I ask just as quietly, feeling the intimacy of the moment wrapping around us.

She studies my face for a long time before saying with a shrug, "I don't know. I can see your eyes, I guess." She ducks her head again, making me wonder what she's really thinking.

"Liar," I whisper, tucking a piece of hair behind her ear. Her head lifts, her eyes meet mine again, and she licks across her bottom lip, causing my eyes to follow the sultry movement.

"Okay, I lied, but the reason just sounds so stupid now that I think about it."

"Tell me," I say on a squeeze, tilting my head lower until our eyes lock again.

"I like thinking I'm one of the few people who sees you like this."

Pulling her toward me with my hand wrapped around the back of her neck until we're sharing the same breath, I tell her softly, "I like that reason," before covering her mouth with mine, licking across her bottom lip, pulling it between my lips and tasting her on my tongue. When her tongue touches mine timidly, I lift her, hearing her squeak as I adjust her on my lap to straddle me.

"Jax," she exhales heavily, leaning back to look at me.

Seeing the trepidation in her eyes, I run my hand over her hair, settling on the underside of her jaw then back up to wrap into her hair. "Slow, Ellie. I promise we'll take it slow."

"Slow," she repeats against my mouth as I pull her forward. Sweeping my tongue between her lips, I groan when her hands slide from my chest to my hair and her fingers move through the stands.

Dragging her tighter against me with one hand on her ass and the other in her hair, I pray I don't come in my pants like a sixteen-year-old kid that's never had a chick on his lap before.

Slipping my hands up the back of her shirt, my fingers roam over her smooth skin. Her tongue moves lightly against mine as her hips circle. I don't even know if she understands what she's doing to me, and to herself, as her core bumps against my erection.

Moving my hands, I still her hips while pulling my mouth away from hers, groaning, "We have to stop."

Seeing the heat in her eyes makes it harder to stay firm, when all I want to do is strip her down so I can explore her body. Shaking my head, I tuck hers under my chin while my heart beats rapidly in my chest.

"Are you okay?" she asks quietly, and I feel her hands on my shirt, running her fingers over the material.

"Yeah, baby." Kissing her head, I tilt her chin up. "You feel like watching TV with me for a bit?"

"Sure," she agrees, and her eyes drop to my mouth, making me smile.

"Just TV, my gluttonous girl," I chide her playfully.

Turning red, she ducks her head again, mumbling, "Sorry."

"Slow, remember?" I ask, running my finger over her lips, gaining her attention once more.

"Slow," she agrees, moving to sit on the other side of the couch. Wrapping an arm around her waist, I yank her back, settling her against my side before picking up the remote and turning on the TV.

OPENING MY EYES, I see the cable box has powered off, leaving on the blue screen that has cast a glow around the room. I feel Ellie's weight against my side, her arm over my waist and her warm breath against my shirt. Smiling, I lean my head back then hear a little voice whisper, "Ax."

Turning my head to look over my shoulder, I see Hope standing in the doorway to the living room, wearing her sleep shirt and pants with the snowman on the front of them. Her long brown hair is down in a mass of wild waves, and her face is soft and sleepy.

"Hey, sweetheart," I whisper as she walks toward the couch. "Are you okay?"

"I had to potty," she whispers loudly, making me smile, then looks at her mom, who's asleep on my side. "Mommy's sleeping," she points out, climbing up on my lap.

"She's tired," I say, watching while she studies me.

"Me too," she says in a whisper, pulling my hand from the arm of the couch and wrapping it around her waist. She then tucks herself into a ball against my chest while her tiny fingers play with mine for a moment until they still. Tipping my chin downward, I find her asleep as well.

At a loss, I kiss the top of her head, letting my lips rest against her hair as I pull in a breath then let it out slowly as I feel my chest crack open, as if they just ripped my heart out and split it amongst themselves. Listening to them breathe, I close my eyes, holding each of them a little tighter, understanding exactly what my mom meant. I would protect these girls with my life. I would die for them. And I will never let anyone take them from me.

Sliding out from under Ellie, I carefully adjust her until she's lying down as I hold Hope against my chest.

"Ax?"

"Shhhh, sweetheart, I'm going to tuck you back into bed," I tell her gently, carrying her up the stairs. Opening her door, I lay her on the bed, tuck the covers up around her, and then kiss her hair again before moving to the door and closing it halfway.

Going back downstairs, I pick up a still sleeping Ellie from the couch and carry her up to her room.

"Jax?" she whispers, clinging to me.

"I'm putting you in bed, baby," I tell her, kissing her forehead as I use my shoulder to open her door. Carrying her across the dark room, I lay her down on the bed, wanting so badly to follow and climb in behind her. Instead, I whisper, "Slow," against her ear when her arms tighten around my neck letting me know she wants the same thing.

Kissing her once more, I pull her arms from me and move to the door before I can't force myself to leave.

"'Night, Jax."

Looking over my shoulder at my beautiful woman, I whisper back, "'Night, baby," closing the door halfway behind me.

It's going to be a test of my willpower having Ellie down the hall from me, especially having seen the way she goes wild once I touch her. Going to my room, I leave the door open, that way I can hear if I'm needed, and then strip down to my boxers and get into bed.

WALKING INTO THE kitchen the next morning, I'm glad to see Ellie alone, and am surprised my sister didn't stay when she came to pick up Hope.

Grinding my teeth. I know men have to hit on Ellie all the time. Fuck, if she was on the opposite side of the street from me, I'd walk to the other side and see if I could get her number. Today, her hair is down in big waves. Her long-sleeved black shirt is tight, with a scoop-neck, making her breasts look even fuller. The jeans she has on are ripped and baggy, with the bottom cuffed, showing off a pair of black boots with high chunky heels that make her ass look phenomenal and her legs look long.

"Morning, baby," I greet her, placing a kiss on her neck as I lift my arm over her head to reach for a coffee cup.

"Morning." She smiles then her head ducks away, but I still catch the blush that has risen on her cheeks.

"We need to talk about something," I tell her, watching her face pale.

"What?"

"Here, up you go," I say, placing her on the counter then pushing her legs open so I can stand between them.

"Jax, what is it?"

"Your mom was arrested yesterday," I explain, watching as her bottom lip goes between her teeth. "My uncle will be calling you today, explaining to you what is going on and when or if you will need to be in court."

"I have to see her?" she whispers worriedly.

"Most likely." I nod, rubbing her thighs.

"My mom is—"

"Your mom has nothing to do with your life now," I say, placing a soft kiss on her lips. "And I'm here with you. You're not alone."

"I'm not, am I?" she asks softly, studying me as her fingers move along my jaw then over my bottom lip.

"Never again, Ellie," I tell her, and her forehead comes to rest against my chin. She and Hope have not only me, but also all of my family. They will never be alone again.

Chapter 6

Ellie

WALKING DOWN THE hall to Jax's office, I stop at the threshold, nibbling my bottom lip while leaning against the doorjamb so I don't fall over.

Jax is sitting at his desk shirtless. His hair is messy, and he has a pair of black-framed glasses on I have never seen him wear before. As I watch him, he lifts his hand and runs his fingers through his hair, causing the muscles of his arms to flex, along with his pecs and abs.

"Hey," I mumble, feeling my cheeks get hot when his eyes come to me and do a head-to-toe sweep.

"Hey, baby." He smiles, motioning for me to come to him.

Shaking my head, I take a step back. I don't trust myself. I know if I get close to him, I'm going to want to kiss him, and then I'm going to want to make out with him. I don't have time to do that and go for a run before I have to get ready for work. And I really need to go for a run since the whole diet thing went down in a burning ball of fire.

"I'm going for a run," I explain hastily, when he gets up from his chair and I notice he has on his nylon shorts that outline a very large erection.

"So come kiss me goodbye."

"I can't." I shake my head frantically, watching him smile.

"You can," he assures me, pressing his knuckles into the desk, making his arms and abs flex.

"I can't. I know I can't," I tell him, taking another step backward into the hall. Then, without thinking, I run for the front door, hearing him run behind me as I swing the door open, and bolt down the steps to the sidewalk.

"Ellie," Jax growls as I jog across the front yard.

"I'll be back," I yell over my shoulder, running faster. Getting to the end of the block, I turn right and spot the park at the end of the street, where I take Hope to play. As soon as I reach the large grassy field, I fall down on my back, panting heavy.

"I'm dying," I wheeze, trying to catch my breath. I have no energy to run again. Really, I have no idea what I was thinking when I said I wanted to start running to begin with. Pulling my phone out of my pocket, I press dial when I reach July's number in my call log.

"Hey, what are you doing? Are you okay? You sound out of breath," she answers.

"I'm pretty sure I just died," I tell her through deep breaths.

"Did you decide to finally start running?" she asks on a snort.

"Yes, and I made it two blocks before I had to rest. Now, I'm lying in the grass at the park, talking to you on the phone, killing time before I have to head back to the house and face Jax," I say through pants while listening to her laugh.

"I don't think Jax will care that you don't run," she mutters.

"I know, but have you seen your cousin? He is—"

"Stop. I don't want to know."

"That's not fair. I don't have any friends who aren't related to Jax. Who am I supposed to talk to about him?"

"You can tell me anything about him except if it has to do with sex, his body, and specifically, his penis."

"That's all the good stuff," I point out, making her laugh.

"Well then, you're going to have to make a new friend."

"Fine," I mutter then say quietly, "I told Hope that me and Jax are dating."

"How did that go?" she asks curiously. She knows how worried I've been about this. I told her the last time we spoke that I was concerned about Hope and explained she had never been around anyone besides family before, and Jax wasn't exactly making it easy for me to keep us a secret from her. When I told her my concerns, she told me I should just be honest with her about us.

I'm still not sure what to think, so even though it's awkward as hell, I talked to Lilly about it, and she said Hope talks about Jax and me all the time. In Hope's eyes, we have become a family of sorts, and even though things are new and she's young, she should know what's happening, because in the long run, it's something that will affect her. After Lilly said that, I told her more about how Hope came to be in my care. Hope knows about her mom and dad, but she has no memories of them. To her, they are just pictures and stories. I don't know what I was expecting, but I didn't expect Lilly to have the reaction she did. Instead of making me feel like less of a mom, she made me feel like I was the best mom in the world for Hope.

"Earth to Ellie," July breaks into my thoughts.

"Sorry."

"It's okay. So what did she say?"

"She asked if she can have a sister, so I think it went okay." I smile at the memory and hear July laugh in my ear. "I told her no, and then she asked if she could get a dog instead."

"Well, you've obviously raised a smart girl if she's already negotiating." She laughs again.

"She's too smart. Are you at work?" I ask, hearing a dog bark.

"Yeah. Oh, now that I'm on the phone with you, I can ask you myself if you're coming to the compound tonight. We're having a get-together. I know Ashlyn was going to try and convince you to come hang out."

"Probably not. I have Hope—"

"You know my mom or any of my aunts would love to watch her."

"I don't know. I hate asking people to watch her. I mean, every time I bring up paying anyone, they ignore me, which makes me feel guilty."

"We're family, girl," she says softly.

"I'll see about it, but I can't make any promises," I tell her after a long moment of watching the clouds go blurry through my tears. It's weird knowing I have this whole group of people to count on, and even stranger that I actually trust them.

"Let me know," she replies just as quietly.

"I will; talk to you later," I say before hanging up and tucking my phone back in my pocket.

Pulling in a deep breath, I let it out then stand up, dust my bottom off, and start walking back to the house. When I reach the corner before the house, I start to jog again so it looks like I was jogging the entire time then head up the driveway, up the front walk, and then push the door open.

"What are you doing?" I squeak as a shirtless Jax pulls me fully into the house, slams the door, and pushes me up against the wall. He drops to his knees, covering my sex with his mouth through the material of my workout pants, pulling so hard my head falls back and my clit pulses against his tongue.

"Jax," I whimper, feeling his hands slide around my hips, pulling my core closer to his mouth. "Wh…what are you doing?" I ask, forcing my eyes to open. Seeing him on his knees, his mouth open over me, causes something deep inside me to start to unravel.

Letting out a loud moan, my hands fist in his hair and my head falls back against the wall with a loud thud.

"Ellie," he groans, pulling me down to straddle his lap. One of his hands wraps around my ponytail. The other trails under my shirt then down over the skin of my belly and under the material of my pants, where one finger slides through my folds, causing my hips to jerk forward.

Placing my hands on his shoulders, our eyes connect, and my heartbeat picks up as the reality of what we're doing hits me. "You're safe with me, baby," he says, reading the look on my face as I feel two fingers circle my clit over and over. Biting my lower lip, I swallow then start rocking my hips forward in sync with his fingers.

"Give me your mouth, Ellie," he growls, nipping at my chin. Tipping my face forward, I kiss him timidly then bite his lip as I feel one finger enter me then two, which causes my breath to catch. "You're tight, baby, so fucking tight and wet," he groans, pulling his mouth from mine while his fingers move ruthlessly inside me. My nails dig into his shoulders and my head drops back again as I cry out, feeling the muscles of my lower body getting tighter and tighter. Then his mouth is on my breast through my shirt and his teeth clamp down on my nipple. My hips buck as the tension building in my core detonates, sending me over the edge, blinding me with white light.

Absently, I hear him whisper, "Shhh, I got you," against my ear as he adjusts me in his lap on the floor. Burying my face in his neck, my body is shaking uncontrollably and tears have filled my eyes. I have never experienced anything like that before. It was like I came out of my skin for a few seconds. Clinging tighter to him, he rocks me against his chest while kissing my hair. Lifting my eyes to his, I swallow, trying to think of what to say.

I mean, do you say thank you for something like that?

"How are you feeling?" he asks softly, tucking some of my hair behind my ear.

"Um…"

"I didn't hurt you, did I?" He searches my face and eyes.

"No, no…it was good."

"Good?" he asks with a smile that looks a little too cocky. "You were convulsing and screaming. Baby, if that was good, I wonder what *great* is like for you."

"It was good." I roll my eyes. I mean, for all I know, it was mediocre, seeing how it was my first orgasm. There could be better, though I doubt that's true. I know the ladies at the salon I worked at were constantly bitching about their husbands and lack of orgasms they received, and it seems to me Jax knows exactly what to do.

"We're going to have to work on that then," he says, nuzzling my neck.

"I have to get ready for work," I breathe, tilting my head back then rolling it so he can kiss up the under side of my jaw.

"Me too," he groans, sounding disappointed.

"I didn't know you wear glasses," I say, opening my eyes and lifting my hand, pushing his glasses up the bridge of his nose.

"I need them for the computer." He smiles. "Do you like them?"

"They're okay." I shrug.

"Just okay?" he asks as his hands move up my sides like he's going to tickle me.

"How can you fit in your car or through doors with your giant head?"

"You haven't even seen how big my head is, baby." He smiles, raising his hips, which causes the large head of his cock to brush against my side, sending goose bumps over my skin.

"You're so cocky," I mutter then press my lips together when I realize how it sounded. "I didn't mean like that." I shake my head when he begins to laugh.

"If we didn't have to work, I'd show you how cocky I am."

"You're cheesy too," I say, fighting back a smile.

"And you're beautiful when you come," he says, getting onto his knees and pushing me back until I'm lying on the hardwood floor with him over me, his hands holding mine above me against the wood.

"Jax," I whisper as his knees slide between mine.

"I love when you say my name like that, out of breath, like you're begging me to kiss and touch you," he says before his mouth lowers over mine, kissing me thoroughly then moving down my cheek to my ear, where he growls, "I'm taking you out tonight, and you need to wear a dress."

"July asked me to go to the shop tonight," I say breathlessly as his mouth moves down my jaw then neck, where he nips me hard enough to sting.

"We'll go there after we have dinner."

"Hope," I whimper as his hands move up my side, under my shirt.

"Mom and Dad'll watch her," he says as his mouth nips my earlobe.

"I hate leaving her," I tell him truthfully.

His face moves to hover over me and his eyes search mine. I see something there that gives me pause and makes me feel warm all over. "You can have a night, baby. We'll pick her up early tomorrow morning."

"Over night?" I whisper, feeling my heart begin to pound against my ribs.

"Over night, but remember we're taking this slow. It's a date then hanging out with friends, and maybe some snuggling if you're nice to me," he says with a peck.

Pressing my lips together to keep from smiling, I mutter, "If they don't mind watching her, then okay." I wrap my legs around his waist while moving my hands over the skin of his back. "But the snuggling is negotiable."

Smiling, he rocks against me, causing his length to rub against me through the material of my pants and a moan to climb up my throat.

Smirking, he murmurs, "I'll convince you to cuddle."

"Maybe," I whisper, finally giving in to my smile.

His face goes soft and his hands frame my face while his eyes move over my hair, eyes, and then mouth. "I like seeing you like this," he says as he kisses my lips then moves his mouth down my chin to my neck. His hands move, cupping my breasts, making my knees weak and my core tighten.

"I have to get ready for work," I moan in both frustration and relief. I don't know if I'm ready to open myself up to him, especially when he doesn't know everything. I don't think there is any way for me to hide the fact I'm a virgin, and once he knows that, he's going to know about Hope. I need to tell him, but I'm so scared.

Knifing off me, he pulls me up to stand, asking, "What time do you get off tonight?" as his hands smooth down my hair and his eyes search my face.

"We close the shop at seven. Is that too late to have dinner?"

"No, and just let me know when you can get lunch, and I'll bring Hope by so we can spend some time with her, since we won't see her until tomorrow."

"I would love that," I say quietly through the tears lodged in my throat.

"Go get ready, and I'll drop you off at work then just pick you up at seven."

"Please...?" I prompt, narrowing my eyes.

"I don't mind staying here and using your body as entertainment for the rest of the day," he says with a shrug, while his eyes sweep over me once more, causing my nipples to harden and the place his fingers just were to contract.

"I...I'm gonna go get...get ready," I stutter out then take off up the stairs, listening to his laughter follow me as I shut the door for the bathroom behind me and lean back against it, breathing heavily. I'm so far over my head it's not even funny.

"THAT WAS JAX Mayson," Kim whispers to me as I set my bag down on my station. "He just kissed you." She blinks at me then looks at the door Jax just left out of. Biting my lip, I nod, because I can't exactly lie. Jax insisted on walking me into the salon, and when I tried to give him a casual goodbye, he grabbed onto the back of my jeans and hauled me against him so he could kiss me in a way that let everyone know we were more than friends. "I thought he's with Mellissa."

Taking a deep breath, I let it out slowly as annoyance washes over me. I don't even think I'm jealous about the whole Mellissa thing really. I'm annoyed she thinks she has some claim over him, when he has made it clear she doesn't. "He's not. I don't know what she's thinking, but I know what Jax has told me, and I believe him."

"Hey, I didn't mean anything by it," she says, wrapping her hand around my arm. "I don't know him; I just know of him, because I've seen him around and she tells everyone they're together."

"It's fine, and I know. It's just crazy. Why would you push yourself on someone who's not interested in you?" I ask, watching as her face loses some of its color. "What's wrong?"

"Do you know Jax's cousin Sage?" she asks quietly, moving to stand in front of the mirror between our stations, pulling her hair up into a high ponytail, and I notice her hands are shaking.

"A little, but really, things have been so busy that every time I've seen him, it's just been hi and bye. Why?" I ask, wondering what she could possibly have against Sage. He's always nice to me, and he's so good with Hope, who loves him.

"I have a sister," she whispers.

"I didn't know you have a sister," I mutter, watching her bite the inside of her cheek.

"We're identical twins, and she's not exactly a good person. Don't get me wrong; I love her, because we're blood, but she's…" She pauses and her eyes meet mine in the mirror once more. "She has some problems."

"Oh." I know exactly what she's saying. I have a whole family full of people with problems.

"My sister had a run-in with Sage before she left town," she says then drops her eyes, along with her voice. "She tried to roofie him when they were at the same bar."

"What?" I breathe, covering my mouth.

"Yeah," she whispers with tears in her eyes. "She was going to get him alone and get his wallet…I don't know exactly, but he caught her when she was trying to mess with his drink. And now he thinks I'm her."

"Maybe you could tell him it wasn't you."

"She left town." She shakes her head.

"If you talk to him—" I try again, but she cuts me off.

"I believe his words were 'Stay the fuck away from me, you psycho bitch' when I tried."

"That's not good," I say as she turns around to face me.

"You wanna know the worst part?" she asks softly, moving to sit in my stylist chair.

"What?" I ask, thinking this couldn't possibly get any worse. She has an evil twin—that's storybook bad.

"I met him the day before it happened." She takes a breath, letting it out slowly. "My car got a flat on Old Fork Road, and he stopped to help me change it. After he got the new one on, he asked me if I wanted to have coffee with him and I said yes. *I never say yes*," she whispers as tears fill her eyes. "I know you're going to think I'm a slut, but I swear I have never done anything like that."

"Had coffee with a guy?" I ask, confused, seeing pain in her eyes.

"No, after we had coffee, we went back to my place, and one thing led to another," she says, waving her hand around, and I understand what she's saying.

"Oh," I breathe, and she nods.

"Then later the next night, he met my sister, and now..." she trails off.

"Now he thinks you're her," I finish her thought.

"Yep." She nods again as her mouth forms a sad smile.

"There has to be a way to prove to him it wasn't you."

"I tried to talk to him, but he refused to listen to me, and honestly, I don't think I care anymore. At first, I was upset, because I really liked him—or what I knew of him—but since then, I have seen him around town numerous times, and he's always with a different girl. Really, he left my place, and the next night he went out to a bar, so that says it all, I think."

"I'm sorry," I murmur, not knowing what else to say right now. I mean, maybe Sage is actually an asshole, 'cause this doesn't seem like something a nice guy would do. A nice guy would at least listen to you.

"It's okay, really. I don't know why I just laid all of that out for you."

"I would like to think we're becoming friends," I tell her softly, giving her a hug. "He's not worth the tears," I whisper as I hear her sob quietly into my shoulder.

"It's not him. I just...I could use a friend right now," she says, pulling away and wiping the tears from under her eyes.

"If you ever want to talk, I'm here," I assure her, giving her shoulder a squeeze.

"You ladies ready to open shop?" Frankie asks, walking out of the backroom heading towards the front of the salon.

"Ready." I smile at him as he passes by then turn to look at Kim, who has pulled out a compact from her bag. "Will you be okay?"

"One thing I know, Ellie, is I will *always* be okay," she says softly, but I understand immediately what she means. Being happy isn't something I found easily until I was blessed with raising Hope. I know how it feels to struggle everyday, never really feeling any true emotions like happiness or joy. *Always just being okay.*

Feeling my throat get tight, I swallow through the pain and press my lips together for a moment. "One day, you're going to find happy, Kim," I tell her softly when I catch her eyes in the mirror in front of us.

"One day," she agrees, putting the compact away before heading to the front of the salon, out of sight. Pulling in a breath, I finish setting up my station then head to the front of the salon so I can take a look at the appointment book. When I walk around the corner into the waiting area, I see Mellissa talking to Frankie.

Ignoring her, I walk behind the reception desk and take out the calendar. Seeing I have a client coming in in twenty minutes who is getting a full head of highlights, I head to the back of the salon and go to the small color kitchen that is set up. I begin getting products out so that when my client comes in, the process will go by much faster. Once I have everything together, I start toward my station, but as I go to pass by Frankie, who is standing at one the shampoo bowls in the back washing Mellissa's hair, I feel her foot hit me just above the ankle, which causes me to go tumbling forward. Dropping the items in my hands, I hit the ground hard, landing on my hands and knees.

"Ellie, are you okay?" Frankie cries, wrapping an arm around my waist and helping me stand.

"I'm fine," I mutter, dusting my knees and hands off as I feel my cheeks grow red with embarrassment.

"Are you sure?" he asks softly, pushing my hair back over my shoulder and searching my face.

"I'm sure. I just hope my knees aren't bruised. Jax and I have a date tonight, and I brought a dress to change into," I tell him loud enough for Mellissa to hear. If she thinks tripping me like we're in middle school is going to scare me into giving Jax up, she has another think coming.

"Oh," Frankie's eyes sparkle, "a date with Jax. Please tell me I get to do your hair."

"Uhh…" I haven't let anyone touch my hair since I was around twelve. I even do my own cuts when I need one.

"You're not scared, are you?" He smiles wickedly, nudging my shoulder.

"You should really let Frankie do your hair, or a least have him cut off your split ends," Mellissa chimes in from her position at the sink, making my teeth grit.

Looking over at her, I give her a fake smile and lie, "That's a great idea. Thanks, Mellissa."

"You're welcome," she says, rolling her eyes and leaning her head back into the bowl.

Picking up the stuff I dropped on the floor, I look from Mellissa to Frankie, seeing he has his eyes narrowed on her. When his eyes come back to me, he asks softly, "Are you sure you're okay?"

"I'm fine." I nod, and he nods as well then gives my hand a squeeze.

"We'll talk about your date later." He winks.

"Okay," I say, but this time I really smile and he grins back while shaking his head then moves toward Mellissa.

Going to my station, I set the items in my hands down on the counter then giggle when I hear Mellissa shriek, "Oh, my God! That's too cold!"

"Karma is a bitch," Kim says, smiling at me in the mirror between us.

"Yes, she is," I agree then laugh harder when I hear Mellissa scream, "You're getting me wet!"

"Mommy," Hope yells as she runs toward me from the front of the salon.

"Hey, Angel baby." I smile, but then frown when I see she has chocolate covering her face from her nose down to her chin.

Picking her up, I look at Jax, who doesn't give me a chance to ask him why he gave her chocolate before he closes the distance between us and kisses me breathless. When his mouth leaves mine, he whispers, "Don't be mad."

"I'm not," I tell him then smile when I hear Hope giggling. "But I thought we were having lunch."

"We are habing lunch," Hope says, happily wiggling out of my arms and climbing into my stylist chair.

"We have to wash your face first, chocolate girl," I tell her, grabbing my purse and pulling out a wet wipe. "Did you trick Jax into buying you chocolate again?" I ask her when I get her face cleaned.

"No, he just gabe it to me," she says, making Jax chuckle and me shake my head.

Standing back up, I look at Jax and whisper, "Pushover."

"I can't say no to her." He shrugs, not denying it, and I roll my eyes.

"Are you ready for lunch, or are you too full from eating chocolate?" I ask Hope, taking her hand and helping her off the chair.

"I'm hungry. I only had four pieces of my candy bar," she tells me, holding up her fingers.

"Oh, you poor thing. You must be starving," I tease, picking her up and tickling her. "Frankie, we're going to go feed this poor, starving child. Do you want us to get you anything?" I ask my boss, who is smiling at us, while Mellissa—foils sticking out all over her head like Medusa waiting for an alien attack—is trying to kill me with her eyes.

"No, thanks. Have a good lunch," he says, laughing.

"Thanks." I give him a wave. "So where are we eating?" I ask Jax.

"I figured we could go to the sandwich place around the corner," he replies, holding open the door for the salon.

"Sounds good," I agree, moving past him through the door with Hope in my arms.

"I want Ax to carry me," Hope says when we reach the sidewalk, causing me to feel something I didn't expect. I never thought I would be jealous, but that's exactly what I feel as Hope holds out her tiny arms toward Jax. Squeezing her a little tighter to me for a second, I almost feel panicked as he takes her from me.

"Hey, are you okay?" he asks, dipping his face toward mine and searching my eyes.

Swallowing hard, I look at him and Hope and know it's completely irrational to feel like I do right now, but that doesn't mean the feelings aren't there as I nod, muttering, "Just hungry."

"Let's get you girls some food," he says, but I can tell he doesn't believe me. I have no idea where this feeling is coming from, but now that it's there, I feel it gnawing at my stomach as we walk down the street, around the corner, and into the small deli at the end of the block.

Once we're inside, we order our sandwiches then take a seat at one of the tables near the front.

"Mom and Dad said they're happy to keep Hope for the night," Jax announces, and Hope smiles at me, saying, "Gwamma said we're going to be vegables and watch the snowman movie." She smiles.

"Oh," I mutter, biting my lip. Maybe this is all a really bad idea. Maybe I'm not ready for any of this.

"Ellie," Jax calls, gaining my attention. "What's going on?"

Oh, God, why do I feel like crying all of a sudden?

"Just hungry," I repeat my earlier lie, and his eyes narrow on me from across the table, but I ignore it.

"Mommy, what's 'being a vegable'?" Hope asks, making me smile.

"It just means to be lazy, Angel baby," I explain.

"Oh." She scrunches up her face and Jax chuckles.

"Mayson, order's up," one of the guys calls from the front of the deli.

"I'll be right back," Jax says, leaving the table to go get our sandwiches. When he comes back, he sets my sandwich down in front of me and my mouth begins to water from the smell of grilled chicken, fresh mozzarella, tomatoes, and basil. Then he mumbles, "Here, sweetheart," to Hope.

He takes her grilled cheese and cuts it into small pieces, which should be sweet, but I find myself snapping, "I'm her mom; I can do that," while attempting to take the knife out of his hand.

"You just eat," he says softly, but I still hear the bite in his tone as he finishes cutting it up for her. Sitting there for the rest of lunch, I can feel Jax's stare boring into me from across the table, but I don't look at him. I either focus on Hope, or my sandwich, which should have tasted amazing, but instead, I don't even enjoy it.

When we get to Jax's truck and I have Hope buckled in, I can once again feel myself fighting tears.

"Bye, Mama," Hope sings.

Giving her a kiss and hug, I fight myself from telling her I will see in a little while, and settle with telling her, "I love you, Angel baby. Be good, okay?"

"Okay, Mama." She grins.

Shutting the door, I squeak when Jax takes my hand, pulls me to the back of his truck, and pushes me up against the tailgate, crowding my body with his and lowering his face towards mine.

"I don't know what the fuck is going on in your head right now, Ellie, but I'm telling you this. You are mine, and Hope is mine. I don't give a fuck how hard you try to push me away; it's not going to happen. We have happened, and I'm not taking a step back, so deal with whatever fucked up shit you have going on in your head and get over it.

Tonight, we're having dinner then spending time with my cousin. After that, I'm taking you home and eating your pussy until you beg me to stop, and then I'm going to keep going until you apologize for your shit today," he snarls then his head ducks, and his mouth latches onto my neck. I feel him pull the skin there into his mouth so hard that I cry out and my legs get weak.

Wrapping my hands around his shoulders, I hold on to keep from falling, when he lifts his mouth away from my neck and kisses me softly. "See you at seven," he says, leading me to the sidewalk. Then he places another kiss on my mouth before going to his truck and getting in behind the wheel. Opening and closing my mouth, I stand there on the sidewalk, watching as he pulls away, then turn around and go into the salon.

"You have a hickey," Kim whispers, covering her mouth while using her free had to point at my neck. Looking in the mirror, I take a deep breath and grit my teeth. Not only do I have a hickey, but I have a huge, dark purple hickey that will likely never go away.

"So classy," I hear Mellissa say from the chair she's in across the salon, and without thinking, I turn and look at her, mouthing, *Jealous,* before pulling out my concealer from my bag and covering the damn thing up.

Chapter 7

Jax

"HEY, YOU," ASHLYN greets quietly with her eyes on Hope in my arms as she opens the door to our parents' house. "Mom and Dad are out back."

"I'll be out in a minute. I'm going to lay her down; she passed out in the truck on the way over here," I tell her, and she follows me down the hall toward my old room, which mom turned into a guest room as soon as I moved out.

Settling Hope on the bed and covering her with a blanket, I press a kiss to her forehead then follow Ashlyn out of the room, asking, "What are you doing here?"

Ashlyn is a receptionist for our family dentist. She got the job a few years ago when she started going to dental school. "Got off work early and just wanted to stop by." She shrugs, but I can tell it's something else from the look in her eyes.

"What happened?" I repeat.

"You know you're annoying right?" she asks, grabbing a bottle of water from the fridge and taking a sip.

"So I've been told. So what happened?" I ask, grabbing a bottle for myself.

"Gregory is selling his practice," she says, and I'm not surprised. Every time I have to see him, I worry he's going fill the wrong tooth, or worse. His glasses have progressively gotten thicker each year, and his hands aren't as steady as they used to be.

"We all knew it was coming. He's what, seventy now?"

"Seventy-two." She nods.

"So you can come work for me. You know I need a receptionist, since things have picked up."

Snorting, she shakes her head. "No, thanks. He sold it to a guy named Dillon. He seems like a dick, but I'd rather work for a dick than my brother until school is done," she mutters.

"So you've met the guy?" I ask her, and she nods again, leaning back against the counter behind her.

"Yeah, he just moved here from New York. I guess in the dental world he's some big shot." She rolls her eyes.

"Did he say you could keep your job?"

"He said he would need to 're-interview' me," she says, using finger quotes. "His words were, 'I don't need pretty objects around to look at. I need someone who knows what they're doing working with me.'"

Frowning at that, I wonder if I should go have a talk with Dillon myself.

"Don't even think about it," she says, reading my face. "He's a dick, but if he thinks anyone can do a better job than me, I'd like to see that person. I've worked with Gregory for the last three years. I only have a year of night classes left before I graduate, and then I can move to another practice."

"Well, if you want me to kick his ass, I will," I tell her, and a smile twitches her lips.

"I can handle him," she says after a moment of thinking about it.

"I do think it's kinda funny there is finally a guy who isn't susceptible to your charm," I tell her honestly. Men normally flock to my baby sister, which is annoying, but also true.

"Well, maybe he will be susceptible to cyanide," she mutters under her breath, which makes me even more curious about Dillon.

"You know I got your back," I tell her, moving out the backdoor to the sunroom.

Mom had the room built onto the house a year ago, when she decided to stop teaching and stay home. Walking through the sliding door, I'm not surprised to find my parents sitting close together on one of the couches, Mom with her feet tucked under her and my dad leaning back against the couch, with his arm wrapped around her.

"Where's my girl?" Mom asks, looking around me for Hope.

"She's in the guestroom. She fell asleep in the truck on the way over here."

"Are you okay?" she asks, tilting her face and studying me.

"I'm good." I nod, sitting down across from them on one of the chairs.

"What happened?" She frowns.

"How do you know something happened?" I ask.

"You have the same look on your face that your sister had when she came in," Mom explains.

"I didn't have a look," Ashlyn complains, plopping down in the chair next to me, and my mom looks at her and shakes her head.

"You did, and then you went off about Dillon the Dick for a good twenty minutes," my dad says, grinning.

"Whatever," she huffs, crossing her arms over her chest.

"So what happened?" Dad asks this time, looking away from Ashlyn to me.

"I took Ellie and Hope to lunch, and Ellie was acting strange. Then she said something that caught me off guard."

"What was it?" Mom asks, pulling her feet from under her and sitting up.

"She was upset that I was cutting up Hope's sandwich, and she said, 'I can do it; I'm her mom,'" I say, pulling my hat off and setting it on my bent knee.

"Honey, that's her baby. She's not used to sharing her. She's had a lot of changes over the last couple months. Just give her some time," Mom explains.

"I'm going slow," I say, slipping my hat back on my head. "I gotta head back to the office, but if Hope needs anything, just call me."

"It will be okay, honey," she says softly as I get up from my chair and lean over, kissing her cheek.

"I know," I agree then mutter, "Later," to my sister, and look at my dad as he kisses my mom's cheek then follows me out of the house to my truck.

"I never thought that I'd ever give this advice to anyone. You know I think your uncles are idiots half the time, but your uncle, Trevor, told me something when I started seeing your mom again," he says, and I raise a brow.

"He told me to push your mom into a corner, not to give her a chance to retreat. At the time, I thought he was nuts, but I think he was right. I know Ellie has had a hard time with everything that's happened, but if she's your Boom, she's your forever. Nothing will change that."

"Thanks, Dad," I mutter as he pats my back.

"I love you, bud,"

"Love you too," I tell him, opening my truck door. "Can you do me a favor and not let Hope eat too much junk food tonight? She had a candy bar already."

"Sure." He nods, but I know he's lying. Shaking my head, I slam my door and lift my chin to him as he steps back so I can pull away from the house.

I'm going to follow his advice. Maybe taking it slow was the wrong move.

GETTING OUT OF my truck, I slam the door, head across the sidewalk, and spot Ellie through the glass of the salon door. I feel my body get tight as I take her in while she stands in the waiting area, talking to some blonde. Her hair is down in messy waves with new red chunky highlights that cascade over her breast. The navy blue dress she has on is molded tightly to every curve of her body, leaving her shoulders bare and hitting her mid-thigh. Moving my eyes down her legs, which seem to go on for miles, I swallow, seeing the cream high heels that wrap around her feet with a million straps ending up around her ankles. Seeing how high they lift her, I know they will put her ass at the perfect height for me to fuck her from behind while she's bent over.

"How the fuck can I go slow when she looks like that?" I mutter to myself, tapping on the glass to get her attention.

When her eyes meet mine, I watch her take a deep breath before moving to the door.

"Hi," she whispers, opening the door.

"You look beautiful."

"I... Thanks," she whispers shyly then looks over her shoulder at the blonde. "Jax, this is Kimberly. Kim this is Jax; I don't know if you've met."

"Nice to meet you," I mutter, giving her a chin lift as I take Ellie's hand in mine and tug her closer to me.

"You too," Kim says, and I hear her laugh, but I can't take my eyes off Ellie and how amazing she looks. Not that she doesn't always look good, but right now, she looks good enough to eat, which is going to make it difficult to share her with anyone tonight.

"Are you going to be okay locking up by yourself?" Ellie asks Kim, picking up her bag from the couch near the door.

"Yep, go have fun and I'll see you on Sunday."

"See you Sunday," Ellie replies quietly then looks up at me and bites her bottom lip, causing my chest to vibrate with a growl. Opening the door for her, I let her walk out before me, just so I can watch her ass, then take her hand again and lead her to my truck, opening the passenger side door for her.

"Thanks," she murmurs, ducking her head again.

Spinning her around to face me, I press her against the side of my truck and dip my head to the side, covering her mouth with mine, fisting one hand into her hair, and pulling her closer to me with the other. Nipping her bottom lip, her gasp of surprise allows me to lick into her mouth, tasting her and mint.

The moment my tongue touches hers, her hands fist into my shirt and her breasts press hard against my chest. As my hat falls to the ground, she pulls my lip between hers and bites hard enough to sting. Moving my hand down over her ass, I rock her into my erection, needing her to feel what she does to me.

"Jax," she whimpers into my mouth as her hands travel up, wrapping around the back of my neck. Tearing my mouth from hers, I rest my forehead against hers, willing myself to stop, when all I want to do is pick her up, place her on the seat of my truck, rip her dress up around her waist and swing her legs over my shoulders so I can feast.

Lifting her mouth closer to mine once more, I shake my head, giving her a squeeze when I see hurt enter her gaze.

"We're going to dinner, and if we keep going, the only thing I'll be eating is you."

"Jax," she moans my name.

"Fuck," I grunt, picking her up, placing her on the seat, and giving her one last kiss before pulling from her grasp and shutting the door.

Picking my hat up off the ground, I shake it out and place it back on my head then take my time walking around the truck, so I can will my erection down enough that I can drive.

Opening the door, I get behind the wheel shutting the door and Ellie's soft voice breaks through the silence, causing my chest to ache.

"My brother's name was Edward. You would have liked him," she says with a sad smile. "He was always doing crazy stuff. He was the guy everyone wanted to be friends with, the guy all the girls wished would take a second look at them."

She pauses, and her voice is barely above a whisper as she says, "He was my best friend." Hating seeing her look so alone, I reach over and unhook her belt then drag her into my lap. Settling herself against me, her eyes search my face then drop to her lap before she continues, "When he met Bonnie and I saw how in love he was with her, I remember thinking everything was going to change. I was going to lose him. He was all I had for so long that I was scared and jealous. I wanted to hate her."

Her eyes meet mine and a soft smile forms on her mouth as she whispers, "Trying to hate her was like trying to hate air. Bonnie became like a sister to me. Her dad was a drunk and her mom was dead. She needed us as badly as we needed her.

She, Edward, and I became a family of our own," she reminisces, and I watch as tears fill her eyes. "When Bonnie found out she was pregnant, Edward was so excited he would tell absolutely anyone. All he talked about was making a better life for his girls."

Her lips press together and her chin wobbles. "Hope was born on July twenty-forth at seven-twenty in the morning, She came into the world screaming at the top of her lungs. *She's still screaming,*" she whispers the last part, leaning her body into mine. "I loved her from the first moment I held her in my arms, but she wasn't mine," she says then lets that hang before continuing.

"On August twenty-seventh, that changed. I was at work when I got a call from the highway patrol. They said Edward, Bonnie, and their daughter had been in an accident and I needed to get to the hospital. I don't even remember getting in my car, or the drive to the hospital. I don't even remember the police telling me Bonnie and Edward were dead. Everything was a blur. None of it felt real, and then they took me to the ICU." She shakes her head. "The doctors and the police both said Hope shouldn't have lived. They said she was lucky to be alive, but because she was so young, her body was still soft, and that saved her life."

"Jesus," I hiss, thinking about a life without Hope and how sad that life would be.

"She had small cuts and bruises on her face and hands, but she was okay. She was awake, and when I walked towards her, I could tell she knew exactly who I was. She knew me, and she was so small and all alone. We were both alone."

Watching as silent tears fall from her eyes, I know how hard that must have been for her, how devastated she must have been.

"I was just nineteen. I didn't know anything about raising a kid, but I knew I wouldn't let Edward or Bonnie down. I knew they would want me to take care of her, to raise her, so after I rocked Hope to sleep in the ICU, I went in search of a social worker, and they told me what I needed to do in order to gain custody of her."

"You're so strong, baby." I kiss the side of her head and breathe her in.

"Hope didn't come from me, but she's a part of me."

"She's your daughter," I tell her softly, wondering how I could have thought otherwise before. My mom was right; you don't have to give birth to a child to love it like your own.

"She knows about her dad and mom, but to her, they are nothing but pictures and stories I tell her. When she's older, I hope I can make her understand Bonnie and Edward loved her more then they loved anything in this world, that they would have given up anything to stay here with her. But until she's old enough to understand that, I'm all she knows."

"I get that," I tell her softly, pressing a kiss to her temple.

"I was jealous she wanted you today instead of me," she says, and I hear her take a breath.

"I know," I say gently then add, "I don't want to take her from you, baby. I just want to be a part of your lives. I want to be one more person she knows who loves her, and I want us to have something solid, so one day we can all be a family."

"Family," she whispers, dropping her eyes again.

"I don't know if you know this," I say, running my fingers along her cheek until her eyes meet mine once again. "Lilly isn't my mother. She didn't give birth to me. My dad dated her when she was in college. Around the time my dad was going to ask her to move in with him, my birth mom, who my dad had a one-night stand with months before, told him she was pregnant. My dad believed he was doing the right thing, and he broke up with Lilly. He didn't want her to be dragged through everything that was happening at the time. He and my birth mother got married, and my dad didn't know he had also gotten Lilly pregnant. My birth mom, who is the definition of crazy, got a message from Lilly that was meant for my dad, telling him she was pregnant, and she replied back that she should have an abortion."

"Oh, my God," Ellie breathes.

"My birth mom and dad eventually divorced, and when I was three, my dad took me to this trampoline place, and Lilly was there with Ashlyn. He knew right away Ashlyn was his daughter, and he thought Lilly tried to keep her from him."

"Poor Lilly," she says in understanding, and my hand moves to wrap around the side of her neck.

"Eventually, my dad won Lilly over and they got back together, but from the moment I met her, I remember thinking I wanted a mom like her. She was the opposite of my mother. So nice, every time she talked to me, she spoke softly and made me feel important. Eventually her and my dad got married and she became my mom. I will always consider her my mom."

"You get it," she says softly, placing her hand against my chest over my heart.

"I get it," I agree.

"I'm sorry about lunch. I…" She pauses, taking a breath. "I just…it's always been just me and Hope. I'm not used to sharing her. I know it sounds selfish, but I don't want her to stop needing me."

"That's not going to happen, baby, and I don't want to take her from you," I promise.

"I know," she says, leaning her head against my chest.

Sitting back, I hold her tighter against me. I know we will still have shit to deal with, but knowing she came right out and told me her problem saved me a shit load of trouble and time.

"Now can I take you out?" I ask, pressing a kiss to the top of her head after a few moments.

"Jax, about us—"

"This is happening, Ellie. I won't stop until every part of you belongs to me, from this," I say, placing my hand over her heart, feeling it pound. Then I run my palm over her breast and down her stomach, over her thigh, and then under the edge of her dress, where I run my fingers over the thin material covering her core. "To this," I finish.

"Jax—"

"No, baby, now slide off me so I can take you to dinner," I interrupt.

"But—"

"Slide off," I rumble, helping her into the passenger seat then buckling her in.

"You're annoying," she grumbles.

"You love it, baby. My fingers are still wet and I barely ran them over your panties." Which is true, but then again, every time I've touched her, she's been wet.

"You didn't just say that." She hides her face behind her hair.

Smirking, I pull her hand to my lap then run her palm over my cock. "You're not the only one," I tell her, hearing her sharp inhale of breath and groan when her small hand tries to wrap around me through the denim covering my erection.

Before I can say fuck it and pin her to the seat, I pull her hand to my mouth and place a kiss against her fingers settling it back against my thigh, so I can start up my truck and put it in reverse.

When we arrive at the restaurant, it's after eight and the lot's still full, which isn't a surprise. Bryson's Steakhouse is the place everyone comes to celebrate. I think I've spent every birthday and special occasion here since I was ten. Shutting down the truck, I hop out and head around to wait while Ellie adds some glossy shit to her lips that causes them look even fuller than they normally do. Helping her down, I wrap my arm around her waist and lead her inside.

For the first time, I realize that the rustic looking décor and lighting give the restaurant a romantic feel. I've never brought a woman here before; I've only ever come with family. Luckily, my dad is good friends with Mani Bryson and was able to get us a reservation on short notice.

"Reservation for Mayson," I tell the maître d', holding Ellie a little tighter when his eyes sweep over my girl and linger a little too long on her mouth then chest.

I've never been jealous; even in school, when I was dating Mellissa and guys would hit on her, I couldn't have cared less. Ellie is different. I can't stand the idea of anyone looking at her, and if someone ever has the balls to touch her, I won't be able to control myself.

"If you'll follow me," he says, picking up two menus and leading us through the restaurant.

Placing my hand against Ellie's back, we cut between tables then stop at one of the booths in the back. My teeth grit when I look to the left and see Mellissa is here with her sister, mom, and dad. Mellissa's dad, Calder, owns one of the most profitable real-estate agencies in the county. If you drive around and see a for sale sign on a house, it's his company's logo normally attached to it. He's an okay guy, but he's a pushover and has babied the women in his life.

Mellissa's mother's job is to stay home and look pretty, and she has raised both her girls to do the same. They expect everything to be handed to them and whatever man they are with to act like their father, giving them whatever it is they want. And if you don't fall to your knees and act accordingly, cue the tears and the bitchiness.

Placing Ellie so that she's faced away from them, I take a seat then raise a brow when the maître d' stands at the head of the table, staring at Ellie again. "You can go," I hear myself growl, and I watch Ellie's cheeks darken as she looks at me and narrows her eyes. Like it's my fucking fault the kid is checking her out.

"Sorry, would you like to see the wine menu?" he asks suddenly.

"No, thank you." I shake my head and feel Ellie kick me under the table before she looks at the guy.

"We'll just wait for our waitress." She says softly and smiles, taking the menu from him setting it on the table. She then watches him walk away before looking at me and growling, "You're so rude."

"Really? And it's not rude to stare at another man's woman when they are obviously out on a date?" I ask as one of the bus boys stops by the table, dropping off water.

"He wasn't staring. He was just doing his job." She shakes her head.

"His job isn't to check out your tits, baby."

"He wasn't," she hisses in anger and annoyance.

"Fuck yes, he was," I growl. "And since those tits, that ass, and that mouth all belong to me, he doesn't get to look at them," I say, watching her chest heave and her mouth open and close.

"Jax, Ellie."

"Fuck," I clip, watching as Ellie's body grows tight across from me then her head swivel towards Mellissa. Turning my head, I say shortly, "Mellissa," through gritted teeth.

"I just wanted to come over and say hi." She smiles her fake smile then looks at Ellie, running her eyes over her. "That dress totally fits you." She sneers. "It's very trailer—"

"Get the fuck away from my table, Mellissa, before you force me to make a scene," I threaten.

"I'm not afraid of you, Jax," she snarls, placing her hands on her narrow hips.

"One more time, Mellissa. Get the fuck away from the table."

"I can't believe you traded me in for some slutty trailer trash bitch."

Like it happens in slow motion, I see Ellie out of the corner of my eye as she wraps her fingers around her glass of water and tosses the contents on Mellissa, who shrieks at the top of her lungs. Ellie scoots out of the booth and storms towards the front of the restaurant.

"You bitch!" Mellissa screams, going after Ellie. Wrapping my arm around her waist, I pick her up, turn her around, and shove her into her dad's arms.

"Put a leash on your daughter, Calder," I tell him. His eyes narrow and his arms lock around Mellissa.

Moving through the restaurant, I see Mani, the owner, walking towards me from the kitchen. "Is everything okay, Jax?" he asks with concern in his tone, looking at me then over my shoulder at the commotion going on behind me.

"I'll call and explain what happened, but right now, I need to go make sure Ellie is okay," I tell him without stopping on my way past the maître d'.

"Sure." He nods.

Pushing through the door, I look toward my truck and see Ellie isn't there. Jogging up the road, I spot Ellie in the distance, walking with her arms wrapped around her body, her shoulders stooped inward and her head bent toward her feet.

"Ellie, stop," I shout, watching her body jerk forward and her head move back and forth. Reaching her side, I wrap my arm around her shoulders and the other under her knees, lifting her to my chest. Hearing her soft sob rips my heart open.

"Please, don't cry. I hate it when you cry," I whisper, pressing my lips to the top of her head, holding her closer against me. When I get her to the truck, I place her in the passenger seat, buckle her in, and then jog around to get in behind the wheel.

"Can you just take me home?" she asks on a quiet sob, wiping the tears away as they fall.

"Yeah, baby," I agree pulling out of the parking lot.

Taking her hand, I pull it toward me, wrapping my fingers tightly around hers, wanting her to know I'm here with her. When we reach the house, I get out and head around to her side, half expecting her to fight me, but her body wraps around mine tightly as I lift her from the truck and carry her into the house. I don't even stop downstairs. I carry her up to my bedroom, lay her in the bed, and get in with her. As soon as I'm settled behind her, she turns in my arms to face me, burying her face against my chest.

"I'm sorry," she says through her tears as I gather her closer.

"You don't need to apologize."

"I shouldn't have let her get to me the way I did."

"She's a bitch, Ellie. You doing that is way better then me laying her out for talking to you like that," I assure her.

"I'm so embarrassed," she whispers painfully.

"You have nothing to be embarrassed about. She shouldn't have come to our table; she should have stayed with her family. And she had no right to talk to you the way she did," I tell her, feeling rage burn through me. Mellissa is lucky she's a chick, 'cause I swear if she were a dude, she would have been sporting a black eye before I walked out of the restaurant.

"You know what makes me really mad?" she asks suddenly, pulling her head away from my chest and looking at me with her big eyes still full of tears.

"What's that, baby?"

"I'm hungry," she says sullenly, making me smile. "I was really looking forward to having dinner with you. Kim said they have the best steaks, and now I will never be able to find out for myself."

"We can go back whenever you want. The Bryson's and my family are tight."

"I'm never going back there," she pouts.

"We will be going back there. It's tradition," I tell her, ignoring her headshake. "Now, do you want to order in and we can watch a movie? Or do you want to go meet up with July?" I ask her, running my fingers through her hair.

"I want to get out of this dress and put on some sweats."

"I'm more than happy to help you out of the dress." I smile, running my hand up her bare thigh.

"Jax."

"Ellie," I reply then roll her to her back and loom over her. I can't believe how beautiful she is, and she's mine. For the rest of my life, this will be the face I look at. Months ago, that thought would have scared me, but it now sends a bolt of excitement through my system.

Dropping my eyes to her mouth, I lean in and place a soft kiss against her lips while running my fingertips up her calf and thigh, hearing her breath hitch.

Moving over her, I place my leg between hers, taking her hands in mine I pull them up and over her head, watching as her chest begins to rise and fall more rapidly.

"I'm a virgin," she breathes, and I raise my eyes to meet hers. "I..." She stops, looking unsure and nervous.

"Shhh, baby, I'll guide you," I tell her gently, kissing her again.

Holding both her hands in one of mine, I run the fingers of my free hand over her cleavage. Her nails dig into the skin of my hand and her chest rises up to meet my palm. Smiling, I slowly pull the top of her dress down, exposing the black lace strapless bra she has on. My zipper cuts into my hard-on as my eyes focus on how perfect she is. Her nipples are visible through the lace, and running my finger over the hard peak and material, I groan when they pucker from the light touch. Sliding the material down under her breast, I lean back and meet her eyes again as I lower my mouth, pulling one hard nub into the cavern of my mouth.

A loud moan leaves her mouth as her eyes close and her head presses back into the pillow. Moving to her other breast, I do the same, feeling her nipple harden against my tongue and her thighs tighten around mine between her legs.

Releasing her hands, I move, placing myself between her legs, wrapping my hands around her breasts, moving from one to the other, licking, sucking, and biting her nipples as her fingers first move timidly through my hair before her nails start scraping across my scalp. Sitting back on my heels, I wrap my hands around the top of her dress and slowly pull the material down her body, loving the way she's watching me, with her eyes glazed over with lust and heat.

Pulling the fabric over her hips, my breath catches when I see the lace of her bra matches the sheer lace covering her center. Picking up her legs, I hold them over one shoulder and unhook her shoes, dropping them to the floor, and then I pull the dress up her legs and toss it to floor behind me.

Sitting up, her hands go to my shirt, and I help her by reaching a hand behind my back and tugging the garment off over my head, dropping it to the ground with her dress.

"I'm not done with you," I tell her, placing my mouth against hers while pushing her back against the bed. Her legs wrap around my hips, bringing my denim-covered cock in contact with the heat of her core. Groaning, I pull my mouth from hers as her fingers unsnap my jeans and her hand moves between the material and my skin. Wrapping my hand around hers, I stop her before she can get her hand around my cock. I'm on the edge of losing it already, and I know if she touches me, I'm going to push her panties to the side and fuck her like an animal. I have wanted this for far too long, but I can't fuck her like I want to. I need to make this good for her. I don't want her to ever have any regrets about giving me her virginity.

"I need to taste you, Ellie. I need it more then I need my next breath," I tell her, kissing down her body, settling myself between her legs. Her eyes watch me closely as I lean in, running my nose along the lace. Her smell is intoxicating; she smells like vanilla, cherries, and Ellie, and that smell has my mouth watering. Taking the flimsy lace in my hands, I rip it from her, seeing her body jerk in surprise and her breathing increase.

"Jax?"

"Christ, Ellie, you're so fucking wet, baby," I tell her, running a finger through her glistening folds and around her clit. Then I place my hands on her inner thighs and spread her open, taking one long lick up her center.

"Oh. My. God," she hisses, and her thighs begin to shake as I lick her again then focus on her clit, pulling the small piece of flesh between my lips and flicking it with my tongue. Looking up her body, her tits are heaving, her head is back, and her hands are covering her eye.

"Ellie, give me your eyes, baby."

"I can't," she cries, shaking her head.

Moving up her body until my face is over hers, I kiss her and pinch her nipples until her hands come off her eyes.

"You're going to watch, Ellie," I rumble against her mouth.

"It's too much," she breathes against my lips, and I run my fingers over her clit, making her hips jerk.

"Get over it," I say, rolling to my back, lifting her easily to straddle my face, and then pulling her hips down roughly onto my waiting mouth.

"Oh, God," she shouts, pressing her hand against the wall in front of her. Keeping our eyes locked, I bury my tongue inside her. Then I use first one then two fingers, pushing them in and out of her slowly until her hips are jerking and she's flooding my mouth with the juices and screaming her climax.

Sliding my hands up her back, I unhook her bra then place her on the bed. Her eyes are glazed over and her breathing is still shallow from her orgasm. Wiping my mouth with my hand, I slip off my jeans and boots and grab a condom from my side table. I slide it under the pillow near her head then slip off my boxers, wrapping my hand around my length, pumping and squeezing the tip, trying to relieve some of the pressure I feel building at the base of my spine. I know I have stamina, but if I get inside of her right now and feel her around me, I'm going to come.

Lying beside her, I wrap my mouth around her nipple and place my fingers against her clit, rolling my middle finger over it then sliding it lower into her wet heat. Her legs spread wider, wanting more as I curl the digit up and hit her g-spot. Hearing her whimper, I move between her legs and grab the condom, sliding it on. As soon as I'm settled between her thighs, her legs wrap around my hips and her arms wrap around my shoulders.

A deep pang hits my chest as I look into her eyes.

"This is really happening?" she asks, making me smile. Nipping her lips, I open my mouth over hers as my hand wraps around my cock, and I run it up and down her folds, listening to her breathe hitch each time I pass the head over her clit.

"Ready?" I ask her, lining up and pressing the tip in.

Nodding, her nails dig into my back as I slide in slowly, inch-by-inch. She's so fucking tight I have to hold my breath to keep from coming.

"Full, I'm so full," she whimpers, and my cock twitches in approval, like it's trying to show off.

"Don't talk, baby," I tell her, pulling out only to slide in farther.

"Jax, oh, God," she moans, lifting her hips higher, taking me deeper, which isn't helping me stay calm.

"Fuck," I clip, pulling out and pushing in slowly breaking through the barrier of her virginity until I'm balls deep, which causes her breathe to hitch and her nails to bite hard into my skin.

Breathing heavily, I kiss her until her body relaxes once again under mine. "Are you okay?" I question, pushing her hair out of her face and looking into her eyes.

"Yes." Her hand comes up to rest against my cheek. "You can move," she says, wiggling her hips.

Tilting my head back, I stretch out my arms and swivel my hips. Her pussy is so fucking hot and so tight that I won't be able to hold off coming for very long. I knew having her was going to ruin me, but I didn't understand how much until I felt her walls ripple around my length, her arms tighten around my shoulders, and her legs clench around my hips like every part of her is trying to hold on to me, to keep me close.

She fits me perfectly. Everything about her was made just for me.

"Jax…"

"I know, baby," I say, dropping my forehead to hers when her walls ripple once more from the slightest movement. "So responsive. You're so responsive, baby. I bet you could come from just my dick, couldn't you?" I ask, swiveling my hips again.

Her reply is a whimper as her walls around my cock tighten to the point that it's almost painful.

"Jesus," I groan, watching her face and feeling her core convulse as her sudden orgasm threatens to pull mine from me. "I need to move, baby," I tell her, adjusting her leg over my arm, putting me at a different angle. Pulling out and sliding in again, her lips part and her walls tighten. Picking up speed, I wrap her leg tighter around me then cover her mouth with mine, thrusting my tongue between her lips as I feel my orgasm climb up my spine, plunging three more times. Then I plant myself deep and pull my mouth from hers, roaring into the room when I feel her clamp down around me as I come hard, sending her into another orgasm.

Rolling to my back so I don't collapse on top of her, I settle her against my chest, still feeling her pussy contracting around my cock.

"I swear, baby. Your pussy is fucking dangerous," I tell her, feeling her body shaking against mine. "It's true. I thought you were going to squeeze my dick off when you orgasmed," I tell her truthfully, and her silent laughter turns into loud giggles that make me smile.

Placing my fingers under her chin, I tilt her face up towards mine. "How are you feeling?"

"Good." She smiles and her face goes soft, softer than I have ever seen it, and I know right then, with her chest against mine, me still buried deep inside of her, our smell surrounding us, I know I'm in love with her. So fucking in love that I want to wrap her up in cotton so nothing can ever happen to her. How the hell are you supposed to survive, when the part of you that you need to live is walking around outside your body?

"Jax?"

"Yeah, baby?" I ask, focusing on her and running my fingers through her hair.

"You got a weird look on your face," she whispers, studying me.

"Just thinking," I tell her softly. I know I'm going to keep pushing us forward, but I don't want to scare her away by letting her know I love her. I need to find a way to get her addicted to me. I need to make her crave me so the thought of not being with me scares her more than any fear of the future does.

"What about?" she asks, sounding unsure.

"You. How perfect you are and how much I want this," I tell her a half-truth, kissing her forehead.

"I want this too," she whispers, and I search her face, seeing something deep in her eyes I hadn't noticed before, but I think it's always been there. Swallowing, I pull her up my body then roll her to her back.

"I gotta take care of this condom."

"Okay." She nods as I pull the sheet from the bottom of the bed and place it over her. Going to the bathroom, I take off the condom and notice a small smear of blood, which reminds me that Ellie is mine, and only mine, bringing the caveman beast inside of me to the surface. Tossing the condom in the trash, I start the bath then go back into the room.

"Come on, let's take a bath," I tell her, pulling her from the bed and carrying her into the bathroom. Stepping into the large tub with her in my arms, I settle her between my legs and run my hands over her as the water fills. Hearing her stomach growl in the quiet room, I tilt her head back so I can see her face.

"You still haven't fed me," she says shyly.

"What do you want to eat?" I ask, running my thumb across her bottom lip.

"Pancakes with chocolate chips," she says, rolling to her stomach so her breasts are in line with my cock, which hardens instantly. Looking down between her tits, her lower lip is pulled between her teeth and her eyes lift slowly to meet mine. The image of her with her hair down, the ends wet from the bath, her skin still glowing from her resent orgasm, and her eyes full of heat, gazing at me with lust, is an image I will use often when I can't take her to bed. Then she shocks me. Her head dips and her tongue touches the head of my cock, licking off the drop of precum that seeped out of the end.

"Oh, fuck," I hear myself groan. "Baby," I breathe as she sits back, her tits rising above the water. Her hand attempts to wrap around me, and she timidly pumps, and then her mouth covers the head and her tongue swirls the tip. Wrapping my hands around the edge of the tub, I try to keep still. I don't want to slam down her throat or grab onto her hair. I don't even know if she understands what she's doing.

Her eyes meet mine as her hand pumps, each stroke killing me slowly. As her mouth lowers, taking me deeper into the depth of her mouth, I flex my muscles, knowing she is going to be the death of me. Her unsure innocence is making it hard to keep my hands locked on the tub.

Feeling myself hit the back of her throat, hearing her gag almost has me coming. "Ellie, fuck, baby. Oh, God." My toes curl and her hand moves faster, like she knows I'm close. "I'm gonna come, baby," I tell her, and her mouth leaves my cock, but her hand pumps. Wrapping my hand over hers, I help her bring me off and use my other hand to pull her forward, covering her tits with my come. "You're gonna kill me," I confess, pulling her to rest against my chest, leaning my head back and closing my eyes, trying to catch my breath.

Feeling myself shaking, I open one eye and dip my chin, seeing Ellie has her mouth covered and her body is quaking with silent laughter.

"Sorry," she giggles when her eyes meet mine.

"You think it's funny that you're gonna kill me?" I ask, and her laughter quiets down and she smiles, shaking her head. "We need to shower," I say, standing and taking her with me.

"Are you mad?" she asks from behind me as I start the shower.

"No, baby." I push her into the shower then move her against the wall, hearing her gasp as her skin touches the cold tile. "Let's see if you're still laughing when I'm done," I say, and dropping to my knees and tossing her leg over my shoulder.

Chapter 8

Ellie

"HERE, BABE."

Glaring at the shirt held out to me, I take it anyways, making sure to tug it with force from Jax's grip, then pull it over my head.

Hearing him chuckle, I pull my long wet hair out of the collar of the shirt and narrow my eyes on him, which only seems to make his smile bigger.

"What?" he asks, pulling up a pair of sweats that are loose and hang low on his hips, showing off the well-defined V of his waist.

"It's not funny," I growl when he begins to laugh louder.

"Baby, I'm not laughing at you."

"You're totally laughing at me," I say, looking around with wide, dramatic eyes, pointing out there is absolutely no one else in the room, or even the house, with us. "And who does that to someone? Who uses sex torture as a way of hearing what you want to hear?" I ask him, feeling my cheeks heat up at just the thought of what happened in the shower.

"Sex torture?" He laughs louder, and I feel a smile on my lips from the sound of it. When his eyes come to me again, I school my features.

"Sex torture, that thing you did when you…when you didn't let me orgasm until I told you what you wanted to hear."

"You're adorable."

"I'm not adorable." I roll my eyes, picking up my towel from the end of the bed.

"You are. Now, are you ready to go have pancakes?" he asks, taking the towel out of my hand and tossing it toward the bathroom on the ground, making me frown.

"I was going to hang tha—"

He cuts me off, lowering his mouth over mine in a brutal kiss that causes my legs to become weak. When his mouth leaves mine and I finally get my eyes open, I find him looking down at me with a very smug smile.

"Now…are you ready for pancakes?" he asks again.

"You're annoying," I tell him, taking a step back and turning toward the door, making a point to stomp down the hall and down the stairs. I notice on the way that something looks different, but I can't figure out what it is. When we reach the kitchen, Jax lifts me onto the counter and starts pulling out the ingredients to make pancakes.

"What happened here?" he asks, stopping in front of me. I absently feel him run his fingers over the skin of my knee, but my eyes are glued to his abs and the outline of his hard-on under his sweats.

"Baby."

"Hmm?" I mumble in a daze, feeling a tingle in my core.

"What happened to your knees? Did I do that?" he asks, sounding concerned, and my eyes move to focus on his fingers that are once more running over one knee then the other. Seeing the bruise; it's not huge, but it's noticeable.

"Mellissa tripped me when I was walking past her at the salon." I shrug, trying not to make a big deal out of it. She already ruined my dinner. I won't allow her to ruin our night.

"What the fuck?" he rumbles as I shake my head, pressing my hand against his chest.

"She's jealous and evil. Honestly, I can't believe you dated her," I tell him, moving my hand up to his jaw and running my fingers over it, gaining his gaze.

"We dated in high school," he explains.

"You still dated her. I can't imagine she was any different back then."

"You're right. She's always been the same."

"So why does she think you're hers now?" I ask. His chest expands on a deep breath, and I can tell he doesn't want to tell me.

"We hooked up."

"You slept with her recently," I clarify, and his jaw begins to tick.

"I hate that you've had to see that part of my past. I hate that it keeps popping up, but I can't change it."

"I haven't asked you to change it. I mean, if my ex-sex partners were popping up all the time, coming to the house, showing up at restaurants and your job, you would have to deal, right?" I ask, watching that tick in his jaw turn into a grind, and his hand on my thigh tightens almost painfully.

"Let's not talk about you being with anyone else," he grits out.

"Why? You wouldn't feel the same way about me that you do now?" I question, tilting my head and raising a brow. "Cause that would be a huge double standard."

"I would learn to deal with it, or I'd end up in jail."

"Well, I guess I'm just a bigger person than you are," I say, pressing my lips together to keep from laughing when his eyes narrow.

"You've got a smart mouth. Maybe I should give you something to fill it."

"Yeah, *food*," I say, pointing at the bowl next to me, and he smiles, but then his face goes serious.

"I'm sorry about Mellissa, baby. I hate that she did that to you, and I really hate that she ruined our date."

"She's not here, so I win." I smile with a shrug, and his face goes soft.

"You're too good for me, Ellie." His hand comes up to rest on the underside of my jaw and his thumb moves across my lips. "Way to fucking good for me, but now that I've had you and I've fallen in love with your daughter, I won't give you up. I will never give you up," he says, leaning in, placing a soft kiss on my mouth, and then moving to the stove before I can reply. I don't want to hope, but God I'm hoping he's feeling for me even half of what I'm feeling for him right now.

"Baby."

"Yeah?" I ask, lifting my gaze to meet his.

"This thing is going to last. We have time, lots of it, to figure it all out. But you and Hope have all of me. Yeah?"

"Yeah," I agree breathlessly, feeling something right settle over me knowing that I'm falling in love with him.

I pray in loving him I will have the family I've so desperately craved since my dad passed away.

Hope would be able to have the family I never did. With that thought, anxiety settles in my gut. If things don't work out, where will that leave Hope? Is it fair to her to give her all of this, only to have it taken away?

"What's that look?"

Licking my bottom lip, I shake my head, murmuring, "Just spaced out."

He moves back to stand in front of me once more and takes my face between his large hands. "Tonight, we have pancakes and watch a movie. Tomorrow, we go pick up Hope from my folks and spend the day with her. The next day, Hope is with me during the day while you're at work, and when you get off work, we'll have dinner together. The day after that, we figure it out, Ellie, but we'll figure it out together."

"Okay," I agree, because I don't know what else to do.

"Okay," he repeats softly then demands, "Now kiss me," lowering his face toward mine, just far enough away that I will need to be the one to close the gap between us. I know this is a test. If I kiss him, I'm saying I trust him. If I don't close the gap, I don't believe in him or us. Lifting up without thought, I press my lips to his. I know this is one of those moments my grandmother told me about, one of the moments when you either have to push your fears aside or let them swallow you whole. I want this, and if this ends up being something beautiful, I know it will have been worth the risk, and if it ends up blowing up in my face, I will just have to survive off of the beautiful moments we make now.

When his lips leave mine and move to press gently to my forehead in a soft touch, I absorb the feeling in my chest and sit back. I watch him move to the stove and turn it on, and then smile as he mixes pancake batter and places the mixture on the pan on the stove top, absorbing everything about this moment. I'm not sure why this point in time seems so important, but I know it is.

"HOW MANY KIDS do you want?"

Shifting on the couch so I can see his face, I feel my heartbeat accelerate from the look in his eyes and the tone of his voice. When we finished eating pancakes, he led me into the living room and settled me on the couch between his legs so that my body was half on his. His legs were settled around me, and he turned on the TV to some scary movie that I knew I would end up sleeping through. "Baby," he says, pulling me from my thoughts.

"I...I don't know. I guess I never really thought about it," I say, rolling to my stomach, placing my hands on his abs, one on top of the other, and settling my chin on top of them. "How many kids do you want?" I ask, studying his face.

"Four, if not more."

"That's a lot of kids," I mumble while my stomach begins to warm.

"You don't want more kids?" he asks softly, running his finger along the edge of my hair then behind my ear.

"I'd like Hope to have brothers and sisters. I know she wants siblings," I confess, watching his eyes darken in a way that I like a whole lot.

"How long would you have to date someone before you married them and had kids?" he asks, dragging me up his body and adjusting me so I'm straddling his lap.

"What's with these questions?" I ask breathlessly as his fingers run between my legs, reminding me I'm not wearing any panties.

"Curious," he groans, palming the back of my head and pulling my mouth toward his as his fingers slide between my folds. He sucks my bottom lip between his lips and nips it with his teeth. "Are you sore?" he asks against my mouth.

"A little," I whimper as the tip of one finger slides inside me.

"Just a little?" he asks, rolling that finger up and over my clit, causing a mewl to climb up my throat, my nails to dig into his chest, and my hips to jerk forward.

"I wish I could slide inside of you, baby, but I don't want to hurt you."

"It's okay," I hiss in distress as his fingers move slowly over my clit and back towards my entrance.

"No," he growls, flipping me over and moving down my body.

"No! No way!" I shout, realizing what he's doing and trying to shut my legs. I don't think I can handle him tormenting me again like he did in the shower.

"Easy," he rumbles, gently pushing my knees apart.

When he nips the skin of my inner thigh, I cry out as his mouth drops down on my core and his tongue licks up my center, ending at my clit, and my hips lift off the couch and my hand grabs onto his hair, wanting to hold him in place.

"Oh, God," I breathe when he pulls my clit into his mouth, flicks his tongue across it, and slides one finger gently inside me. Feeling all of that, all of him, my back arches and the heels of my feet press hard into the couch so I can lift closer to his mouth. His hand on my thigh squeezes almost painfully as his tongue laps up my center.

Squeezing my eyes closed, I know I'm close. My body feels coiled and ready to snap at any moment, and his growl and the hook of his fingers against my g-spot send me over the edge. My body begins to shake and my legs attempt to clamp closed as my orgasm washes over me. Feeling his tongue lick up my center once more and the roughness of his jaw run over my inner thigh, my eyes blink open, connecting with his.

"C'mere," he says, lifting my limp body to his chest and settling me in his lap. Resting against him, it takes a few minutes to come back to myself. My whole body is completely relaxed and the space between my legs is still sending tiny jolts of pleasure through me. Tilting my head back, his chin lowers and his gaze meets mine. He's always looked at me like I'm something precious, like I'm something he wants to protect, but the look in his eyes now is something different. It's warmer and softer, somehow sweeter than anything else I have ever seen from him before. The words *I love you* are on the tip of my tongue, but I can't get my mouth open to say it. I don't want to ruin this.

"I know," he mutters quietly, tucking my head under his chin and breaking our connection. My heart starts to pound harder, and I wonder if he somehow knows what I'm thinking, what I'm feeling. Closing my eyes, I soak in his smell and the feeling of his arms around me, and before I know it, I fall asleep.

Waking up slowly, I smile as last night comes back to me. I had sex. Not only did I have sex with Jax, I had *amazing* sex with him. Opening my eyes, I turn my head and see I'm in Jax's bed, but he's gone. Pushing my arm out from under the covers, I feel across the sheets, noticing they are cool to the touch, like he's been gone for a while.

Sitting up, I look around and really take in his room for the first time. The walls are a grey-blue that is masculine but still soft. The room is almost the exact shape as the room Hope has been sleeping in, with a large, curved window that juts outward, and has a seat under it that has a large cushion on top of it. So if you wanted to sit and read, you could do it comfortably.

Between the door to the room and the bathroom is a tall, dark dresser. The front of the drawers look like black leather and have unusual silver handles. Another dresser with the same style leather drawers is on the opposite side of the room. That one is long with a large mirror on top of it, and a flat metal-looking dish with some odds and end in it sits on top of the dark surface.

Looking to my right then left, I see there are matching side tables on either side of the bed, along with lamps that curve in an unusual shape and are the same dark silver as the handles on the drawers. Leaning back against the headboard and feeling coolness hit my back through my shirt, I turn and look over my shoulder. The back of the bed is the same black leather as on the front of the dressers, with tucked pieces that have dark silver buttons in the material.

Pulling the blanket up, I wonder if his mom helped him decorate, and that makes me smile. The comforter matches the furniture perfectly, with dark grey, black, and white rivets that shoot through it. Hearing banging downstairs, I roll to the side of the bed and put my feet on the floor, trying to be quiet as I make the bed, picking up decorative pillows from the floor, along with a dark grey throw, and placing them on the bed.

Once I have the bed made, my clothes picked up out of the bathroom, and toss the towels from last night into the hamper, I head down the hall to the bathroom I have been using. I take care of business quickly then go across to my room to grab a pair of panties and sweats, putting both on before heading down the stairs, where I see Jax at the bottom. Shirtless and wearing a pair of shorts, his body is bent double as he hammers something into the floor.

Moving quietly to the last step from the bottom, I look down at my feet then turn to look over my shoulder. That's when I see the stairs now have a dark grey-colored carpet running down the center of them.

"Did I wake you?"

Pulling my gaze from the stairs behind me, I look at Jax and my eyes drop to his chest and abs, which are covered in a fine sheen of sweat.

"No," I say absently then look behind me again at the stairs, remembering last night I thought something looked different; I just couldn't figure out what it was at the time. "When did you do this?" I ask, turning to look at him while pointing at the stairs.

"Started on it yesterday, but I wanted to finish it before Hope came home today. She scares the shit out of me every time she runs down the steps."

"She scares you when she runs down the stairs, so you're putting in carpet?" I ask just to clarify as something warm washes over me.

"I was going to do it anyway," he says, running his hand over his head and looking around.

"She scares you when she runs down the stairs…so you're putting in carpet?" I repeat, and his face goes soft and his hand reaches out toward me.

When I take his hand, he pulls me flush against his body then kisses me softly grumbling, "I was hoping to have this done before you woke up, so I could come wake you."

"It's okay. I can help," I murmur against his mouth as his arms band around me tighter, allowing me to feel his arousal against my

144

stomach.

"I'm almost done. Why don't you go make some coffee and call July back. She's called a few times, but I told her you were sleeping."

"Was she okay?"

"She was wondering why we didn't show last night," he explains.

"Oh," I whisper, feeling my face heat, which makes him smile.

"Call her back. When I'm done, I'll make us breakfast, and then we can go pick up Hope."

"Sure." I nod, pressing up on my toes and placing a kiss on his mouth then pulling myself away from him to head into the kitchen.

Finding my bag on the counter, I pull out my cell, seeing July sent three texts, all of them from when she was probably drunk. Most of them don't make much sense, but all of them make me smile. Pressing call on her number, I put my phone to my ear and pull down a coffee cup, filling it before going to the fridge to get the cream.

"I called you," July answers almost right away.

"I know, sorry. I just woke up."

"It's fine. I was worried about you last night. I heard your dinner plans got shot, because of Mellissa."

"How did you hear about that?" I ask, dumping some cream and sugar into my coffee and stirring.

"It's a small town, and word travels fast."

"I'm so embarrassed. I shouldn't have let her get to me, but she made me so mad," I tell her honestly, while going back to the fridge and pulling out the carton of eggs and some left over steak from a few nights ago, along with cheese and a diced onion and pepper.

"She had it coming besides, She's just jealous that Jax is in love with you and not her," She says and I feel my heart flutter.

"How did last night go? Your texts were a little hard to understand." I say changing the subject.

"That's what happens when you try to outdrink a giant," she mutters, and I hear Wes say something in the background, and then July tells him to be quiet because he was supposed to take care of her. "So what are your plans for the day? Do you want to go shopping with me and Ashlyn? I guess her new boss is a jerk and told her she can't wear skirts or dresses to work anymore."

"Are you kidding me?" I ask. Ashlyn told me a little about her new boss, but I didn't know he was such an ass.

"Yeah, but I think he has a thing for her."

"Isn't he engaged?"

"His fiancée's in New York. Ashlyn overheard him on the phone with her, and she was complaining about the size of the house he had chosen for them."

"What?" I whisper while breaking the eggs into a bowl and beating them.

"Yeah, my guess is things are not so good for him, and he sees sweet Ashlyn so close yet so far away, so he's taking his women problems out on her."

"How old is he?"

"I think around thirty. Have you seen him? He's gorgeous," she whispers, and I hear a loud smack then her say, "Honey, I just mean he's a good-looking guy."

"July, don't piss me off," I hear Wes growl, and I smile when July starts laughing.

"I'm gonna have to call you back," she squeals in laughter right before the phone goes dead.

Giggling and shaking my head, I set the phone down on the counter next to me and start chopping up the steak. Then I turn on the stove and put the meat in a pan, along with the onions and peppers, then put another pan on the stove. I go back to the fridge and grab the butter, cutting off a slice and placing it in the pan before dumping some of the eggs on top of it.

"What are you making?" Jax asks, coming up behind me and wrapping his arms around my waist, kissing the skin below my ear.

"Omelets." I smile then laugh when his teeth nibble on my earlobe.

"Smells good," he mumbles absently.

"I do know how to cook," I tell him, leaning into his embrace and tilting my head farther to the side, while his mouth travels down toward my shoulder and his hand moves under my shirt to cup my bare breast.

"If we didn't have to pick up Hope, I'd have you for breakfast," he whispers against the shell of my ear before nipping it then licking over the sting as a flood of memories from last night come back to me in a rush, causing my knees to get weak. Looking over my shoulder at him, I wonder if I can talk him out of breakfast and into a shower.

"Don't look at me like that, baby. I know you're still sore, and I don't want to hurt you."

"You won't," I assure him, dropping my eyes to his mouth, watching as a smile forms on his lips.

"You like my mouth?" he asks with a smirk.

Shrugging, I look back at the stove, lifting some of the steak, onions, and peppers from the pan on the opposite burner and tossing them over the eggs. I then grab a handful of cheese, muttering, "It's okay."

"Just okay?" he asks, licking along the pulse of my neck, and I can tell he's smiling.

"I don't really have a reference point, but if I had to give you a rating, it would be around a seven," I say, hoping he will try to turn that seven, which is actually like a hundred, into a ten.

"A seven?" he asks in disbelief.

"Yeah, but like I said, I don't have a reference point. If you want, I can go find someone else to do it and see if your rating goes up." I shrug again then squeak when he spins me around, picks me up, and tosses me over his shoulder before turning off the stove and carrying me up the stairs to his room where he drops me onto the bed then proceeds to prove he's definitely not a seven.

"AX, CAN I hab a sister?" Hope asks as soon as we walk into Jax's parents' house.

Feeling my mouth fall open, I look at Jax's mom, who is covering her mouth trying not to laugh, and then to Jax's dad, who has his lips pressed tightly together while watching my daughter.

"Maybe one day, sweetheart, but really, I don't think you get to choose. You may get a brother," Jax tells her, picking her up.

"Do I hab to ask God or Santa for a sister, Mama?" she asks, scrunching up her face, looking at me.

"Oh, lord," I breathe, glaring at Jax when he laughs.

"Do you want to show your mom and Jax what you made them?" Lilly chimes in, helpfully changing the subject of babies.

"We made cockporn balls," she cries happily, wiggling out of Jax's hold while I watch horrified as she runs past us toward the kitchen.

"Cockporn Balls?" Jax asks, raising a brow at his mom, who rolls her eyes and smacks him on the chest playfully.

"Popcorn balls," she says then comes to me, sliding her arm through mine and dipping her face toward my ear, where she whispers, "We heard about last night. Are you okay?"

"Sheesh, did everyone hear about it?" I whisper, feeling my face heat in embarrassment. I know this is a small town, but seriously, this is getting ridiculous. Kim and Frankie both sent me texts making sure that I was okay because they had also heard about what happed last night.

"No, Mani was worried about you, and he called to ask Cash if he heard from Jax. He wanted to make sure you guys were okay and to let us know he told Mellissa and her family they were no longer allowed at the restaurant."

"Now I feel even worse than I did before," I mutter, feeling my stomach twist.

"Don't feel bad. We heard what she said to you. In fact, a whole lot of people heard it, and I know that quite a few of them are disgusted by the way she acted and have pulled the houses they had listed with her father."

"I don't think that makes me feel any better," I say as my anxiety begins to increase. I hate what happened last night, but I don't think there is any other way for this to go. I just don't think Mellissa's dad should be punished, just because Mellissa is evil.

"If you're talking about Mellissa, we're not talking about her to-day," Jax says, coming up and wrapping his arm around my waist. "We're taking Hope to the park and out for pizza. We're not going to discuss Mellissa, or even think about her," he states firmly, giving my waist a squeeze while looking pointedly at his mom.

"When did you turn into your dad?" she asks him softly, shaking her head.

"Mom, don't get all mushy on me right now, okay?"

"I'm not getting mushy," she mutters, swiping under her eyes, but I can tell she was totally going into mushy mommy mode.

"Jesus," he grumbles, releasing me and taking his mom into his arms, giving her a hug, and a kiss on the top of her head.

"Here's your cockporn ball, Mama," Hope says happily, coming over to me, carrying a large, unwrapped, oddly shaped popcorn ball and handing it to me, causing the candy coating to stick to my hand. "I love cockporn balls," she tells me, licking the palm of her hand that is covered in candy.

"Angel baby," I say softly, getting down to her level and taking her candy-covered hand into mine so she will focus on me.

"It's popcorn," I tell her slowly. I have no idea where she got the whole cockporn thing, but that is definitely not something I want her saying in public, or ever, for that matter. I can just see us going to a movie and her yelling, 'I want COCKPORN!' at the top of her lungs in the middle of a packed theater.

"I know, cockporn." She nods, licking her palm again.

"No, Angel. POP-corn," I tell her, pronouncing each syllable.

"COCK-porn," she says slowly back, like I'm deaf, and then places her hands on her hips.

"Oh, geez," I mutter, giving up, looking at Lilly, who is fighting laughter, and ask her, "Do you have a bag for this?" while holding my hand upside down, showing the ball is stuck to my palm and now looks like a penis and balls.

"I do." She giggles then looks at Jax, who is looking at Hope like she's the cutest thing in the whole wide world. It's as if he missed everything that just happened and the fact she's saying cockporn.

"Do you want to go to the park, sweetheart?" he asks her, picking her up.

"Yes! Can you push me on the swing?"

"Sure, and after the park, we can go have pizza for dinner."

"Can we have fwozen yogut?" she asks, looking at him and batting her lashes. His eyes come to me, and all I can do is roll mine. She has him wrapped around her tiny little finger, and she knows it too.

"If you eat all your dinner, then yes," he tells her as I head to the kitchen, where I find Lilly wrapping up popcorn balls with saran wrap.

"Thank you for keeping Hope," I tell her, walking over to the sink and washing the sticky mess off of my hands.

"We love her, and you, though you should know she has been talking nonstop about getting a sister."

Shaking my head, I pull a paper towel off the roll then take a seat next to her and start helping her wrap the remaining popcorn balls.

"Ever since I told her Jax and I were dating, she has been asking me that everyday."

"We wouldn't be upset about that. I mean, you guys have lots of time to date and get to know each other, but when you do have more babies, you can always depend on us to babysit."

"Thanks," I tell her, feeling awkward. Jax and I are still so new. Even if I feel like I have known him forever, the truth is we still have so much to learn about each other, and I want to wait for more kids.

"Did you hear me?"

Focusing on Lilly, I shake my head then murmur, "Sorry, no."

Smiling, she looks toward the living room, and I turn my head to look over my shoulder at Jax, who is talking to his dad, with Hope still in his arms and her head resting on his chest. "Normally, on Jax's birthday, we have dinner as a family, but I didn't want to make plans if there was something you had planned."

"When is his birthday?" I ask her, feeling horrified I had no idea his birthday was even coming up.

"Oh, Wednesday," she says, wrapping another ball.

"I have to work."

"Don't worry about it. We can make reservations for dinner on Saturday if you want."

"What about a surprise party on Monday or Tuesday?" I ask her, and her face lights up.

"He hates surprises," she grins then mutters, "Let's do it," as Cash steps into the kitchen.

"What are you guys whispering about?" he asks, going to the fridge, grabbing a beer, and leaning back against the counter.

"Nothing, just wrapping up all of these cockporn balls," Lilly whispers loud enough for him to hear, causing him to chuckle and me to laugh.

"You ready to head out, baby?" Jax asks, settling his hand on my shoulder when he walks into the kitchen.

"Yeah," I say, getting up and hugging Cash and Lilly both, telling them thanks again for looking after Hope and watching them hug her before we leave the house.

WHEN WE PULL up to the park, I look through the front window of the truck. The park we normally go to is just a couple blocks from the house, and there are only a few kids who go there to play. This park is the opposite. The whole place is overrun with kids, with most of the parents sitting around the tables outside of the large sand area, talking and not really paying much attention to what their children are doing. Waiting for Jax to open my door, I hop down then grab Hope's jacket from the front seat.

"I want you to stay in the play area, where I can see you. Do you understand?" I ask, getting down on my haunches, zipping up her jacket and putting on her hat.

"Yes, Mama," she says excitedly, bouncing up and down as she watches the kids who are running around laughing. She's never been to a park this large before, and I'm a little worried with so many kids around that I'll lose sight of her.

"What did your Mom just say, Hope?" Jax asks, sounding so much like a dad that I'm a little caught off guard.

"She said to make sure she can see me," she tells him, and his hand comes out to cup her cheek.

"Good, sweetheart," he says, and she smiles up at him then raises her glove-covered hand to his as I stand up. Taking his opposite hand, we walk along the concrete path then stop when we reach the play area, which has been dug out with smooth logs built up around the edge, keeping the sand separate from the grass surrounding it.

"Can I go on the swide?" Hope asks, pointing to a slide that has two other kids on it, one boy and one girl, both around the same age as

Hope.

"Sure, Angel," I say, and she lets go of Jax's hand, jumps down into the sand, and runs across to the slide. "She'll be okay," I tell Jax, feeling his hand tighten around mine when she stumbles before righting herself and taking off again.

"I feel like there is a constant ball of worry in my chest when it comes to her. I'm always wondering if something's going to happen, if there is something I can prevent from happening. Is that normal?"

"Yeah, but it gets easier after awhile," I say as his arm lifts to wrap around my shoulders so he can haul me closer against his side. Seeing Hope head up the stairs for the slide, I smile and wave when she reaches the top then watch as a little boy smiles at her and allows her to head down the slide before him.

"Did that kid just flirted with her," Jax asks, sounding annoyed and surprised.

"He's just being nice," I tell him, watching as Hope glides down the slide and lands with her feet in the sand before running back to the stairs again.

"No, he's flirting," he complains then growls when Hope reaches the top of the stairs, and the little boy says something to her that causes her laugh to ring out loudly above the noise of the park. "You're telling me he's not flirting?" he asks, and I feel my mouth drop open as the boy pulls something out of his pocket and hands it to Hope. She smiles at him then leans in, and I know she's going to give him a hug or a kiss, but Jax's ear-splitting whistle causes everyone to turn and look at him, including Hope and the boy.

"Let's go to the swing," he shouts to Hope, whose brows pull together before she says something to the boy and hands him back what he gave her then, slides down the slide, and runs to us.

"Can my new fwiend come wiff?" she asks when she reaches us.

"No," Jax says immediately, and my hand gives his a squeeze. "Not right now, sweetheart," he tells her more gently, taking her hand and leading her toward the swings, which just so happens to be on the opposite side of the park, far away from the boy.

"SHE'S ASLEEP?" JAX says, and I turn, looking from him to Hope and smiling, because she had just been talking excitedly about the park moments ago, but is now asleep with one elbow on the table, holding up her head, while the other hand holds her piece of pizza.

"The park wore her out." I giggle as her head dips suddenly, causing her eyes to spring open.

"Are you tired, Angel?" I ask, wrapping my arm around her so she can rest against me.

"No, my eyes are just wazy," she mumbles, and I hear Jax laugh from across the booth.

"I'm gonna get a box for the pizza and we can eat at home." Jax says, sliding from the booth and stopping at my side, dipping his head toward me, placing a kiss against my lips before straightening to his full height and going to the front of the pizza shop.

Adjusting Hope so her body is on the bench, I feel something prickle across my skin, and the fine hairs on my body stand on end. Looking around, I don't notice anyone out of place, but something about the feeling is unsettling.

"You okay?" Jax asks, coming back to the table, carrying a box. Looking around again, I shake off the feeling.

"Yeah, just heebie-jeebies," I tell him, and his eyes search my face before he looks around like he knows exactly what I'm talking about.

"Wait here," he commands, dropping the box to the top of the table and moving through the small restaurant then out the door. My heart pounds as I wait for him to come back. I don't know if someone is watching us, or if I have a reason to be worried, but when Jax comes back inside, I breathe a sigh of relief. I don't know what I would do if something happened to him.

"Is everything okay?" I ask, seeing the look on his face and the way his body seems to be strung tight, like all of the muscles in his torso are larger than they were before he went outside.

"It's fine," he says, but his tone and demeanor are saying something completely different. "Let's go," he states, picking up Hope and adjusting her in his arms. "When we get outside, you need to stick close."

"What was it, Jax?" I ask, trying to keep the wobble out of my voice, which is difficult, because I'm so scared.

"There was a note on my car."

"About me?" I ask, looking at Hope. I would die if anything happened to her.

"As soon as I get you two home, I'll call my uncle."

"Jax," I whisper, feeling my insides begin to fill with adrenalin, which is making me want to take Hope and run as far and as fast as I can.

"Nothing will happen to you or Hope. Now, I need you to listen to me and do what I say."

"Okay," I agree with a nod, picking up my bag from the booth and swinging it over my shoulder.

"Come on, baby," he says, taking my hand and leading me out of the restaurant to his truck that is parked right out front. Getting into the back with Hope, I watch Jax run around the front of the truck to the driver's side then look around, trying to see if anything is out of place, but I don't notice anything.

When we pull up to the house, Jax takes us inside and gets us settled in the living room before leaving with his phone to his ear. Looking down at Hope, I pray Jax, unlike everyone else I know, is able to keep his word.

Chapter 9

Jax

"YOU GUYS GONNA be okay?"

"Yeah, Ellie's freaked, but I think since she knows this had nothing to do with the guy who kidnapped her, she's gonna sleep a little easier," I tell my Uncle Nico, looking toward the stairs, where Ellie disappeared with Hope a few minutes ago.

I hate that she was scared at the restaurant, that I couldn't reassure her things would be okay, but my only thought was to get her and Hope out of there and home. I'm not too worried that Mellissa will do anything while I'm around, but I'm still not going to risk anything happening to either of my girls. "When will Mellissa get served with the restraining order?" I ask, going to the fridge, grabbing two beers.

"I know one of the judges in town, and I'll make sure it happens tomorrow morning," he says as I grab the bottle opener and pop the top on both before handing him one, leaning against the counter behind me, and taking a long pull. "I don't think she will do anything to hurt Hope or Ellie," he adds, and I feel my jaw clench.

"I don't think so either, but I'm not taking any chances. The chick thinks she has some kind of hold on me. Even after I've made myself clear on more than one occasion that there is nothing between us, nor will there ever be. Her insisting differently only tells me she's whacked, and in this day and age, you can't turn your back on crazy."

"I agree. It's better to be careful," Nico agrees.

"I don't know how my dad did it," I mutter, taking another pull from my beer, watching as my uncle's face changes slightly. I know he understands what I'm talking about. He helped my dad get back Ashlyn after my biological mom kidnapped her when she was little.

I still remember being scared when she took Ashlyn right from our backyard when we were playing hide-and-seek. Even as scared as I was, I still found my way into the back of the pickup truck, where I hid under a tarp. When the truck stopped at an old house in the country, I ran across a field to an old farmer's house and told him what happened, and he called my dad. Thankfully, the guy my biological mom was going to sell Ashlyn to was actually an undercover agent, but if he hadn't been, things could have turned out completely different.

"The idea of Hope and Ellie being in any kind of danger sends me into a panic I'm not used to feeling."

"Love does that to you, makes you feel unsure and unsettled. To this day, I worry about your Aunt Sophie and your cousins. I don't think there is a minute or second that goes by when I'm not wondering if there is something I can do to make sure they're safe and taken care of. You just gotta know that shit's gonna happen; things that are out of your control are going to occur, and the only thing you can do is be thankful you're all together when the dust settles," he says, just as the scent of Ellie hits me, letting me know she's close. As soon as she walks around the corner into the kitchen, her gaze locks with mine and I feel my face go soft.

"Is she asleep?" I ask her as she comes toward me.

"Yeah, she didn't even want to take a bath, so I know she's beat," she mumbles, walking to my side and taking the beer from my grasp, putting it to her mouth and taking a pull before looking at my uncle and saying, "Thank you for coming over."

Uncle Nico's lips twitch. "No problem," he says, setting his beer on the counter. "I'm gonna head out. I'll call tomorrow after Mellissa has been served with the restraining order. If you need anything, just let me know."

"Will do," I say, wrapping my arm around Ellie's waist and following him to the front door.

"We need to have dinner soon, your aunt Sophie has been on the girls' asses about settling down since you met Ellie. I'm hoping if she can get some Hope time, she'll chill out. I'm not ready to be a grandpa yet." He grins as Ellie giggles then leans in and presses a kiss to her forehead, muttering, "Everything will be okay," to her before giving me a chin lift as he opens the door then shuts it behind him.

"I can't see him as a grandpa either," Ellie says, smiling at me. "He's kinda a badass."

"He is a badass," I tell her, taking her hand and leading her into the living room, where I settle her on my lap.

"Are you okay?" I ask, taking the beer from her hand and setting it on the side table next to the couch.

"Yeah, but you still didn't tell me what the note said," she complains quietly, lifting her head to look at me.

"You don't need to worry about it."

"Don't do that; don't make me feel like I have no control over my life or the things that effect me and Hope," she says, and my mouth opens to speak, but she covers it with her hand. "I know you want to protect us. I get that, but I need to know what's going on. You can't just expect me to follow you blindly, not when Hope and I are involved." Taking her hand off my mouth, I adjust her on my lap so she's straddling my waist and take her face gently in my hands.

"I don't like that I'm the reason this is happening. I hate that, because of my bad decision, she thinks she can fuck with me and, in turn, fuck with you. I don't want any of this to touch you or Hope. I don't want you to have to worry."

"I'm already worried. You rushed me and Hope out of a restaurant like the mob was after us," she says, making me fight a smile.

Pulling her toward me, I place a soft kiss against her mouth then lean back, studying her face. "The note didn't say much."

"Jax," she growls, pushing against my chest and trying to get off my lap.

Flipping her to her back, I pull her hands above her head and hold her down. "It said, *When she's gone, you'll come back to me*," I snarl, feeling the anger from reading the words the first time build back up in my system.

"Oh, my God," she says as the color drains out of her face.

"That's why I didn't want you to know what it said. That look on your face right now is the reason I wanted to keep that shit from touching you."

"I knew she was crazy, but I didn't know how crazy she was," she breathes in distress as her body stills under mine.

"She won't touch you or Hope. Nothing will happen to either of you."

"She's crazy," she repeats.

"I'm going to call her dad in the morning. I know he doesn't want this kind of attention, especially after what happened the other night at the restaurant. Hopefully he will be able to talk some sense into her."

"I can't believe her," she whispers, looking over my shoulder before meeting my eyes once more. "What kind of woman does that? I mean, I know Kim told me about her twin trying to drug Sage, but this isn't like that. She's not trying to rob you," she says, and I rear back, 'cause I have no idea what the fuck she's talking about. "She wants you and thinks if I'm gone, you will go back to her. She's seriously insane, and I mean insane…like she needs medication and a psychiatrist, maybe even a straight jacket."

"What happened with Sage?" I ask, ignoring her rambling.

"Uhh…" She freezes then pulls her bottom lip into her mouth.

"What happened to Sage?" I ask again.

"I don't think it's my place to tell you," she whispers, trying to sit up.

"Tell me," I demand, holding her wrist firmly against the couch.

"You're such a jerk."

"Ellie."

"Fine, but I think if Sage wanted you to know this, he would have told you himself."

She's probably right, but I don't give a fuck. "Tell me," I repeat.

Huffing then narrowing her eyes, she says, "Kim has an evil twin sister. Kim liked Sage, and they…" She pauses, turning red. "They hooked up, but then the next night she and Sage…you know…Sage went out, and Kim's sister tried to drug him. So Sage now thinks Kim is crazy, but she's not; her evil twin is."

"What the fuck?" I say, releasing her and sitting back on the couch, trying to wrap my head around this.

"I know it's totally messed up, and I feel bad, 'cause I think Kim really liked him before he called her a b-word and told her she was crazy," she says, sitting up then moving over me, grabbing the beer from the table, pressing it into my hand, and then lifting it to my mouth. "I'm going to talk to Sage about it, but I haven't been able to be alone with him," she says, and my eyes meet hers and narrow. "Don't even start that caveman business. He's your cousin. I mean, he's good-looking, but—"

"Stop," I growl, setting the beer back down.

"What? I'm just saying he's a good-looking guy." She shrugs, but I see the smile she's trying to hide.

"You think it's funny to make me crazy?" I ask her, and she shrugs again. "You're lucky I love you," I say without thinking, and her breathing stops completely then she moves off the couch before I can catch her.

"I…I'm going to go…go shower then go to bed," she stammers, leaving the living room in a rush, and I hear her feet pounding up the stairs.

Running my hand over my head, I mutter, "Fuck," under my breath then pick up the beer and finish it off before getting up, shutting down the house, and setting the alarm. Heading upstairs, I hear the hall shower running in the hall, so I turn out the light and wait in the dark for the water to turn off and the door to open.

As soon as she steps into the hall, I cover her mouth with my hand and whisper, "Don't wake Hope," into her ear before dragging her down the hall to my room.

Closing the door behind me halfway, I push her onto the bed then crawl on top of her with my legs between hers. The only thing separating us is the small towel she's wearing and my jeans.

"Jax," she says, and I hear the fear and worry in her tone. Reaching over, I turn on the lamp next to the bed so I can see her face.

"I don't care if it's too soon to tell you. I don't care if you think we need more time. I'm not going to pretend I don't love you."

"Jax," she repeats, but this time there's a softness in her tone that wasn't there before.

"I love you, Ellie. I loved you before I even knew who you were. I have no idea how this works. I have no idea how it's possible to find someone who was made just for me, but you were. You were made for me. You're everything I never knew I wanted. You and Hope complete me, and it doesn't matter if I tell you now or a year from now, because my feelings will still be the same. You were meant to be mine," I say, watching as tears slip from the corners of her eyes, into the hair at her temples.

"It's too soon," she whispers.

"It's not."

"We don't even know each other."

"I know enough to know how I feel."

"It's too soon," she repeats softly, searching my face as her fingers intertwine with mine.

"It's not," I say again, leaning in to kiss her then pulling back enough to reveal, "Time's only going to make what I feel now stronger, what *you* feel stronger." I kiss her, rolling to my back and adjusting her to rest on top of me.

"I love you too," she says so quietly I barely hear her over the loud pounding of my own heart. "I didn't think it was possible to feel this way."

"You have me, Ellie. You and Hope both have me, always," I tell her, running my hand over her wet hair while listening to her softly cry. "I promise we'll be happy."

"I'm already happy," she whimpers, and I feel her body shudder against mine. Holding her a little closer, I listen as her tears stop and her breathing evens out then roll her to the side, adjusting her until she's under the covers, and I get out of bed.

Going down the hall, I open Hope's door and walk across her almost dark room then crouch down next to her, laying my hand on her chest, feeling the rise and fall under my palm before kissing her forehead and going back down to my room. Slipping off my jeans and shirt and climbing into bed behind Ellie, I fall asleep.

"You have to be quiet, Angel," I hear Ellie say then feel wiggling and a warm small hand land on my face.

"He's snoring weally loud," I hear Hope whisper loudly then hear her giggle. "He sounds wike a monster."

"I thought that you were still tired," I hear Ellie whisper as I open one eye then the other and dip my chin down, seeing both Hope and Ellie's eyes on me. Hope is on the opposite side of Ellie with her arm across her mom's neck and her hand resting against my cheek.

"Morning," I rumble, and Hope giggles, but Ellie's eyes go soft.

"Morning. I was going to get up to let you sleep," Ellie says.

"It's okay," I tell her, leaning in and pressing a kiss to her forehead then raising my hand to run it over Hope's hair.

"Can we have Skittle pancakes?" Hope asks, and I feel myself smile when her mom's face pales at just the idea of Skittle pancakes.

"I don't think so, sweetheart," I tell her.

"Oh," she pouts.

"How about we have eggs and toast?" Ellie suggests, rolling to her back.

"But I want pancakes."

"We can't have pancakes everyday, Sweetheart," I tell her gently, putting my elbow in the bed and resting my head in my hand.

"Why not?"

"If we have them everyday, they won't be special," Ellie tells her, pulling her to lay against her chest, and I notice she now has on the shirt I wore yesterday, which is a good thing, since Hope came into the room.

"Oh," Hope says then looks at me. "Is that why we can't have birthday cake everyday?"

"Exactly," Ellie confirms with a smile.

"Can I have a sister?"

"Lord," Ellie whispers, and I chuckle then say, "Maybe one day."

"Can I have a dog?" she asks after a few seconds.

"How about a time out?" Ellie asks her.

"I don't want a time out." She frowns.

"Go brush your teeth, sweetheart, then we'll go and make breakfast," I say.

"Okay," she pouts, kissing her mom then me and standing up on the bed, jumping twice before landing on her bottom on the edge and sliding off the side, onto the floor, and running out of the room.

"She's persistent," Ellie murmurs, and I roll onto her, caging her in underneath me.

"I say we just give her what she wants," I mutter into the skin of her neck, hearing her sharp intake of breath.

"It's way to soon for a baby," she whimpers as I slip my knees between hers and run my hand up her thigh, cupping her ass and pulling her core closer to my erection.

"Maybe," I say, nuzzling against her ear then biting it, loving the moan that comes after.

"Jax," she whispers, running her hands up my back while lifting her knee and wrapping her foot around the back of my thigh, bringing me even closer. Grinding against her, I cup her breast then lean forward so I can lick over her lips.

"I'm done!" Hope yells from somewhere down the hall, making me groan in frustration. Rolling to my back, I hear Ellie laugh and I lift my head to glare at her as she gets out of bed and walks to the door.

"I'll see you downstairs." She smiles then looks down at my lap and laughs.

"See you downstairs," I agree, wrapping my hand around myself, trying to relieve the pressure before rolling out of bed and heading to the shower. I turn the water to cold and get in, killing my hard-on after a few painful minutes before turning the water to hot and washing up quickly.

When I get downstairs, Ellie is dressed and her hair is up on top of her head in a bun that fits the outfit she's wearing. The black, form-fitting, long sleeve t-shirt dress goes down past her knees, where it's met with black tights and black knee-high boots with a low heel.

"Where are we going?" I ask her, seeing she's dressed for the day.

Turning to look at me over her shoulder, she replies, "Work. We talked about this yesterday. You said you'd watch Hope."

"That was before last night," I remind her quietly.

"I'm still going to work," she responds then looks at Hope, who is sitting on the counter, watching us. "She won't bother me there." She goes to the fridge and gets out a carton of eggs.

"Ellie," I say harshly, watching her eyes turn hard.

"Jax," she retorts in the same harsh tone, walking over to the counter and telling Hope she can crack the eggs to scramble them.

Pulling in a deep breath, I let it out slowly, trying to calm myself. "Fine, I'll have one of the guys there all day."

"That's ridiculous," she grumbles as I help Hope break the eggs into a bowl then hand her a fork before kissing her nose when she smiles.

"Accept it or stay home," I tell her, trying to keep the frustration out of my tone in front of Hope.

"Fine," she huffs, slicing off a piece of butter into the pan on the stove.

"Fine," I agree, reaching around her to get a coffee cup then dip my face close to her ear. "Are you still sore?" I ask, feeling her shiver against me.

"No," she breathes after a few beats.

"Relish that feeling, baby, 'cause tomorrow, you wont feel the same," I say, placing a kiss on her neck before pulling the skin there into my mouth, biting down until she gasps.

"Please don't have Sage come to the salon," Ellie says after we've eaten breakfast and are finishing up putting away the dishes that we just washed. "I don't want to make it awkward for Kim."

"I'll send Tallon," I tell her, but I know I'm going to have to talk to my cousin. Really, I'm surprised he hasn't brought up what went down with him and Kim before. It's not like him to keep something like that to himself.

"I still think it's ridiculous to send anyone."

"And I would rather be safe then sorry," I tell her, drying off my hands then leaning back against the counter and pulling her to stand between my legs. "I need to know you're safe," I say, and she studies my face for a long time before letting out a breath.

"Okay, but only for today."

"I'm not negotiating with you, Ellie, not when it comes to you or Hope's safety."

"Having a boyfriend who's a badass is annoying," she mumbles under her breath, making me smile.

"You'll get used to it eventually," I promise her, running my hands up the curve of her waist.

"If you're done bossing me around, can I go finish getting ready for work and make sure Hope hasn't painted herself or another wall?" she asks, referring to the last time we left Hope alone and she started painting the wall in her room with glitter nail polish.

Feeling my brows pull downward, I look her over and ask, "I thought you were ready."

"I still need to do my makeup, and I want to get Hope dressed before I go. No offense, but the last time you watched her and she wore her green Christmas tights and her frozen dress, I was a little embarrassed."

"She wanted to dress herself." I shrug, grabbing her ass and pulling her closer. "And you don't need makeup, you already look beautiful."

"You're such a guy." She smiles, leaning up and kissing my jaw.

"I want a real kiss before you go," I say, hauling her tighter against me and dipping my face towards hers.

"Boss—"

Cutting her off, I cover her mouth with mine and swipe my tongue across the seam of her lips, groaning when her lips part and her tongue slides across mine, leaving behind the taste of her and coffee. Pulling away slowly with one last kiss, I smile when her eyes flutter open and her hands reluctantly release my tee.

"Tonight," I tell her, watching her eyes heat and feeling her body melt into mine.

"CAN YOU PAINT my nails, Ax?" Hope asks, coming into the kitchen, where I'm standing and going through surveillance for one of the local businesses that's been having a slew of break-ins over the last two months.

"I…" Looking at the polish in her hand, I know this will be disastrous, even worse than her doing it herself, which is bad, considering she had polish covering her and her clothes the last time she did them. "How about we go get your nails done?" I say instead.

"Weally?" she breathes happily.

"Sure, sweetheart, then after, we can go see July at the vet."

"Yay!" she screams, dancing around in circles, making me laugh.

"Go get your coat and shoes," I tell her, and she runs out of the kitchen. Shutting down my laptop, I grab my hat from the counter and pick up my keys, putting them in my pocket.

"I can't find my coat." Going to the front hall and opening the door for the coat closet, I pull out her jacket that is hanging on one of the lower hooks.

"Did you even look?" I ask, handing her the coat, knowing she never looks for anything; she always just says she can't find whatever it is she's looking for so that someone will get it for her.

"I looked everywhere but there," she says seriously, making me fight back a smile.

"Do you know where your shoes are?" I ask.

"Yep," she says, running to the living room and coming back a few seconds later with a pair of sparkly, red, kids' plastic heels on that remind me of *The Wizard of Oz*.

"I don't know if you should wear those," I tell her, watching as she attempts to walk in the shoes, which are too big and are only made for playing dress-up.

"But they wook pretty," she states, looking down at herself and tapping the toes of the shoes together.

Knowing Ellie won't be happy if she wears the heels, I go to the front door and pick up her tall, rainbow-striped rubber boots and ask, "How about these instead?"

"But I wike dese ones," she insists as her bottom lip wobbles and tears fill her eyes.

"Don't cry, sweetheart. You can wear them, but we'll take these just in case."

"Okay," she says with a smile as the tears dry up instantly, letting me know I just got played.

Walking into the nail salon thirty minutes later, carrying Hope, because she can't walk in her shoes, I wonder if this was a huge mistake. There is nothing but women inside, and by the way they are all looking at me, you would think I just walked into a speed-dating meet-up.

"How can I help you?" an older woman asks, looking at me then Hope, who has suddenly gone shy.

"She would like to get her nails painted," I tell her.

"Oh," the lady says, smiling at Hope. "Do you know what color you want?"

"Pink," Hope says, laying her head against my shoulder.

"How about I show you some of the pinks we have, and then you can pick your favorite?" the lady asks with a gentle smile.

"Okay," Hope replies as I set her on the ground so she can follow the lady in her sparkly heels to a large display of polish. Feeling heat on my back, I turn around, noticing a few of the women in the salon have their eyes on me, and most of them have an approval there that is making me uncomfortable. Turning and going to Hope, I watch as she doesn't only pick pink, but purple and sparkles as well, before handing the colors off to the woman, who then leads her over to one of the chairs.

"Would you like a massage while she gets her nails done?" a younger girl asks, coming up to me.

"No thanks," I say, trying to be polite while taking a seat in the chair next to Hope.

"Are you sure?" she asks, and I feel my jaw grind as her eyes wander over me.

"I'm sure," I mutter, turning away from her watching the woman doing Hopes nails glare over my shoulder before turning her attention back to Hope.

"It's nice of your dad to bring you here to get your nails done," the woman doing Hope's nails says, and my body goes tight. If Hope someday decides to call me Dad, I will be all for it, but I don't ever want her to feel like she has to, or make her feel awkward about it.

"He's always nice to me. He even wet me wear my sparkewe shoes today," Hope tells her, tapping her feet together, causing the shoes to fall off and hit the ground.

"I bet you have him wrapped around your little finger, don't you?" the lady asks, smiling at Hope then me.

"No." Hope giggles.

"You do, honey," she says to Hope then smiles at me and winks before painting her nails, only to have to fix them three times before they dry. Once we leave the salon and arrive at the veterinarian clinic where July works, it's just after two and the lot is half empty.

"Can you carry me?" Hope asks when I set her on her feet in the gravel parking lot.

"How about we change your shoes?"

"I want to show Juwy my sparkle shoes that match my powish," she tells me, holding up her now glitter-covered fingers for me to see.

"Okay, hop on," I tell her, bending down for her to hop on my back so I can carry her across the lot. Once we reach the entrance, I let Hope down then open the door, which chimes when we enter.

"Hey, is everything okay?" July asks, coming out of one of the back rooms, tucking in her shirt, followed by Wes.

Smirking at her, she rolls her eyes as I say, "Your dad said you had some puppies dropped off here yesterday, and I wanted to show Hope."

"Puppies?" Hope smiles, tilting her head back to look at me, then looking at July, she asks, "Can I pet them?"

"Of course you can, honey, and I love your shoes," July tells her, running her hand over the top of her hair.

"How's it going, man?" I ask Wes, giving him a handshake while July talks to Hope about her nails.

"Was gonna to call you as soon as I left here," he says quietly, looking at Hope and July.

"Everything good?"

"We need to talk," he states, pulling his eyes from the girls.

"Ellie gets off work at five. You got time to meet up after that?"

"I'll be with the guys at the shop," he says, leaning back against the counter behind him.

"Should I bring my uncle?" I ask, knowing if this has anything to do with the girls, then my Uncle needs to know since it's his case.

"Bring him along."

"We'll be there," I mutter, feeling myself grow tight.

"You getting a dog for Hope?" he asks, changing the subject looking over at Hope and July.

"She's been asking for a sister," I tell him, shaking my head.

"Jesus." He smiles.

"I know." I smile back, mumbling, "She might be a genius, 'cause every time she asks for a sister, she asks for a dog right after."

"Smart kid." He chuckles.

"I'm fucked," I tell him honestly, turning when I hear Hope laugh.

"Get her the dog then give her a sister," he says, patting my shoulder.

"Plan on it," I say, and his eyes crinkle as he shakes his head. "I'll see you later."

"Later," I agree, watching as he goes to July, telling her something that makes her blush before kissing her then putting out his fist for Hope to bump with hers before leaving.

"What do you say we go see some puppies?" July asks, and Hope jumps up and down in her heels, causing the *click clack* to bounce off the walls before taking her hand and following her down the hall towards the back of the clinic. Going out a set of double doors she leads us into a small room with a bench along one wall.

"Sit on the floor and I'll be right back," July says, and Hope sits on the floor while I take a seat on the bench, resting my elbows on my knees, watching as she smiles at me excitedly. A moment later, July comes back into the room with two puppies, one in each hand. One is dark brown, and the other is cream-colored, both wiggling in her grasp.

"They're so cute!" Hope cries as July sets the puppies on the ground, and they immediately go to Hope and begin climbing all over her. "What are their names?" Hope picks one then the other up, holding them close to her face so they can lick her.

"I haven't named them yet. Do you want to help me?" July asks, and Hope lets go of the one in her hand then picks up the other.

"This one is Chocolate Chip," she says, holding the brown one in a hug that has me worried for the small puppy.

"And this one?" I ask, picking up the cream-colored pup that isn't as hyper as the other.

"Pancake." She smiles then giggles as Chocolate Chip crawls up her chest, forcing her to her back so he can lick her face.

"Do you know what kind of dogs they are?" I ask July, who takes a seat next to me on the bench as Pancake burrows his way into the crook of my arm.

"We think a lab mix, but there isn't really any way to tell for sure without a DNA test," she says, smiling at Hope, who is barking at Chocolate, making him bark back. "Chocolate's a boy, and Pancake's a girl. They are both sweet." She gives me a knowing look.

"Ellie is going to kill me," I say, watching her grin.

"She won't be able to kill you when she sees how cute they are," she singsongs, running her hand over Pancake's body.

"Two puppies," I mutter to myself then look at Hope, who's laying on her back, watching as Chocolate walks backward, dragging her red sparkly shoe around.

I'm so fucked.

"Where do I sign?" I sigh, and July's face lights up.

HEARING THE FRONT door alarm beep, I look at Hope and place my finger to my mouth, telling her to be quiet as I make my way to the hall toward Ellie.

"Hey, baby. How was work?" I ask her as she shuts the door behind her and takes off her jacket.

"Good, not too busy, and nothing happened," she says, looking at me with triumph.

"I know. I talked to Tallon, and I also spoke with Mellissa's father, who told me that he was going to send Mellissa to stay with her aunt for a while," I tell her, watching as a look of relief passes through her eyes.

"Oh," she says, and then her eyes move over my shoulder when Hope yells, "No! Don't eat that, Pancake!"

"What's going on?" She frowns, when I move to stand in front of her.

"Before you get upset, just know this is better than the alternative," I tell her then block her again when she tries to move past me.

"Jax," she growls, but before I can say anything else, the sound of little paws hitting the hardwood floor followed by the sound of tiny feet echoes through the room. "You didn't," Ellie says, and Chocolate Chip runs to her feet and jumps up on his back legs, pawing at Ellie's black boots.

"Don't be mad," I say, leaning down and picking up Chip. "How can you be mad at this face?" I hold the puppy close to my cheek.

"I can't leave you alone with her, can I?" she asks, fighting a smile as Hope steps from behind me, holding Pancake. "Two? You got two puppies?" she asks, seeing Pancake.

"Surprise!" Hope sings, and Ellie's eyes go to her then move back to me as she shakes her head. "Aren't they cute, Mama?"

"Very cute, Angel," Ellie replies as I feel something warm soak the front of my tee. Looking down, I groan while Ellie and Hope both laugh. Setting the puppy down on the floor, I rip my now soaked shirt over my head then smirk when Ellie's gaze drops to my abs.

"I gotta go shower, and head out to meet my uncle and Wes," I say, watching her face change. "Everything's okay," I assure her, reading her face, reaching out and running my fingers over hers. "When I get home, we'll talk."

Nodding, she pulls her bottom lip between her teeth before saying, "Okay, when you get home."

"I'll be back down in a second," I rush out, jogging up the stairs and hopping into the shower quickly. When I make it back downstairs, I find both Hope and Ellie in the living room, sitting on the floor, playing with Chocolate Chip and Pancake, both of them with smiles on their faces.

"I'll be back," I say, walking into the room and crouching down, kissing Ellie then leaning over and pressing a kiss to the top of Hope's head.

"What do you want to do for dinner?" Ellie asks, and fuck me if that simple-ass question doesn't do something to me.

"Whatever you want, baby. If you don't feel like cooking, I'll cook when I get home, or we can go out to eat."

"I'd like to eat something that tastes good, and no offense, but the only thing you make with flavor is pancakes," she says, making me smile.

"You don't like chicken breasts and steamed vegetables?"

"If you add butter and mashed potatoes with gravy to that then yes," she retorts.

"So do you want to cook?"

"I'll cook, and then unwrap you a bar or something," she says with a grin patting my abs.

Shaking my head I wrap my hand around the back of her neck and pull her toward me kissing her, saying, "I'll eat whatever you cook, babe." Then I stand, saying goodbye to Hope before leaving the house and heading out to my truck.

"So what do you got?" I ask, taking a seat next to Uncle Nico, Sage and Tallon in one of the metal folding chairs around a large table in the middle of the compound's open court. Taking in the other men at the table, I notice Z, Mic, Everett, Harlen, and Wes all have the same look on their faces.

"You know we've been keeping our ears to the ground, and there's always a lot of chatter, most of it never panning out. But last night, Everett made contact with a source online. This person told him they had a lead about our guy, and then they sent over a name. When we did a simple search online, we were able to pull up a picture of a Yury Letov," Wes says, and Mic slides a piece of paper across the table with the mug shot of a guy on the front of it toward me.

"He was in Tennessee when July was kidnapped, but has since disappeared," Mic adds as my uncle picks up his phone and starts to send someone a message.

"I haven't showed July this picture yet. I know that's going to be the quickest way to find out if this is the guy, but I hate pulling this shit back up when she's finally starting to relax," Wes says, and I know exactly what he's saying. Ellie's not jumpy anymore. I don't see the constant worry in her gaze, but I know I don't have a choice in this matter. I have to show her.

"Fuck," I growl, ripping my hat off and running my hand over my head then down my face. "I don't want to have to show Ellie this, but I know if she finds out I kept it from her, she's going to be pissed, especially when she wants to help."

"Do you want me with you when you show her?" my uncle asks, and I shake my head.

"No, I won't show her until after Hope goes to bed. I'll send you a message when I get her answer."

"I'll talk to July tonight too," Wes says, sitting back and crossing his arms over his chest.

"If this is the guy, it will be a lot easier to find him with a name attached to his face," Tallon says, looking down at the picture.

"But this isn't the guy who purchased Ellie," I remind them, and Wes's jaw goes hard.

"If we find him, he may know who the buyer was." Mic adds.

"I still can't believe some sick fuck is buying virgins," Z grumbles from across the table.

"You and me both," I growl, hoping like fuck that we catch this guy before any more women are taken. There is still no lead on the woman whose family contacted us when she was taken weeks ago. The only thing we know is she was meeting a guy she met online for dinner. The day she disappeared, so did her profile, along with the profile of the man she was meeting and their online conversations. It was like it never happened.

"We're going to catch these guys. They will fuck up, and that's when we'll shut them down," my uncle says, standing then looking at Wes and me. "Let me know what the girls say, and we'll figure out the next step after that."

"Will do." I nod, watching him walk off, followed by Tallon, then I stand as well. "I'll call after I talk to Ellie," I say, watching Wes grind his jaw and lift his chin before getting chin lifts from the rest of the guys and leaving.

"YOU WANNA TALK to me about what went down with Ellie's coworker?" I ask my cousin Sage, leaning back against my truck outside of the Broken Eagle's Bike Shop.

"There's nothing going on. We hooked up; she's whacked; I told her to stay away; end of story."

"She told Ellie she has a twin, and she's the one who did what she did."

"Heard that. Don't buy it." He shrugs, but I see something in his eyes that says he's lying, or at the least that he doesn't know what to believe.

"Have you ran a check on her?" I ask him softly, crossing my arms over my chest, watching his eyes go hard.

"Have I ever gotten involved in any of your relationships?" he asks, pointing a finger at me then growling "Fuck no, I haven't. So drop it."

"This isn't about that and you know it. I've met Kim. She seemed nice, and definitely didn't look like the kind of girl who would drug someone she was interested in."

"I love you like a brother, but I'm telling you to stay the fuck out of it."

"Run a check," I say, watching his eyes flash.

"I ran a check; she's an only child. So like I said, leave it the fuck alone," he growls, storming off toward his car.

Watching him go, I shake my head, opening the door for my truck then pausing before getting in and looking in his direction. "Whenever you get your head outta your ass, I'm here," I yell at his back, watching his shoulders sag before I hop into the cab, start up my truck, and take off toward home, where I know Ellie and Hope are waiting for me.

Chapter 10

Ellie

SITTING CROSS-LEGGED ON Jax's bed, I stare down at the picture in my hands, feeling something ugly creep over me. Even though I remember the night July and I escaped from the house we were taken to, and even though I can still recall every single scary moment, I could never fully remember the faces of the men who had taken me. But now, looking at the picture in my hand, memories begin to flood back, more detailed than they ever were before.

"Hey, you're safe here, remember?" Jax says gently, and I feel his fingers under my chin, bringing my eyes to his. "I promise nothing is going to happen to you."

"I could never really picture his face until now, but it's him," I say, licking my bottom lip, feeling my pulse speed up and my hands shake.

"That happens sometimes. The rush of the moment clouds everything, making it hard to remember anything clearly, but then something will happen and the fog will clear, making it easier to remember," he says, and that's exactly what this feels like. When they asked me and July if we could help them make a sketch of the assailant, neither of us we're able to paint a clear enough picture for the sketch artist and they had to give up.

"So what does this mean?" I ask, holding up the piece of paper then dropping it down onto my lap.

"Wes is showing this to July tonight. If she says the same thing you have, that this is the guy, then we will start tracking him," he says as dread fills my chest.

"I don't want anything to happen to you," I say, watching him smile, which pisses me off. "I'm serious," I growl in annoyance.

"I know you are, and that's what makes it so cute," he says, taking the paper out of my lap and tossing it to the floor. Then he crawls over me, pushing me to my back in the bed. "Do you think she's asleep?" he asks against my ear as he settles himself between my spread legs, allowing me to feel his erection through the material of his jeans and the thin cotton of my sleep shorts.

"She was half asleep when we finished reading her book," I murmur as he licks up the side of my neck, pulling a moan from the back of my throat.

"I think you need to be punished for all your back-talking today. What do you think?" he asks, causing my core to convulse, my knees to tighten around his hips, and my hands to wrap tightly around his shoulders.

"Okay," I agree without thinking then close my eyes when I feel his chest vibrate with laughter against mine. "I mean no," I retract, letting my legs fall open and my hands slip from his shoulders.

"Sure you do," he says, raising his head above mine, smiling down at me and, not for the first time, I'm struck by how absolutely gorgeous he is. Lifting my hand, I run my fingers over the scruff along his jaw then over his bottom lip, remembering how it feels against mine every time he kisses me.

"The first time I saw you, my world stopped," he says, catching me off guard, and my gaze goes to his. "Nothing else existed but you, and then it stopped again when I held Hope for the first time. And since that moment, there have been a million pauses, each one giving me something beautiful to remember," he explains, and I feel my vision go blurry with tears. So I do the only thing I can: I lift up and press my face into his neck, where I whisper, "I love you," while wrapping my legs and arms around him, soaking in the feeling of being in his arms.

"Let me check on Hope, baby," he says, pressing a kiss to my temple after a few minutes. Letting him go, I roll to my side and watch as he leaves the room and walks down the hall, coming back a few seconds later and pulling off his shirt when he enters the room. "She and the puppies are asleep," he whispers, leaving the door cracked behind him, then he turns on the monitor next to the bed that will let us know if she wakes as he toes off his boots and unhooks the buttons of his jeans.

Captivated by his torso, I blink up at him when he commands, "Loose the shirt," so softly the words are barely audible. Looking at the door, my eyes fly back to him when he growls, "Now," in a tone that has wetness gathering between my legs. Reaching for the hem of my shirt, I slowly slide it up my thighs then belly, pausing below my breasts when his eyes grow darker. Swallowing hard, I pull it over my head and drop it to my side, feeling my hair slide over my breasts.

"So perfect," he rumbles, stepping toward the bed, running a single finger over one nipple then the other. "Now the shorts."

Pulling my lower lip into my mouth, I sit up on my knees and pull my small sleep shorts down over my ass then sit to the side, pulling them off and dropping them onto my shirt.

"Are you wet?" he asks, pulling me to sit back up, with my knees in the bed in front of him. Nodding, because the words are locked in my throat, I feel his fingers slide down the middle of my chest, over my belly then my pubic bone, through my folds, collecting wetness before circling my clit. Causing my hips to jerk forward and my hands to land hard against his bare chest. "Easy, baby," he says, gathering the hair at the back of my head into his free hand, forcing my head back and my eyes to meet his.

"I love this pussy. I love how wet you are." He nips my bottom lip hard as two fingers plunge into me. "I love how tight it is," he growls against my mouth, pulling those same two fingers out, only to thrust them back in. "I love how I can feel it begging for me to fuck it," he says harshly before swiping those fingers over my clit in a tight circle as his hand in my hair tightens and his mouth covers mine in a brutal kiss. That has my hips rotating, fucking myself on his fingers so hard I feel the walls of my core clench.

"Not yet," he groans, pulling his fingers away and bringing them up between us, swiping one over my bottom lip, which feels swollen then licking over it. "Lay back and spread your legs for me."

Oh, God.

Doing what he orders, I lay back and timidly spread my legs then bring my hands up, covering my breasts.

"Unless you're going to pull on your nipples for me, don't cover them," he demands, and my hands fall away to my sides as his slide down over my knees and inner thighs, where I feel his thumbs pull me open. Feeling my body shake with nervousness and excitement, I watch his face lower and his tongue come out, licking between my folds then curling around my clit, tugging it between his lips.

"Jax," I whisper as my back arches, and my hands move back to my breasts, cupping them and pulling my nipples between my fingers.

"Show it to me, Ellie. Let me watch you as you come in my mouth," he commands as his fingers move and two slide deep inside me, curling up and hitting that spot that pulls a mewl from deep within my chest. Pressing my tiptoes into the bed, I raise myself higher and grind myself against his mouth, coming so hard the world shatters around me, causing stars to cloud my vision and heat to race through my system like wildfire.

Coming back slowly, I hear the sound of plastic ripping then feel the weight of him settle over me. "So fucking perfect," he says as our eyes meet, and he slides slowly into me, stretching and filling me. Pressing one hand into the bed near my head, his other wraps around the back of my thigh, pulling it tighter and higher against his side, causing the head of his cock to rub against my g-spot with frightening accuracy.

"Harder," I beg into his mouth as his lips cover mine and his hips pick up speed. "Please, harder," I tell him again when I realize he's holding back.

Pressing my head into the pillow, I lift my hips with each of his thrusts, scrape my nails down his back, and then hold onto his ass, feeling the power of each movement as he slams into me over and over. Closing my eyes, I open them when he flips us over, settling me on top of him with his hands on my ass.

"Ride me," he growls, rocking up into me.

"Jax," I breathe, unsure, and then moan when his hands lift and drop me onto his length, bumping against something that sends a bolt of pain and pleasure through my core. "Oh, God!" I breathe, lifting my hips, falling over and over until my center begins to clench hard. As he fists my hair in his hand, my back arches, and my hands leave his chest and grip the hard muscles of his thighs behind me. His hips buck up into mine, and his free hand cups my breast, pulling my nipple, sending a spark to my womb that sets off my second orgasm, which sends me into orbit.

Letting my hair and breast go, his hands grab onto my waist and hold me tight against him as my name leaves his mouth. Falling against his chest, I feel his heart beating hard against mine and his chest moving in unison with my own as we both attempt to catch our breath.

"I gotta take care of the condom, baby," he says gently, rolling me to my back and kissing me as he pulls out slowly, making me instantly miss him and my limbs to tighten around him, not ready to lose his weight.

"How do you feel about getting on birth control?" he asks, pushing my hair out of my face and pressing another kiss to my sensitive lips.

"I thought we were using condoms," I whisper when his mouth leaves mine.

"We are, but if you get on birth control, we won't have to."

"Oh." I bite my lip and tighten my thighs around him once more at the idea of nothing between us.

"Oh." He smiles then murmurs, "Unless you want to give Hope her sister, then we can forgo all forms of birth control."

"I'll make an appointment with the doctor," I say, rolling my eyes.

"Just giving you options, baby."

"I don't want to have a child until I'm married," I say quietly, dropping my eyes from his, only to feel his finger press up under my chin.

"We can make an appointment for the courthouse instead."

"You're so ridiculous." I giggle, knowing by the look in his eyes he is completely serious.

"I'm going to marry you one day, Ellie, and then I'm going to adopt Hope so you'll both have my last name," he says, causing the air to rush out of my lungs and my body to jolt.

"Jax."

"Gotta take care of the condom, baby, then make a couple calls," he says, rolling off me and out of bed, coming back a couple minutes later with a warm rag, which he uses between my legs before tossing it into the bathroom. Going to his dresser, he grabs a pair of sweats that he pulls on, while I slip back on my shorts and shirt.

"I should go back to my room," I say, watching him grab the picture from the ground and his cell phone from the top of the dresser.

"Stay here," he says, coming toward me, forcing me back into the bed.

"Hope," I murmur softly, looking into his eyes then to the door.

"Is fine." He cages me in with a hand on each side of me in the bed. "I'll be back, so just try to get some sleep," he says, kissing my forehead then lips and leaving the room.

Rolling to my back, I look up at the ceiling and feel a smile form on my lips as my eyes grow heavy.

LIFTING MY COFFEE cup to my mouth, I look at Jax over the rim and fight the urge to laugh at the look on his face as Hope tells me about her day with him yesterday. I guess in all the excitement with the new puppies, she forgot to tell me about her and Jax going to the nail salon and wearing her costume heels around town. But my sweet Angel is telling every detail now, and each of those details is causing Jax to look at me pleadingly.

I'm not even mad at him for giving Hope her way. I know he can't help it. Looking at her now and knowing what she had taken from her, I want to give her everything her heart desires. But as a mom, I know that's impossible and will only lead to problems down the line.

"It sounds like you had a good day, Angel," I tell her, watching as she spins back-and-forth and side-to-side on the bar stool she's sitting on, eating her breakfast.

"I love Daddy Ax days." She grins as my heart stops and my eyes fly to Jax, who has a look on his face I can't decipher.

"I..." He clears his throat then looks from me back to Hope. "I love spending time with you too, sweetheart."

"I know, 'cause I'm da best." She nods then dips her spoon into her cereal, shoving a large spoonful into her mouth like she didn't just rock my world.

"Hello?" is yelled as the front door opens and shuts, and I look from Hope towards the door to the kitchen and watch Ashlyn walk in wearing a pair of simple black ballet flats, dark grey slacks, and a black blouse. It all looks good on her, but isn't what she normally wears, and I wonder if this is the work uniform her new boss requested.

"Hey, princess," she greets Hope with a kiss to her cheek then turns to look at her brother then me. "Am I interrupting something?" she asks, and I shake my head, knowing I won't be able to talk to Jax until later tonight about Hope calling him Daddy Ax. Not that I really want to talk to him about it. I don't know what I will do if he says he doesn't feel comfortable with her calling him that.

"Nope, but I love your outfit," I say, watching her eyes roll.

"My boss is an asshole," she mutters as her nose scrunches up in disgust.

"Asshole is a naudy word," Hope chimes in helpfully, making her cringe.

"Sorry, honey," she tells her, watching as Hope shrugs then takes another bite of her cereal.

"I gotta head out," Jax says, placing his cup in the sink and shoving his keys into his pocket. "I won't be back until dinner."

"We'll be here all day," I say, leaning up on my tiptoes when his arm bands around my waist.

"Be good."

"Maybe." I smile, watching his eyes darken right before his head dips and he whispers, "Or don't," kissing me softly then letting me go. Placing his hand on the top of his sister's head, he rubs it roughly, messing up her hair and making her shriek before going to Hope and kissing her forehead.

"Men are jerks," Ashlyn grumbles, running her hand down her hair, trying to tame it. Then, she looks toward the front door and back to me when we hear it close, signaling Jax's departure. "He's gone," she whispers.

"Go brush your teeth, Angel, then come back down and I'll tell you what we're going to do today," I tell Hope, watching her scoot off her chair and run for the stairs. "Did you bring the stuff?" I ask looking at Ashlyn, referring to the decorations for Jax's surprise party.

"They're in my car." She smiles, and I feel excitement bubble up inside me.

"What time is everyone getting here?"

"Around five. I'll be back at three to help set up," she says, going to the coffee pot and pouring herself a cup. "Are you sure you don't want me to pick up a cake?" she asks, going to the fridge and getting out the cream, pouring some into her cup.

"I'm sure. I figured Hope and I could make him one."

"He'll love that," she says as her face goes soft.

"I hope so," I mutter. This whole family thing is still kind of new to me, but this is what I have always wanted, and this is what I want Hope's memories to be filled with.

"Have you talked to July today?" she asks, changing the subject and leaning back against the counter.

"We talked this morning," I say, wondering if she knows about us confirming that the picture was of the guy who had gotten away.

"She told me that you guys identified the other assailant."

"We did," I say quietly, looking toward the hall in case Hope comes back down.

"Are you okay?"

"I'm glad we know who he is and that there is now a chance of him getting caught," I say then drop my voice. "But it doesn't feel real anymore. It feels like something I made up in my mind, like it never really happened."

"I think that's because you know you're safe."

"Maybe, but I worry I've let my guard down too much, that this is all to easy."

"Maybe it's your turn for easy," she returns as I hear Hope's feet on the hardwood floor and watch her run past the kitchen doorway. Then I hear the sound of her being followed by little paws a moment later, letting me know she let the puppies out of their pen in the living room.

"You got a puppy?" Ashlyn asks, and I fight back my smile.

"Your brother got Hope two puppies," I mutter, holding up two fingers as Hope runs into the kitchen, followed by Chocolate Chip and Pancake.

"Wook at my puppies, Aunty Ashwyn!" Hope cries excitedly, and I notice she put her tutu on over her pajama bottoms.

"Oh, my God," Ashlyn whispers, looking at me.

"I know." I shake my head, watching her bend down to pick them up. "Careful, we need to take them out again. Last night that one peed on Jax," I say, pointing to Chocolate Chip, who barks at me.

"No." She laughs.

"Yes." I nod, going to the backdoor, opening it for her, and following her down to the grass, where we watch as both puppies run around and play until finally handling their business. When we get back inside, I tell Hope what we're going to be doing today, while Ashlyn goes to her car, coming back a few minutes later with her hands full of bags and a promise to be back at three.

Shutting the door behind her when she leaves, I turn to look at Hope and ask, "Are you ready to bake?"

"Yes!" She yells making me smile.

LOOKING DOWN AT the phone in my hand, I angrily type out the words: **We are never having babies,** to Jax before pressing send.

I don't care if I'm being irrational. Taking care of Hope and two puppies has put things into prospective for me today. I'm completely exhausted, the house is messier than before I cleaned it this morning, and Jax's birthday cake—which is sitting on the counter in the kitchen—is burnt and completely lopsided. I want to cry and sleep for a week, but I still have to attempt to decorate then cook for and host his surprise birthday party.

Feeling my phone vibrate in my hand, I look down and fight back the smile I feel creeping onto my face as I read his message: **Babies are**

easier than puppies.

Hell no, they aren't, I text back, pressing send as I walk into the living room, where I find Hope asleep in the crate with both puppies curled around her. Snapping a picture, I send it to him, saying: **Okay, this is definitely cute,** before taking a seat on the couch, needing to rest for a minute.

BLINKING MY EYES open when I hear Hope say, "She's sleeping," I come face-to-face with Ashlyn, July, and some guy I have never seen before.

"Is everything okay?" I ask, sitting up and looking around.

"I used my key and found you all asleep," Ashlyn says as the guy picks up Pancake from the floor when she jumps up on his leg.

"Oh, what time is it?"

"Just after three. If you want to sleep, we can handle everything," she offers gently, studying me.

"No, it's okay," I tell her, standing up from the couch and giving July a hug when she comes to my side.

"That's Doctor Hottie," July mutters into my ear before letting me go. She's not wrong; the guy is good-looking. He's tall with dirty blond hair that's tied back away from his face in a man-bun, with a strong jaw covered in stubble, and green eyes that stand out against his tan skin.

"I'm Dillon," he says, turning to look at me.

"Uh…nice to meet you," I reply, looking at Ashlyn and wondering how he ended up here.

"Mom invited him," she tells me, rolling her eyes.

"Oh…well, that's nice."

"Yeah…nice," Ashlyn grumbles under her breath then looks around. "I'm going to start getting things set up." Then she looks at Dillon, saying, "Why don't you fill the balloons? You seem to have a thing for helium."

Watching him, his eyes change as he looks at her muttering, "Sure, babe," before dropping his gaze to Hope and asking, "Do you want to help me fill the balloons?"

"Are you Aunty Ashwyn's boyfwiend?" Hope asks, tilting her head to the side and studying him.

"Hope," I say, watching Dillon smile, showing off two dimples.

"We're just friends," he tells Hope as Ashlyn snorts, folding her arms across her chest.

"Um...I think we're going to need to get another cake," I throw in, trying to break the awkwardness that has seeped into the moment. "I burnt the one I made."

"I'll go pick one up from the store," July says, taking Ashlyn's hand and pulling her out of the living room.

"Thanks," I call to her back, hearing her say something to Ashlyn about "Being nice."

"Are you weally not her boyfwiend?" Hope asks, and I can't help it; I cover my face and laugh.

"HE'S HERE," I say, turning off the light, which causes the roomful of people to instantly go silent. Walking to the front door, I meet Jax as soon as he comes inside then take his hand without saying anything and start to lead him, chuckling, down the hall behind me toward the living room, where everyone is gathered.

"Did my mom come pick up Hope?" he asks, spinning me suddenly and pushing me up against the wall. Before I can answer him, his mouth comes down on mine, silencing anything I was going to say and making me forget we have a roomful of people waiting for us.

"Surprise!" The loud roar sounds through the house, and he pulls away just enough to see my face.

"Surprise," I whisper, watching his face go soft then laugh when Hope runs to us, yelling, "Happy Birthday, Daddy Ax," before throwing herself against us.

Picking her up, he smiles then wraps his arm around my shoulders. "Thanks, sweetheart," he tells her, kissing her forehead.

"Happy Birthday, honey," Lilly says, coming over and kissing his cheek.

"Thanks, Mom."

"Happy Birthday," Cash says, patting his son's back.

"Thanks, Dad. Thank you all. This is definitely surprising." He laughs, leaning over and pressing a kiss to my hairline, making all the stress of the day worth it.

"I'M READY FOR my real gift now," Jax says, coming into his room and closing the door halfway before taking off his shirt. The party was a hit and everyone had a good time. I even caught Dillon and Ashlyn laughing together a few times, which was unexpected, since there seemed to be some major tension between them. Jax even insisted on eating a piece of the cake Hope and I made him, which was sweet, considering he could have ended up in the hospital.

"I already gave you your gift," I say with a laugh as he pushes me back into the bed and pulls my shirt off over my head.

"I love that gift, baby, but the one I really want is right here," he says, shoving his hand down the front of my shorts, in between my legs, making me gasp.

"You can have that one too," I moan into his mouth before giving him exactly what he wants, though I'm pretty sure I was the one who got the best gift of all.

Waking up, I roll over and see Jax is gone then lift my head and look at the clock. It's after eight-thirty, and I don't have to be at work until eleven today.

Hearing giggling coming from down the hall, I slip out of bed and make my way quietly to Hope's door, where I find her wearing her pajamas, and Jax shirtless, wearing sweats, sitting at the small table his mom had gotten for her. Leaning against the door, I watch Jax take a drink of his coffee, while Hope places a piece of toast on a small plastic plate in front of him.

"Thank you, princess," he tells her, picking up the piece of toast, taking a bite, and smiling when Hope giggles.

Lifting her glass of orange juice, she takes a sip then looks at her doll that is pulled up next to the table in her stroller. "Would you like some milk?" She asks placing a plastic bottle in the dolls lap, making Jax laugh.

Last night, after Jax made love to me, he told me he loved that Hope called him Daddy, and I know if my brother had a say in the kind of man Hope would consider her father, Jax would be that guy. Feeling tears burn the back of my eyes, I move quietly across the hall to the bathroom and get into the shower, letting the water wash away my happy tears.

"KIM, ARE YOU okay?" I ask, knocking on the bathroom door, when I hear her getting sick.

"I'll be out in a minute," she calls back, and I hear the toilet flush and the water turn on. I know exactly what is going on, because I heard the same thing when Bonnie was pregnant with Hope. And everyday I have worked with Kim in the last week, she has gotten sick.

"Kim," I whisper when she walks out of the bathroom, holding a paper towel to her mouth. Handing her a bottle of water, I wrap my arm around her shoulders. "What's going on?"

"It's not what you think," she says, shaking her head and turning to face me with tears in her eyes.

"Are you sure?"

"Yes," she says, pulling me into the bathroom and shutting the door behind us, and then she lowers her gaze to the floor, shaking her head.

"What's going on?" I ask gently after a long moment.

"Two years ago, I started to get sick, and I found out my kidneys were in the beginning stages of shutting down."

"Kim," I whisper, grabbing onto her hand.

"That was also when I found out I was adopted and that I have a twin sister. My sister is obviously a match, but every time things get tough, she takes off."

"Oh, my God," I whisper, covering my mouth, not understanding how her twin could possibly leave Kim to face this alone, not when she needs her.

"I'm trying to get her to come back here. This is where my doctors are, but if she refuses, I may have to leave and follow her again."

"I'm going to talk to Jax," I tell her, knowing Jax will help track her sister down.

"No, I know Sage works with him, and I don't want him to know what's going on. I don't want anyone to know. My parents were approached by my sister a few weeks back, and she told them if they gave her the money she's asking for, she would come back and help me."

"She wants money?" I hiss.

"She had a hard life. Her mom—my biological mom—is a mess" she defends.

"I had a hard life, Kim, but family is family. You don't do that to family."

"I need her," she whispers in pain.

"I know she's your sister, but seriously, she's a bitch."

"When I get better, it won't matter anymore," she says, and I hope

192

she's right. I hope her sister steps up before it's too late.

"I'm here for you, whatever you need, even a kidney," I tell her honestly, watching her give me a sad smile.

"Just don't tell anyone. I'm working this out on my own."

"You don't have to be alone," I tell her softly, pulling off a piece of paper towel and handing it to her when tears start falling from her eyes.

"I have my parents," she whispers before opening the door and leaving me in the bathroom trying to think of a way to tell Jax without actually telling him, but come up with nothing.

Chapter 11

Jax

WATCHING ELLIE AS she moans and her head presses back into the pillow I lick, and circle her clit again.

"You're so goddamn sweet, Ellie. I swear I want to eat you for every meal," I growl against her core, feeling her tighten around my fingers.

"I...I don't think that's very nutritious. Not for every meal, anyways," she mumbles, and I can tell by her tone she's serious.

"Baby." I chuckle, resting my forehead on her lower stomach then look up the length of her body at her beautiful face.

"Why are you laughing?" she asks, and I know she's still drunk, judging by the glazed look of her eyes.

Climbing up the bed, I roll to my side and place my hand over her pussy, slipping my fingers into her.

"You're cute when you're drunk," I tell her, nuzzling her ear.

"I'm not drunk," she lies, circling her hips and forcing my fingers deeper. I know she's drunk, 'cause I watched her and July both taking tequila shots, trying to outdrink Harlen who compared to them is a giant.

I have no idea why July thought it would be a good idea for her and Ellie to try and team up against the man, but she did, and the rules were for every drink they took, he took two. Both the girls were wasted before the bottle was empty, while Harlen got up and walked off, muttering, "Amateurs."

"You know what tonight is?" she asks, looking up at me and biting her bottom lip.

"What's that, baby?" I ask, tilting my head down and pulling her nipple into my mouth, making her back arch and my fingers slide deeper inside her.

"No more condoms," she breathes, and my body stills.

"You went to the doctor?"

"Yeah, it's right here," she says, showing me the inside of her arm, where there's a lump and a small bruise. "It lasts three years," she adds, licking over her lips.

"So I have to wait three years to put my kid in you?" I frown studying her arm.

"We have two puppies and an almost four-year-old to keep you occupied."

"I'm not waiting three years, Ellie."

"Can we not talk about that right now?" She pouts, placing her hand over mine and pressing my fingers back inside her, which makes me smile.

"We'll talk about it when you're sober."

"Less talk, more action," she whimpers, riding my hand. Watching her, mesmerized as she gets herself off on my fingers, I wait until she's finished coming then kick off my boxers, move myself between her legs, and pull them up around my hips.

"Jesus," I groan, sliding inside her, feeling the wet heat of her walls clamp down on me. No fucking way will I be able to hold off, feeling all of her for the first time, while she looks at me with wonder in her eyes.

"I love feeling you inside me," she moans, and I feel my toes curl.

"Fuck, baby," I growl then flip her to her stomach and pull her hips up high. I slam in deep, so deep I feel the wall of her cervix against the tip of my cock, then do it over and over again, listening to her cry out as her walls clamp down around me. Wrapping my hand around her waist and one beneath her chest, I pick her up, impaling her on me as my fingers roll over her clit.

"Jax."

"I'm here, baby. Give it to me," I tell her, taking her mouth with mine and planting myself deep inside her, feeling her walls contract around me as she comes again. Waiting until her orgasm passes, I clench my teeth then push her face into the bed and hold her in place by the back of her neck, sliding in and out of her slowly at first, feeling my cock drag along her walls, then fuck her so hard the bed shakes under us, and her scream fills the room as I plant myself deep inside of her, coming on a groan.

Resting my forehead against her back, I listen to her breath come out in harsh pants that match mine before pulling out slowly and rolling to my side, bringing her with me, roaming my hands over her stomach and breasts.

"What time are we picking Hope up in the morning?" she asks when we catch our breath, and I can hear the sleep in her voice.

"We'll go in the afternoon. Mom wants to take her and the puppies to some class they have at the pet store."

"I still think your mom's crazy for wanting to take Hope *and* the puppies."

"She loves having Hope, and Hope wouldn't agree to sleep over unless the puppies went along for the night," I tell her, running my hand over her hair.

"Do you ever think about your real mom?" she whispers, catching me off guard, while her fingers draw absently on the skin of my arm, and I wonder if this is the alcohol talking, or if this is something she has been thinking about.

"Sometimes," I say, letting out a deep sigh. "Sometimes I wonder how she could have cast me aside the way she did," I confide honestly, feeling a pain hit my chest that is always present when I think about Jules.

"I know that feeling. You're lucky to have your dad and Lilly. I wish I had a parent I could share things with. I wish my dad was still alive," she chokes out as wetness hits my bicep. Turning her in my arms I hold her closer against me.

"You have a family, baby," I whisper, tucking her head under my chin.

"You know the sad part?" She sniffles.

"What's that?"

"I would forgive her. If she came to me and apologized, I would forgive her, because I want to have that relationship with her. I'm so twisted that I would accept her back into my life if she apologized to me," she whimpers, and I feel my heart break for her, because I know exactly what she's feeling.

"You're not twisted, Ellie. It's ingrained in us from the time we're little to love our family, to want to be close to them. It's human nature, baby."

"I hate her."

"Shhh…" I soothe then tell her how much I love her, how much Hope loves her, and reassure her over and over what she means to me, while listening to her heartbreaking sobs until she finally cries herself to sleep. Getting out of bed, I go to the bathroom and wash myself off then take a wet towel to the bed and clean Ellie up before tucking her under the covers.

Grabbing my laptop from the top of the dresser, I walk across the room and take a seat in the chair next to the window. I've been keeping track of Jules since she was released from prison a few years ago, and I know she lives a couple hours away, near her mom and brother. Listening to Ellie tonight made me realize it's time for me to face my demons, and finally get some much needed closure.

Pulling up her address online, I send myself a text from my computer with her information then shut down the laptop and set it on the chair. Going back to bed, I climb in behind Ellie and pull her body flush against mine, hearing her mumble, "I love you," making me smile before I drift off to sleep.

"HEY, MAN, WHAT'S up?" I greet Evan as he steps into my office and takes a seat across from me in one of the two chairs in front of my desk.

"Dropping this off," he says, reaching over and handing me a folder that has my brows drawing downward.

"Who's this?" I ask, opening it up and pulling out a stack of papers, all of them referring to a guy named Lane Diago, who is some low-ranking drug dealer in Alabama.

"That's your cousin's man," he grits out, and my eyes meet him, seeing something in his gaze that causes my eyes to narrow.

"June?" I ask, and he nods while sitting back and running his hand down the beard he's grown over the last few months. "Do you know how long she's been seeing this guy?" I ask. I forgot all about Sage asking him to look into this a few months ago.

"My guess: about five months, give or take."

"You wanna tell me why you look like you just got punched in the gut?" I ask, studying his face.

"Nope," he says, crossing his arms over his chest. "What are you going to do about that?" He nods toward the folder that's still in my hand and blanks his expression.

"I'll deal with it," I tell him, and his jaw ticks.

"You need to tell her to drop him. He's gonna end up getting her in trouble, or worse."

"Like I said, I'll handle it."

"Whatever. Are we still heading to Kentucky tonight?" he asks, changing the subject.

"Yeah, we'll head out after eleven," I mutter, giving him that play, seeing he's not going to tell me what the fuck is eating at him, or why he seems so pissed about this to begin with.

"I'll be here," he says, getting up and walking out of the office, closing the door behind him. Evan is still a wild card. I know he's smart as fuck and a hard worker. I also know about his history in the military and how he was the only one to survive when his unit was attacked, but everything else about him is up in the air, and seeing he is keeping something from me doesn't sit well.

Picking up the folder, I flip through it and shake my head. June's going to be pissed we're checking in on her, but knowing my cousin, she has no clue the kind of man she's been spending time with, and if she did, she would probably lay his ass out.

Setting the folder down on the desk, I lean back in my chair and cover my face. Last night, when I told Ellie I was heading to Kentucky with Wes and the guys to check out a lead, I could see it in her eyes that she was worried, but I could also see relief that this shit may be over soon. Since her mom was in jail awaiting trial and we were on Yury's trail, I hope like fuck that with us tracking him down, it will lead me to the man who purchased her to begin with, and we could finally put all of this shit to rest.

Standing, I shut down my computer and shove the file for June in my desk before walking out the door, coming face-to-face with Sage.

"I was just coming in to see you," he says then dips his head toward my office. "Can we talk?"

"Sure," I agree, swinging the door back open, walking across the room from him, and crossing my arms over my chest.

"I wanted to say I'm sorry for the way I left things the other night. I know you're just trying to help."

199

"I understand," I tell him, uncrossing my arms.

"I'm gonna talk to her," he says, shoving his hands in the front pockets of his jeans.

"Good."

"We cool?"

"You don't even have to ask that shit. We're family," I confirm, watching his body relax.

"You ready for tonight?" he asks, studying me.

"Yeah, Ellie and Hope are staying with my parents. If the lead pans out, we'll call your dad and have him come in."

"Are you and Wes going to be able to keep your cool if it *is* him?"

"Not sure," I tell him honestly, knowing what the guy did to Ellie and July.

"I've got your back, whatever happens," he mutters then looks at the door. "I'm gonna head out. Do you need anything before I go?" he inquires, opening it and stepping out into the hall.

"Nah, I'll see you tonight," I say, following behind him out of the building pulling the keys out of my pocket and locking the door as he walks across the parking lot to his car. Getting in my truck, I head over to the salon to meet Ellie for lunch then stop by my parents' to say goodbye to Hope before going home and getting ready to head to Kentucky.

Standing in the dark hotel room, I move the curtain to the side once more and place my binoculars to my eyes, zooming in on the room across the lot from us.

The lady at the front desk confirmed the guy we're looking for is staying at this hotel, and after Mic spoke with her, she placed each of us in a room that would give us all a different vantage point.

"See anything?" Wes asks, pulling up a chair next to me, and I swear I see the curtains in the room I'm watching move. But if the room is the same as this one, the AC unit is under the window, and that could be causing the flutter.

"Not yet," I mutter, squeezing my eyes closed then looking through the lenses again, seeing the same thing, only this time, the movement is slightly more pronounced than it was before.

"Send Harlen a text and ask him if he's seeing anything from his vantage point," I tell Wes just as his phone rings.

"What's up?" Wes asks then stands. "Are you sure?"

I pull the binoculars away from my face and let the curtain slide closed, watching as he walks toward the door.

"What's going on?" I ask him, seeing that he's going to leave.

"Mic said he heard banging and moaning coming from the room," he says.

I run my hands over my face, knowing this shit could go south real fucking fast if the moaning is nothing more than someone in the room on the other side of him getting off, since this hotel is one that is known for cheap hourly rates. We set up Mic and Sage in the room next to the one Yury is supposed to be occupying then Harlen and Evan in the middle, while Z stayed in the truck outside the entry of the hotel's parking lot.

"Fuck, let's go," I say, following Wes down the open second floor walkway of the hotel. Once we reach the door where Harlen and Evan are, they come out and follow behind us. There's no way to go unnoticed. The hotel is open, with the doors of the rooms leading outside to the parking lot. When we make it to the room, I stop and pull out my gun and press my ear to the door.

Hearing nothing, I'm about to move on to the room Sage and Mic are occupying, when I hear banging and what sounds like someone attempting to scream. Without thinking, I step back and kick the cheap door with my boot, sending wood splintering off in every direction. Holding my gun out in front of me, I scan the room then my eyes land on a gagged naked woman sitting on the floor, with her hands and ankles tied and her back pressed to the AC until under the window.

"Fuck," I breathe, seeing the bruises covering her small form. "It's okay," I say, walking towards her, shoving my gun away and pulling my knife out of my pocket. Removing the gag first from her mouth, her head lowers and a loud sob rips from her chest as I cut the ties that are keeping her in place. "It's gonna be okay." I tell her, taking off my jacket and using it to cover her up.

"He's coming back," she says, lifting fright-filled eyes up to meet mine. "He's going to kill me when he comes back."

"You won't be here when he does," I assure her, picking her up and handing her off to Harlen, who is standing close to my side. "Get her to the hospital," I tell him then look at Wes, who's barely keeping it together, then to my cousin. "Call your dad and let him know what's going on."

"On it," he mumbles, stepping to the back of the room.

"Mic, see if you can close the door," I say calmly, and Mic's eyes darken with fury as he goes out to the walkway and kicks off the broken pieces of wood then comes back inside, closing the door behind him. Standing in the room, I look around, seeing the place is a mess. There are clothes, empty food containers, and beer bottles thrown around the room, along with open condom wrappers, which cause rage to burn through every cell of my body.

"Keep it together," Sage says, coming up next to me. My dad's on his way, and this guy maybe the only lead we have to find the one who wanted Ellie."

"I know," I agree, but that doesn't stop the images of me putting a bullet between Yury's eyes from entering my thoughts.

"He just pulled in," Wes says low, walking to the door and holding his phone in his hand, typing something back on the screen before shoving it in his pocket. Pulling his gun from the back of his jeans, he flips off the light. "How pissed is Nico going to be if I shoot this stupid fuck?" he asks, and I grin then move to the side of the door.

Placing my back against the wall, I hear the sound of metal and someone walking up the concrete stairs that lead to the second level. When we finally hear keys jingling, I swing the door open and shove my gun into Yury's face.

"Honey, I've been waiting for you," I growl, grabbing his shirt in my fist and pulling him into the room. Once he's inside, Wes kicks him to his knees as I put my foot to his back, forcing him face-first into the dirty carpet. "Try it, and I'll fucking shoot you," I snarl, restraining his hand he's trying to get to his back, where he has a gun.

Locking his hands behind him, I use one of the plastic zip-ties from my pocket to bind them together then search him for any weapons. He not only has the gun from his waistband, but there's also one in the ankle of his boot.

"I didn't do anything," he says as Sage helps me sit him on the edge of the bed.

"Yeah? How about we play *Let's Make a Deal?*" I say as his eyes scan the room, and I know he's looking for the woman.

"Fuck you. I didn't do anything," he repeats when he doesn't see her.

"Tell me who paid you to pick up Ellie Anthony."

"I'm not telling you shit," he shouts, spitting at my feet. Seeing Wes step up to my side with his gun in his hand, I look at him then back to Yury as Wes holds his gun next to his right ear.

"Talk, motherfucker," Wes growls, and Yury's eyes lift, going to Wes before meeting mine again.

"I don't know who he is. He always has one of his men do the pick-ups." He grins then scans the room once more. "You don't know who you guys are fucking with."

Putting a bullet in the chamber of my gun, I cock it back and place it against his knee. "Who do you contact when you have a pick-up?" I ask again, placing my face inches from his.

"Fuck you," he snaps, and I let off a round in his knee that has him falling forward, groaning.

"I asked you a fucking question. Who do you contact when you have a pick-up?"

"Nah, cous'. Alive, remember?" Sage says, putting his hand on my gun when I raise it to Yury's temple.

"He doesn't deserve to live," Wes growls, and Yury's eyes turn to him.

"This is bigger than you and me," Yury says, moving his gaze to mine. "Shoot me, motherfucker. I'm dead anyways."

"Tell me who your contact is," I demand, watching something work behind his eyes then his nostrils flare.

"All I got is an email," he says, dropping his head as something that had been strangling me since Ellie walked out of the woods toward me unravels.

Taking a step back, I take my cell phone out of my pocket and begin typing in the information he gives me. Then we wait until my uncle shows up, who says nothing about the fact that Yury's bleeding everywhere.

GETTING IN MY truck and starting it up outside of the hospital, where I stopped to check on Avalee, the woman Yury had kidnapped, I lean my head back against my headrest and close my eyes. Harlen is staying with her at the hospital until her family is able to get into town. She is still asleep and would be in the hospital for a few days while she recovers from the worst of her injuries, then she'll be going home with her parents, who live in Mississippi. She wouldn't talk to the police without Harlen with her and refused to let him go, even when the doctors explained they needed to examine her, leaving them no choice but to sedate her.

From what Harlen was able to gather before they drugged her, her friends had been insisting she get out and date, so she downloaded a dating app onto her phone and met Yury. They chatted for a couple of days before she finally agreed to meet him for coffee, and that's when he took her. Knowing how similar her story was to the other woman who was still missing Tallon did a search of the dating app site and found nothing. Avalee's profile had been erased along with any chats she had with Yury leading up to their meeting. Now that there was a correlation between the two cases there was a chance the other woman could be found.

Lifting my head and looking out the windshield, I put the truck in drive and head out of the parking lot towards the highway. When I spoke with Ellie earlier and explained to her what went down, I could hear her cry in relief and sadness as I told her about Avalee. I knew she could understand to an extent what Avalee had been through, and that shit killed me. No woman should ever have to understand something like that, and there is no fucking way a woman should ever have to experience that shit firsthand.

Getting on the highway, I make a last second decision and turn in the opposite direction of home. I need to talk to Jules. I can't figure out why it's so important to talk to her after all these years. I just know something in me needs to put that part of my past to rest so I can fully move on.

It doesn't take long to reach the town she's now calling home, and when I pull up in front of the small house that is located on a street with homes similar in size, I'm surprised to see how well kept it is. The grass of the front yard is cut low, and the flowerbeds out front look like they have recently been tilled, like they are just waiting for flowers to be planted. Putting my truck in park and getting out, the front door opens just as I'm making it around the hood.

"What are you doing here?"

Taking in Jules for the first time in over twenty years, I'm taken aback by how different we look. I don't know why I thought there would be some kind of resemblance, but looking at her now, I see there's none.

"I don't want any trouble," she says, letting the metal storm door close behind her with a whoosh as she steps out onto the small front porch, wrapping a long blue sweater tighter around her waist.

"I'm not here to cause problems," I say, moving to stand at the bottom of the stairs below her. She's aged well. I knew from rumors that she was a beautiful girl, and time has surprisingly been good to her. Her dark brown hair is cut just above her shoulders, and her creamy skin hardly shows any sign of wrinkles. I don't know why I pictured her weathered and warn, but I did. "Really, I'm not sure why I'm here," I confess, placing my hands in the pockets of my jeans and leaning back on the heels of my boots.

"Go home, Jax," she instructs quietly, turning her back on me and opening the door.

"Why?" I ask without thinking, watching her body jolt and her eyes come back to me over her shoulder. Holding my breath against the pain I see there, I question, "Why did you do it? Why didn't you love me?" I whisper the last part, which seems to be the question eating away at me most.

"I didn't even love myself," I hear her say before she walks back into the house without a second glance, closing the door behind her.

Pulling my hands out of my pockets, I walk back to my truck and get inside, where I stare at her house for a long time. I didn't expect her to invite me in for cookies, but I thought she would at least give me something but then maybe she just did.

Putting my truck in reverse, I pull out of her driveway then look at her house in the rearview mirror. Ellie was right; I was lucky as fuck to have the parents I have. There has never been a day I haven't known they love me, and I promise myself right then that Hope and any other kids Ellie and I have will feel the same way. They will never have to guess or wonder when it comes to my love for them.

"IT'S YOUR TURN," I tell Ellie, rolling to my back and covering my eyes with my arm when I hear whimpering and barking coming from Hope's room down the hall.

"You wanted puppies," she mumbles, and I pull my arm off my eyes to glare at her as she pulls the covers up over her head.

"The puppies want to go outside, and I'm hungwy!" Hope yells a minute later.

"Three years," Ellie mutters from under the blanket, making me smile and shake my head, knowing she's referring to how long her birth control implant is good for.

It's been two weeks since we found Yury, and in that time, he confessed to the murders of three women, one of them being Vanessa Commerce, the woman who had gone missing months ago. Even though her family was mourning her loss, they were relieved to have closure and to know her murderer was off the streets and behind bars where he can't hurt anyone else. Avalee had also been in touch with Harlen. She explained she was doing okay then asked for July and Ellie's numbers after she found out they had also gone through a similar situation, though not as severe as what she endured. Ellie and July had both talked to her a few times and had plans to meet up once Avalee felt a little stronger.

"Do you want me to go?" Ellie asks, peeking out from under the covers, bringing me out of my thoughts.

"No, baby, sleep," I say, pressing a kiss to her forehead and slipping out of bed, I walk down the hall to Hope's room, where I find her trying to unhook the latch on the dog pen while Chip and Pancake jump up on the door, trying to get to her.

"Good, you're here." She sighs then points to the puppies. "They want out."

"I see that," I confirm, laughing as I open the gate, allowing both puppies to rush out of the crate and circle her feet, which sends her into a fit of giggles.

"Let's get them downstairs before they have an accident," I tell her, picking both wiggling puppies up and carrying them downstairs, hearing her follow me out the back door of the kitchen, where I stand shirtless in the cold, vowing to have a fence put up and a doggie door put in soon so that I won't have to do this shit forever.

Opening the back door, Hope yells, "Good morning!" to Ellie, who is standing in the kitchen, wearing my shirt as she runs past her to the living room, followed by both puppies barking at her feet as I close the door behind me.

"Three years, huh?" I say, and she gives me a knowing smile then places her hand to my abs and leans up, kissing my jaw, pressing her tits against me, making me want to lift her to the counter and tell her good morning in a completely different way. Fisting my hand in her hair, I tip her head back and dip my mouth closer to hers.

"Daddy Ax, Chocolate Chip is eating the couch!" Hope yells, breaking the moment and making me groan.

"Definitely three years," Ellie says, letting out a breath against my mouth and dropping back down to her feet.

"Three years," I mutter, kissing her once before leaving the kitchen and heading to the living room, where I find Chip eating the edge of the couch. Luckily it's leather, so the damage is minimal.

Going upstairs after making a phone call, I stop and frown as I watch Ellie hang up clothes in the closet of the room she chose when she first came to stay with me...a room she hasn't slept in for weeks.

"What are you doing?"

Jumping, she turns to look at me then holds up a shirt on a hanger. "Putting away my laundry."

"Why the fuck are you putting it away in here?" I frown, looking at the closet and seeing it's full of her clothes.

"Um…"

"What the fuck, Ellie?"

"I—" she starts, but I hold up my hand, walk over to the pile of laundry on the bed, and pick it up, carrying it down the hall, where I toss it on the bed then turn to face her.

"You sleep in here. Your shit should be in here."

"Are you asking me to move in?" she asks quietly.

"Jesus, Ellie, what the fuck? Did you think you were going to move out?" I growl, watching her eyes narrow and her hands go to her hips.

"I don't know." She flings her arms out then swings them around. "You never asked me to live with you. I'm not a mind reader!"

Placing my hands on my hips, I lean forward, getting in her space. "You already fucking live with me. I didn't think this was something we needed to fucking talk about."

"Well, we did. I mean, you haven't said anything about it until now, how was I supposed to know."

"You live here, Ellie; you sleep in my bed, in *our* bed. Hope sleeps in her bed down the hall from us, and will until she eventually moves out to go to college, so go get your shit and hang it in there," I say, pointing to the closet in *our* room. "Or wait until I get home in a couple hours, and I'll help you move it."

"You could ask me nicely if I want to live with you," she grumbles.

"It's not something I need to ask you. It's already done. Now I gotta go, so stop being difficult and give me a kiss before I leave."

"I don't feel like kissing you now." She frowns.

"To bad," I rumble, closing the distance between us, fisting my hand in her hair, taking her mouth in a brutal kiss that has my cock pushing hard against my zipper and her nails digging into my scalp before pulling away.

"Hang your shit in the closet," I command, pressing one last kiss to her mouth before stepping away, smiling as I leave the room and head down stairs where I find Hope hanging over the edge of the couch upside down.

"Daddy Ax," she says when she spots me standing in the doorway.

"Hey, sweetheart, I have to leave for awhile, so help your mom out while I'm gone, okay?"

"Okay," she says, flipping over then standing.

"Be good."

"I will. Wuv you," she says, wrapping her arms around my legs, and fuck me if that isn't even better than her calling me daddy.

"Love you too, sweetheart," I murmur, running my hand over her hair, kissing her forehead then placing my hat on my head and heading through the front door.

Chapter 12

Ellie

AFTER HANGING THE last of my clothes in the closet, I walk down the hall to check on Hope, when I hear the puppies barking. I know they were asleep with her the last time I checked in on them, so I have no idea what's gotten them so riled up. Entering the room, it takes a second for my brain to register what I'm seeing, but when I do, adrenaline and fear floods my system.

"Put down my daughter," I say, but I'm not even sure if the words are loud enough to hear as I stand across the room from the man I met briefly at the zoo, holding a crying Hope in his arms.

"Mama!" Hope cries, bringing my attention to her as she holds out her hands to me.

"It's okay, Angel baby. It's going to be okay," I choke, reaching out for her, but I drop my hands back to my sides when his hand moves up to wrap around her throat.

"Do you ever wonder how children can be so innocent, even when growing up in a life of sin?" he asks, kissing the top of her head while his eyes roam over me from head to toe.

"Please, give her to me. I'll do whatever you want, just please let her go."

"Such devotion; to a child who's not really yours." He shakes his head.

"She's mine," I whisper, wanting so badly to rip her from his grasp, but knowing there is no way for me to do that without getting her hurt in the process.

"Now she belongs to me, and so do you," he states calmly then looks over my shoulder and lifts his chin to whoever is behind me, but there is no way I'm taking my eyes off my daughter, not when he still has his hand wrapped around her tiny neck.

"Please, let her go. She's just a baby," I beg.

"She's coming with us," he says firmly, running his hand over her hair almost affectionately, causing bile to burn the back of my throat.

"Please don't do this," I choke out. "Whatever you have planned, please don't do this. We can work something out."

He starts to move around me, and I reach out trying to grab Hope, who's now screaming and kicking, but he turns his body so that she's farther away from me, and then looks at the man who is standing in the doorway of the room. "Take her down to the car. We'll be there in a moment."

"No, please don't!" I scream, trying to get Hope from him, only to be grabbed around my waist and chest and pulled back into a solid torso so hard that the air is pushed out of me. "Please don't hurt her," I beg the man holding Hope as he leaves the room with her screaming and kicking in his arms and the puppies barking at his feet.

"No one will hurt her. She will live a life free from the sins you have shown her," he says near my ear as I feel his arousal press into my back.

"No," I breathe, feeling tears fill my eyes when I hear what sounds like one of the puppies cry out and a loud bang as if it hit the wall. "Please don't do this," I whimper, trying to get away from him, but he's strong, way too strong for me, even with the moves Jax taught me I can't get free.

"You're mine, Ellie. I own you."

"No."

"Yes," he snarls, biting my neck so hard I wouldn't be surprised if he broke the skin."

"Please don't," I whisper as my legs give out underneath me and his hands wrap around my breasts, squeezing painfully tight.

"Your virginity was supposed to be mine, but you gave it away," he growls, moving his hands from my breasts to my neck, squeezing so hard the oxygen in my lungs gets trapped as stars and tears blind me.

Trying once more to free myself, I only manage to claw skin off his arm with my nails, but it does nothing. His grip never lessens, and I feel myself become weaker as I attempt to breathe. "I may not be able to take your virginity, but your womb is mine. You'll give me a baby before I'm done with you."

"No!" I shake my head in denial as darkness clouds my vision.

"Who are you? Where's Jax?" I hear a woman's voice ask, but it sounds like I'm under water, and then I'm released, falling to the floor and gasping for air. Feeling a sharp pain across the side of my face, it takes a moment to realize he's smacked me.

"You'll do as I say or you'll die," he threatens, pulling out a gun and pressing it to my forehead. Nodding, I agree as he yanks me roughly up to stand then drags me stumbling behind him out of the room, still trying to catch my breath.

Reaching the bottom of the stairs, a woman I have never seen before is standing in the doorway with her chest heaving as she blocks the man with Hope in his arms from going outside.

"Where is Jax?" she yells then her eyes fly to me as I dizzily stumble down the last step and hit the wall with my shoulder.

"Get into the house now, or I'll put a bullet in her," the man next to me says, roughly pulling me against his chest and placing the barrel of the gun against my temple. Watching her step into the house, tears fill my eyes and drop silently down my cheeks.

"Put her down and go check to see if we have drawn attention to ourselves," the one holding the gun to my head says, and the man holding Hope nods, setting her on the ground then walking back towards the kitchen as she runs to me.

"It's okay," I tell her, picking her up and tucking her against my chest as she sobs into the crook of my neck.

"You guys can go. We won't say anything," the woman offers, coming toward Hope and me. "I won't let them say anything; just please leave and we'll put this all behind us," she pleads.

"Shut the fuck up before I shoot you," he says, and Hope whimpers, tucking her small body tighter against me.

"No one's outside. We can go," the guy who left moments ago says, coming back into the hallway near the front door.

"She's coming," he says, pointing to the unknown woman.

"Let her and Hope stay. I'll do whatever you want," I whisper, trying to get Hope to let me go so I can hand her to the woman.

"She's coming!" he roars, and the front door swings open.

"Jax," I whisper, seeing his eyes pull down in confusion, as he takes in the scene then fly to the woman in the room.

"What the fuck are you doing here, Jules?" he asks, and my mind registers Jules is his mom, the one he went to see.

"No!" Jules shrieks, running toward Jax when the man near the door pulls out his gun. Swinging Hope in the direction of the kitchen, a loud bang fills the room.

"Run," I tell her, unwrapping her from me and putting her on the ground, pushing her toward the kitchen. "Now!" I scream, watching her look at me with tears soaking her face before running off.

Looking around frantically for anything I can use as a weapon, I run to the stand near the front door and rip out one of the drawers, causing papers to flutter down around me as I bring it up over my head and down hard, hitting one of the men over the head. Jax wrestles with the other one, trying to get his gun away from him. Hitting the guy on the floor again and again, a shot goes off and my body jerks from the sound, and then another goes off and wetness splatters across my face. My eyes start to go to the man at my feet, but Jax's hand tilts up my chin.

"He's dead, baby. Go find Hope."

Swallowing, I look around, feeling like I'm outside of my body.

"Ellie, be strong for just a little longer and go get our baby girl."

Dropping the drawer still clutched in my hand, I nod, and his eyes search my face for a brief moment before his body turns away from me as he goes over to Jules. He bends over her, pressing his fingers to her neck and a hand to her chest, where red has soaked through her shirt. Stumbling down the hall into the kitchen, I see Pancake hiding in the kitchen under the counter, so I pick her up and hold her to my chest as I make my way through the open backdoor just as three cop cars pull into the driveway, their sirens and lights blaring.

Looking around frantically for Hope, I run past the police cars, ignoring them telling me to stop, and then I see Hope next door, standing in the yard with an old woman and man.

"Hope!" I scream, and her head turns toward me.

"Mama!" she cries, running to me as I drop to my knees, letting Pancake fall from my grasp to the grass as Hope hits my chest hard, rocking me backwards.

"Oh, God, Angel! Are you okay? Are you hurt anywhere?" I ask, pushing her away so I can check her over.

"Ma'am, who's in the house?" an officer asks, crouching down next to Hope and me.

"Jax. His mom was shot; she needs an ambulance," I say, and he yells over his shoulder at someone.

"Are the assailants still inside?" he inquires.

"They're both dead," I tell him, watching his face soften before he looks away and gives instructions to the men behind him. He then picks Pancake up from the ground and nods toward one of the cars.

"Come with me and get cleaned up then you can wait in the cruiser while we get everything worked out," he says gently.

Helping me stand with Hope in my arms, he leads me over to one of the cruisers and gives me some wipes that smell like alcohol. It burns as I wipe down my face and hands. Then he opens the backdoor, assisting me inside before dropping Pancake onto the seat next to us and shutting the door.

"Where's Chocolate Chip?" Hope sobs, gathering Pancake between us.

"I don't know, Angel," I murmur, holding her against me, watching the front door of the house as policemen and paramedics go inside. Then I see Jax walk out the front door, holding Chip in his hands as he scans the yard. I bang on the glass of the door and his eyes come to me, and he jumps down the steps and runs toward us.

As soon as he reaches the car, he swings the door open and gathers Hope and me in his arms. "I'm so fucking sorry...so fucking sorry," he repeats over and over, while he rocks us against him.

"It's okay. We're all okay," I cry, leaning back to see his eyes. "We're okay," I echo as his eyes close and his forehead touches mine.

"She's dead," he whispers, squeezing us tightly, and my heart breaks.

"DO YOU NEED anything else?" Lilly asks, standing in the open doorway of Jax's old room with Cash's arm around her waist.

Placing Hope on the bed, I tuck her in under the covers and press a kiss to the top of her head. After answering a few questions from the police and getting things settled, I knew there was no way I would be able to stay at the house. Not tonight, and probably not for a long time. I couldn't even force myself to go into the house to get the clothes and stuff we would need to hold us over for a few days, and I don't know what Jax packed.

"We're okay, Mom," Jax tells her, wrapping his arms around her, and his dad gives them another hug, one of the many he's given them since they found out what happened. I think Lilly and Cash are still in shock. No one besides me knew Jax had recently been in contact with Jules, and I don't believe anyone would have guessed she would've given her life for his, knowing their past history.

"Thanks again for letting us stay here," I say quietly, taking a seat on the bed and rubbing my eyes.

"We're family," she says, and my eyes fill with tears.

"Are you sure you all want to sleep in here?" Cash asks.

"I need my girls close," Jax explains quietly, moving his gaze to the bed, where Hope is a sleep, then to me.

"Whatever you need, bud," Cash says, and I hear the rawness in his voice, which only serves to make the pain in my chest expand. "Get some sleep and we'll see you in the morning."

"Night," I say, getting off the bed, hugging Cash then Lilly, and watching Jax do the same before closing the door.

"Are you tired, baby?" he asks as I go to the suitcase in the corner of the room and grab one of his shirts.

"Yes, but I don't know if I'll be able to sleep," I tell him as I take off my clothes I put on after the shower I took when we got here and put on his shirt.

"I fucked up today."

"You didn't," I whisper, sitting on the side of the bed, watching as he trades his jeans for a pair of sweats.

"I did, Ellie," he argues quietly, coming to stand in front of me, running his hand over the bruises on my throat.

"He was crazy, Jax, and now that he's gone, all the women he's held hostage are free from him. They have a chance to start over; their children have a chance at a normal life," I tell him, feeling sorrow wash through me for those women and their children and what they have yet to face.

After the medical examiner ran the prints of the dead men, they found out the main guy's name was Tobias Benedict. He was the son of a prostitute who lived in the mountains of Tennessee on a six hundred acre plot of land, which he had turned into a compound of sorts. He had reportedly said he spoke to God and that God told him it was his duty to bring forth pure children into the world, and his offspring would lead in the war against evil at the end of times.

He had a harem of women, all of them he had either kidnapped or bought, and they were all virgins, who he then had children with. I was stunned when Jax's uncle told us he had over two hundred followers who all believed him. But knowing the world we live in, and how badly some people want to believe in something, anything, I know it's possible.

"You were almost taken from our home. I could have lost you and Hope, and I would've had no way to find you," he says, getting down on his knees in front of me, wrapping his arms around my waist and resting his head in my lap.

"You would have found us." I whisper, forcing his eyes to meet mine then holding his face in my hands. "You wouldn't have stopped until you did," I say then drop my forehead to his. "I don't want to play what if, not when we're here together, not after what happened," I whisper, closing my eyes, feeling his arms wrap around me.

"You're right," he says quietly, pressing his mouth to mine briefly.

Opening my eyes to meet his, I see pain and regret in his gaze that makes it almost hard to breathe. I hate that he feels so at fault for something completely out of his control.

"I love you," I whisper as he helps me get into bed and adjust Hope between us.

"I love you too, both of you," he says, turning off the light, casting the room in darkness. Lying there, I listen to him and Hope breathe, trying to sleep, but my brain refuses to shut off, and I can tell he's having the same problem, because his fingers on my waist move continuously. Finally, light finds its way into the dark, and I'm able to fall asleep.

Waking up, I look across the expanse of the bed and panic when I see Jax and Hope are both gone. Sitting up, I put my feet to the floor then sag in relief when I see Hope is in the room across the hall from me, sitting on the floor, playing with both puppies and her doll. Grabbing my sweats, I put them on and walk across the hall, taking a seat next to her on the floor.

"Hey, Angel Baby," I greet her quietly, seeing she's not her normal happy, hyper self and that she hasn't really acknowledged me.

"Are the bad men gone, Mama?" she asks, and my heart breaks as I pull her into my arms, settling her on my lap.

"Yes," I whisper into her hair, breathing in her scent.

"They hurt Chocolate Chip," she tells me, and I press my lips together to keep from crying.

"I know, Angel, but remember Aunt July said he would be okay," I assure her. Chocolate chip had one of his legs broken and was now sporting a cast, but July said he would be fine; it would just take a few weeks for him to heal.

"Can we go home?" she asks, tilting her head back to look at me.

"In a few days." I nod, running my fingers through her hair as she lays her head against my chest until she eventually gets up and begins playing with the puppies. Watching her for a long time, I don't get up and leave until I hear her laugh. That sound lets me know she will be okay.

"Why didn't you tell us you were going to talk to Jules?" I hear Cash ask as I walk around the corner into the kitchen, seeing Jax and his parents, along with Ashlyn, sitting at the table and drinking coffee.

"I didn't want to bring up old shit for you guys. Really, I don't know what I wanted from her," Jax replies, rubbing his hands over his face. "When I saw her, she didn't talk to me. I don't even know why she was at my house yesterday," he says in a voice full of pain as his eyes come to me and he holds out a hand in my direction. I take it, and he pulls me into his lap and wraps his arms around me, placing a kiss on the side of my neck.

"I'm glad she was there," Lilly says softly, and I nod in agreement, turning in his lap and running my fingers over his jaw. If she weren't there, things would be completely different right now. I don't even want to imagine how terrible things could have turned out.

"I GOT IT," Jax yells from downstairs when the doorbell goes off.

"Okay," I yell back, smiling at Hope when she laughs. It's been three weeks since everything went down, and last night was the first time we've stayed in the house since then. It was terrifying walking through the front door, but Jax, along with his cousins and uncles, had painted and made some changes while we stayed with his parents, and also had the alarm system repaired and updated. Making it easier to deal with coming home.

"Are you ready to go hunt for Easter eggs, Angel?" I ask Hope, who has been sitting on the vanity in the bathroom, watching me put on makeup.

"Yep." She grins, fluffing out her poufy eggshell-blue dress around her then kicking up her feet, clicking together her plastic, glittery dress-up shoes, which she won't be wearing when we leave the house. "Can I have makeup?"

"A little." I smile, dabbing her cheeks then eyes with a brush then let I her use my lip-gloss after I do.

"You look pretty, Mama."

"So do you." I smile at her, lifting her off the counter and setting her on her feet. "Go make sure the puppies are okay and change your shoes so we can leave."

"But I want to wear my princess shoes." She frowns.

"If you want to get lots of eggs, you have to be able to run fast, so you need your other shoes."

"Okay," she grumbles, leaving the bathroom with me shaking my head.

Going to the closet, I slip on my heels then look at myself in the mirror once more before going downstairs, where I find Jax sitting in the living room with his elbows on his knees and his head in his hands.

"What happened? Who was at the door?"

Lifting his head slowly, his eyes meet mine and his hand holds out a slip of folded paper to me.

"What is it?" I whisper, and he shakes his head. Taking the paper from him, I unfold it then move to sit on the couch when I see it's a letter from his mom.

Dear Jax,

To say I was surprised to see you standing outside of my house would be the understatement of the century. For years and years, I thought of what I would say to you if we ever met face to face, but being in your presence and seeing up close the pain I caused you made it too real.

I could make a million excuses and tell you a million lies, but the truth is I was a selfish coward. I'm sorry for the pain I caused you and your family, and if it were possible to go back in time, know I would do a lot of things differently. All except for giving birth to you.

The first time I saw your dad hold you, I knew that was what love was supposed to look like, and even though I was jealous at the time, I now understand how wrong I was for feeling that way.

I was lucky for a brief moment to see something so beautiful and to know I helped bring it to life.

I know we will never be close, and I have made peace with that, but I wish you the best and hope you find your own piece of beautiful.

XX Jules

"Oh, my God," I breathe as tears fall onto the bottom of the shaking paper in my hands.

"That's why she was here; she was bringing me that letter. Her mom found it in her belongings when she got her stuff back from the medical examiner," he says, clenching his jaw.

Getting off the couch, I walk to where he's sitting, settle myself on his lap, and then hold his face between my hands. "I'm so sorry, Babe," I whisper, watching his eyes close briefly before meeting mine again.

"She saved my life, and because of her, you and Hope are still here."

"I know," I agree, pressing my mouth to his then leaning back to search his face while my hand stays wrapped around his jaw and my thumb moves over his chin.

"I've hated her for so long, and now I don't know what to feel."

"I know it's not easy after everything that happened, but I think you'll feel better once you find a way to forgive her," I tell him quietly, running my fingers over his lips.

"How do I do that?" he asks, looking lost.

"I don't know," I confess, feeling tears fill my eyes. "But I'll help you."

"I'll help too, Daddy Ax," Hope says as she runs into the living room and climbs onto the chair with us. "What are we doin?"

Laughing, Jax presses a kiss to her hair then smiles at her. "You're doing it, sweetheart. You and your mom both are."

"I'm a good helper." She smiles, making us laugh.

"You're the best helper there is, Angel baby," I say, kissing her forehead then Jax before getting off his lap watching Hope kiss his cheek before getting off his lap and pulling him up, tugging on his hand.

"Are you ready to go Easter egg hunting?" he asks her.

"Yes, I'm going to get all the eggs," she yells happily, running toward the front of her house. Taking his hand before he can follow her, I take a step toward him and lean up, wrapping my hands around the back of his neck, bringing his face closer to mine. "I would do it all again, even the scary parts, as long as I knew Hope and I would have you in the end. I would do it all over again," I tell him honestly.

"Baby." He shakes his head, resting his forehead against mine.

"It's the truth," I murmur, and his arms tighten while his mouth drops down to mine, kissing me gently.

"Wet's go, people!" Hope yells, breaking into the moment, making us both smile.

"MARRY ME."

Opening my eyes to look at Jax through the moonlit room, I feel my mouth go dry. "What?"

"I had this whole fucking thing planned of how I was going to ask, but I don't want to wait any longer. Marry me, Ellie," he says, picking up my hand, settling something cool and heavy on my finger.

"Jax."

"We'll go to Vegas next weekend."

"Oh, my God." I shake my head, feeling my throat close up.

"We can take people with us or have a party when we get home, but

I don't want to wait."

"Okay," I whisper, pressing myself flush against him and balling my hand into a fist, afraid the ring will disappear if I don't.

"What?" he asks against my forehead, where his lips have landed.

"When I was younger, I saw a commercial where this couple rented a convertible and got married at a drive-thru. Do they really have that?" I ask, and his face dips toward mine.

"I'll find out."

"Okay," I murmur then tuck my head under his chin.

"You don't want to see your ring?" he asks with a smile in his tone as his arms band tighter around me.

"I already know it's perfect," I whisper as tears fill my eyes. I know it's going to take a while for all of us to heal, but I know, with time, things will get a little better everyday, and in the end, as long as we have each other, nothing else will matter.

Epilogue

Ellie

Three years and seven month later

"WHAT THE HELL are you doing?" Jax roars, placing his hands on the back of my knees. Setting down the box of cereal on the shelf in the cabinet, I roll my eyes. I swear if he's not roaring, he's growling. "I asked you a damn question, Ellie Mayson."

"I'm putting away the groceries," I say, turning around to face him. Then I get down on my knees and swing my legs around so that I can take a seat on the countertop, which I had used a chair to climbed up onto so I could put away some of the extras I bought in the cabinets close to the ceiling.

"I told you I'd go shopping," he says, wrapping his arms around me, pulling me against his body, and then sliding me carefully to the floor. "I also told you that if you needed to put anything away up there," he says, pointing to the cabinets, "I'd do it when I got home. Are you even listening to me?" he frowns, moving his face closer to mine.

"Sorry, what?" I ask, blinking up at him. Since I got pregnant, he's been bossier than ever, and half the time, I tend to zone him out when he's talking about what I can or can't do.

"Ellie, you're seven months pregnant, not two anymore."

"I'm being careful. I'm not doing anything the doctor hasn't said is okay for me to do. You need to relax, Jax. Hey, that rhymed. *Relax, Jax* should be a slogan." I smile and his frown grows deeper.

"The doctor told you it's okay to climb up on the countertop?" he asks, ignoring my joke and placing his hands on my ever-growing belly, rubbing gently.

"No, but—"

"I don't want anything to happen to you or my boy."

"Fine, I won't climb on the counter anymore," I give in, knowing he won't stop until I do.

"Between you and Hope, I'm going to turn gray by the time I'm thirty," he says as his hands wrap around my back, settling on my ass.

Leaning up and kissing his chin, I say softly, "I'd like to remind you it was your bright idea to get her bunk beds, knowing she loves jumping on the bed.

"How was I supposed to know she would think it's okay to jump off the top bunk?"

"Because she's crazy and a thrill seeker. I wouldn't be surprised if she goes skydiving and bungee jumping when she gets older."

"Stop talking," he says, making me laugh.

"It's true, and this guy is going to be just as rambunctious, judging by the way he plays soccer with my bladder."

"At least he's stopped making you sick."

That's true. The first four months of my pregnancy were spent in the bathroom. Most days, I couldn't even make it to work because of how sick I was.

"How long do we have before Hope gets off the school bus?" he asks, changing the subject.

Looking around his shoulder at the clock on the stove, I smile. "Long enough for me to take advantage of you," I tell him, placing my hands on the button of his jeans.

"You're just going to use me?" He grins.

"Don't worry. I promise you'll enjoy it," I tell him as his hand wraps into my hair and his mouth lands on mine. Lifting me carefully to the countertop, he slides my maternity dress up around my hips and runs a finger over my clit.

"You're swollen and wet baby."

"I know." I swallow, letting my head fall back as his fingers slip inside me.

"Lean back on your hands and spread your legs," he commands, and I place my hands behind me on the counter and spread my legs as he unhooks his jeans then pulls down the top of my dress, exposing my breasts, which are now super sensitive.

"I love seeing you pregnant," he says as his eyes darken further.

"Jax," I breathe as his fingers slide through my folds once more then the head of his cock lines up and he slowly pushes deep inside of me.

"Fuck you're so fucking hot," he growls, leaning forward, pulling my breast into his mouth, which sends me over into a sudden orgasm that has me screaming his name and wrapping my legs tightly around him. "Jesus, baby." He rams into me three more time, planting himself deep and coming.

Trying to catch my breath, I lie back against the counter then moan as he pulls out and helps me sit up.

"Go lay down, baby," he says, holding my face gently between his hands. "I'll take Chip and Pancake with me to the bus stop to pick up Hope."

"Are you sure?"

"I know you haven't been sleeping well," he says running his fingers under my eyes.

"That's your son's fault," I point out, making him smile as his hands move to hold my stomach.

"Not much longer and he'll be here, and I can help you when he's trying to keep you up."

"I can't wait to meet him," I say, placing my hands over his.

"Hope is still annoyed he's a boy." He smiles and I laugh. "She'll get use to it eventually."

Jax

THERE ARE A few times in my life I can look back on and know exactly what Jules was talking about: Every time my dad gave me a pat on the back or a word of advice when I needed it. The moment Lilly looked at me the way a mother looks at her son, with pride in her eyes. The first time I saw Ellie and knew I was seeing my future when I looked at her. The day Hope called me Daddy, and the day I signed her adoption papers.

And then today, the day my son was born and took his first breath.

Lifting Jasper from his sleeper, I pull down the edge of the blanket Ellie wrapped him tightly in, turning him into a baby burrito, as Hope had joked, and run my finger over his chin. I can't believe I helped create this tiny human, that Ellie and I made something so perfect. He has his mom's cheeks, but he is all me. Bringing him up to my chest, I press a kiss to his forehead and breathe him in. Walking him across the room to where his mom and sister are talking quietly, I sit on the side of the hospital bed, pressing a kiss to the top of his head before placing him in Ellie's arms. I watch her face soften as Hope leans in to kiss his cheek, giving me one more pause, one more beautiful moment.

Five years later

"MOM, DAD, I demand a sister!" Hope screams at the top of her lungs from somewhere in the house as Ellie looks at me from across the kitchen table.

"One more?" I ask, grinning, and Ellie rolls her eyes.

"We are not having any more babies. I still don't quite know how I ended up with the last one," she mutters, and I look at Toby, who is sitting in his highchair, shoving noodles into his mouth...or attempting to, anyways. "Not that I would change him for the world, but still." She smiles at him, running her finger over his chubby cheek, gaining a one-toothed smile from him.

"Mom, Dad, I'm serious. I want a sister," Hope says, stomping into the kitchen, followed by both dogs, Jasper and Edward, who are both singing, "*Hope and Ty, sitting in a tree.*"

"The baby shop is closed, honey. Besides, if you had a sister, you would have to share your room," Ellie says, while my eyes narrow, listening to the boys singing.

"Who's Ty?" I ask, and Hope's face turns red.

"I can't wait until I can move out!" she yells, stomping off, presumably to her room, where I hear the door slam.

"Who's Ty?" I ask Ellie, and she rolls her eyes then hands me Toby.

"Who's Ty?" I ask my boys, and they just look at me before taking off to cause chaos somewhere else.

"Do you know who Ty is?" I ask Toby, who pats my cheek and babbles something I can't make out.

Ellie

"SHHHHHH," JAX SAYS, covering my mouth with his hand, which only makes me giggle louder, because he's the one who slammed me up against the kitchen wall so hard the cabinets shook when he found me getting a late-night snack. Wrapping my legs tighter around his hips, I moan against the palm of his hand as the fingers from his free hand slide between my folds.

"No panties and you're wet," he groans, and I feel the head of his cock slide over my clit then down to enter me slowly.

"Oh, God," I breathe, feeling his thick length fill me then the head rub perfectly against my g-spot. "Harder," I plea as my head falls back against the wall and his hand drops from my mouth.

"No, just like this," he says, moving slowly, so slowly it feels like torture as one of his hands cups my breast and the other palms my ass.

"Harder," I beg, using my hands on his shoulders to lift myself up and then drop down on his length.

Stilling and pressing me harder against the wall, his mouth moves to my ear, where he growls, "I'm fucking you, Ellie, not the other way around." Then he covers my mouth with his hand, pressing my head firmly against the wall as he slams into me again and again, sending me over the edge then planting himself deep, groaning his orgasm into my neck.

"You have to carry me upstairs," I tell him breathlessly, coming back to myself.

"I already carried you upstairs," he chuckles, and I feel the bed underneath me as he lays me down.

"Oh," I mutter, feeling my eyes grow heavy as he gets into bed and rolls me to face him.

"Who's Ty?" he asks, and my body starts to shake with laughter as I bury my face against his chest, ignoring his question. Most days, I still can't believe this is my life, that I have a man like Jax who loves me and our family so completely…even if he is a little crazy.

The End

P.S. Alycia Jax is all yours girly

Until June

Coming 2016

LOOKING AT MY reflection in the mirror across from me, I cringe. My hair is a disaster, there are bags under my eyes, and the nightgown I have on isn't even one of the cute ones I normally wear. It's the one my sister December got me as a joke, but I wear it occasionally, even if it was made for a woman three times my age, because it's comfortable. Resting my elbows on the desk in front of me, I run my fingers through my hair, pulling the strands back away from my face, staring at the table I'm sitting at.

"I hate men," I whisper into the empty interrogation room, where I was told to wait over an hour ago after the police kicked in my door and dragged me from my bed. Lifting my gaze, I look at myself in the mirror once more and vow that whenever I get out of the mess my ex-boyfriend has gotten me into, I'm going to learn how to be a lesbian, even if I'm not sure that's actually possible.

Acknowledgment

First I want to give thanks to God without him none of this would be possible.

Second I want to thank my husband. I love you now and always.

Blue – You're the best dog ever.

To my editors. Kayla, you know I adore you woman. Thank you for all your hard work and for being an editing rock star. Jennifer thank you for your keen eyes and hard work.

Thank you to my cover designer and friend Sara Eirew your design and photography skills are unbelievable. I love that you accept my craziness and that you know what I'm looking for even when I just have a vague idea. This cover is one of my all time favorites. (I say that every time don't I?)

Thank you to TRSOR you girls are always so hard working, I will forever be thankful for everything you do.

To every Blog and reader thank you for taking the time to read and share my books. There would never be enough ink in the world to acknowledge you all but I will forever be grateful to each of you.

XOXO Aurora

About The Author

NEW YORK TIMES & USA TODAY BESTSELLING AUTHOR Aurora Rose Reynolds started writing so that the over the top alpha men that lived in her head would leave her alone. When she's not writing or reading she spends her days with her very own real life alpha who loves her as much as the men in her books love their women and their Great Dane Blue that always keeps her on her toes.

For more information on books that are in the works or just to say hello, follow me on Facebook:

www.facebook.com/pages/Aurora-Rose-Reynolds/474845965932269

Goodreads

www.goodreads.com/author/show/7215619.Aurora_Rose_Reynolds

Twitter

@Auroraroser

E-mail

Aurora she would love to hear from you Auroraroser@gmail.com

Sign up now for Aurora's Alpha-Mailing list where you can keep up to date with what's going on.

http://eepurl.com/by57rz

And don't forget to stop by her website to find out about new releases, or to order signed books.

AuroraRoseReynolds.com

Other books by this Author